A Messenger So Dark

the sequel to *Instant Messenger*

Joel Pierson

iUniverse, Inc.
Bloomington

A Messenger So Dark
the sequel to *Instant Messenger*

iUniverse books may be ordered through booksellers or by contacting:

iUniverse
1663 Liberty Drive
Bloomington, IN 47403
www.iuniverse.com
1-800-Authors (1-800-288-4677)

ISBN: 978-1-4759-1931-8 (sc)
ISBN: 978-1-4759-1932-5 (e)

Printed in the United States of America

iUniverse rev. date: 4/26/2012

Acknowledgments

Thanks to Scott Schirmer, filmmaker extraordinaire, for lending me the jumping-off point and inspiring the scenes in Silver Spur.

My ongoing and sincere gratitude goes out to Juliet Youngren, who has become my one-person writers' group this time around. She always manages to bolster my self-esteem while keeping things from venturing into absurdity.

Thanks to Marcus Chait, for keeping the Hollywood dream alive for the whole Messenger series.

And, of course, thanks to Dana, my without-whom, my sine qua non, for always being my biggest fan. Can't wait to map out the next one with you.

About the Author

Joel Pierson is the author of numerous award-winning plays for audio and stage, including *French Quarter, The Children's Zoo, The Vigil, Cow Tipping,* and *Mourning Lori.* He also co-authored the novelization of *French Quarter.* How he has time to write is anyone's guess, as he spends his days as editorial manager at the world's largest print-on-demand publishing company. Additionally, he is artistic director of Mind's Ear Audio Productions, the producers of several popular audio theatre titles and the official audio guided tour of Arlington National Cemetery. If that weren't enough, he also writes for the newspaper and a local lifestyles magazine in his hometown of Bloomington, Indiana. He stays grounded and relatively sane with the help of his wife (and frequent co-author) Dana, and his ridiculously loving dogs.

The Messenger Series

Don't Kill the Messenger
The Messenger Adrift
Messenger in a Battle

The Prequels

Instant Messenger
A Messenger So Dark
The Messenger Conflicted (coming winter 2012–13)

And then shall befall the messenger days
fraught with darkness, sorrow, and trial.
His faith shall turn to doubt, hope to despair,
Powerless to stop the great scourge upon his people.
One doubted shall rise, one trusted shall fall,
And the messenger shall be lost, even unto himself.

—Found in a cave outside of Jerusalem, 1763
Author unknown

Chapter 1

This woman hates me.

As I stand on the front stoop of the home of Mrs. Elaine Maxwell of Tuckahoe, Virginia, looking into her eyes, all I can think is, *For reasons I can't fully understand, this woman hates me.* Upon further consideration, it's not a complete mystery. I did arrive unannounced and uninvited, ring her doorbell, and warn her out of the blue of impending danger to her children. Now she stands there, staring at my face as I look back at her in silence. She's looking for the catch, the hook, the angle. She's doing what people do when I warn them of danger: trying to figure out why I'm doing this and how I could be trying to scam her.

"You want to tell me that one more time?" she says with controlled disgust evident in her voice. "I want to make sure I heard you right."

"Ma'am, I promise you I mean no harm to you or your family. It's just very important that your children not be out playing in your back yard at 6:02 this evening. They can be in the house, at a friend's house. Anywhere but in your back yard."

"And why is that?"

"Because …" I pause for a much-needed deep breath. I was hoping I wouldn't have to tell this part, but she requires an explanation. "Because at 6:02 this evening, a car traveling too fast through the alley behind your home is going to run into a telephone pole, knocking it over into your back yard and exposing your children to live electrical wires that will injure or kill them."

Her expression does not change. "What is this?"

"The truth," I reply honestly. "A truth that for some reason I've been allowed to know and compelled to tell you. I don't want anything from you, and as soon as you have enough information to make the right decision, I'll leave and never bother you again."

"Who sent you here?"

"I think God sent me."

"I don't believe in God," she says quickly.

"Yeah, neither do I, really. That's what makes this whole thing so messy."

"I'm not letting you in."

"I'm not asking."

Still she looks at my face, as if the truth of my statement will appear, tattoolike, on my forehead. To my knowledge, nothing appears; my eyes, my face simply represent what I believe to be an honest forecast of things to come.

"That's all I have to do? Keep them out the yard?"

"Yes. Until the crews come to repair the lines."

"Why would you do this?" she asks. "Come here and tell me this?"

"I'm trying to figure that out. Best answer I can come up with is because I should."

She nods without answering. That's all I need.

"If you're clear on the particulars, I'll go ahead and leave," I tell her.

"I … I suppose I should thank you."

"I'll understand if you don't."

"Thank you," she says, and as I walk back to my car, I don't know if it's for the information or the understanding. Doesn't really matter. Nor do I know if she'll follow my instructions. *That* matters, but I can't let it influence my actions. I've said what I came to say, and now it's time to leave.

I open the driver's door and climb inside. "Did it go all right?" a voice asks me.

Genevieve Swan. The woman I may very well love; I'm still working out the details on that decision. She's lovely; it's not a matter of that. Plus, she's intelligent, funny, fiercely loyal, and powerfully attractive. It's just that we've only known each other for a little over two weeks, and I'm not the type to fall in love easily. Or at all. In the days before the messages came, I was far too busy running my company to even contemplate romance. But now everything's different. Now my life is about waiting for the next assignment—the warnings from points unknown, compelling me to deliver them or suffer unbearable pain.

In the midst of that unfathomable situation, into my life strode Genevieve—confident, trusting, accepting of my incredible tale. Yes, we've only known each other about two weeks, but the things we've seen in those weeks have brought us together, and now I can't imagine going through this without her.

"It went as well as can be expected," I reply.

"Are you coming back at 6:00 to make sure they listened?"

"No, I can't. We're expected in Washington, and we've already lost a day because of this assignment." I start the engine. "Besides, we have to meet your sister back at your house."

"We've got almost two hours before she arrives," Genevieve says as I pull away from the curb and take us back toward Richmond, toward Genevieve's home.

"Is she going to like me?" I ask.

"I'm not sure," she replies honestly. "I gave her only sketchy details about what I was about to do, and she sounded a bit suspicious. I think it'll be a good idea for you to put on your most charming demeanor when you meet her, given that you're taking her little sister away."

"Great. I love a challenge."

"Play nice. This is all very new to her. She's not used to me being in a relationship, let alone something like this."

The end of the drive does not leave me much time to prepare, as Genevieve's sister arrives a bit early. I'm in the living room, trying not to pace as Genevieve lets her in and they hug in the foyer. The words "He's in here" are my indicator that it's time; smiles and charm.

"Alison, this is my very dear friend, Tristan Shays. Tristan, this is my sister, Alison Swan."

"Nice to meet you," I say with hand outstretched, as smilingly and charmingly as I can muster.

"You too," she replies, accepting my hand.

Alison is what polite society terms "a handsome woman." She is not what impolite society labels as "hot," but she has an earthy sturdiness to her that would serve her well as a farm wife or other bucolic calling. And as I'm thinking these things, I'm hoping like hell that psychic abilities don't run in their family and she's not reading my thoughts at this very moment. A quick look at her eyes shows no daggers, so I think I'm safe.

"Why don't we sit?" Genevieve suggests. "I have sweet tea. Does anyone want any?"

Alison and I both accept, and Genevieve disappears into the kitchen briefly. I sit on the living room sofa, while Alison takes a wing chair opposite, in the interrogator position—a role I hope will not become necessary tonight. Essence of awkward silence perfumes the room while sister and I are its sole occupants. I'm silently hoping that Genevieve pours quickly, so that we don't have to start the conversation without her. Mercifully, she returns within two minutes, glasses in hand. After distributing two and keeping the third for herself, she joins me on the sofa—close enough that it doesn't escape Alison's notice.

"So," Genevieve begins energetically, "first of all, thank you for agreeing to stay at the house while I'm away. You're really helping me out. I think you know where everything is kept. Bills are paid automatically each month, so you won't have to worry about that. And I'll be reachable by phone if you have questions or problems."

"Okay."

"Well, I'm sure you must have questions about what's happening, so now's a good time to ask."

Alison just sits for a moment, maybe wondering where to start. Then she begins, "I don't know, Gen …" *Strange, I never thought to call her that, natural as it sounds.* "When you called me and told me you needed me to house-sit, I thought you were taking a week's vacation. But when you said you'd be gone indefinitely—and then just casually added that there's a new man in your life—I wasn't sure what to think. No offense or anything, Tristan. You might be a millionaire with a heart of gold; I don't know." Genevieve and I simultaneously stifle a laugh at her accidental accuracy. "But this is my little sister we're talking about, and I'd kind of like to know what's going on to make her leave her home indefinitely to be with you."

Genevieve replies gently, "Ali, I understand your feelings, and I know that the short version of what's happening sounds absurd. But I think that once you hear the long version, you'll understand why I'm doing this. Tristan is my friend. He may be more than that; we're still working out the details. Even though I've known him for less than three weeks, we've been through some remarkable things together. He's the owner of a corporation in Maryland that makes LEDs; you know, those little lights. Well, he was running his company and living his life like he always did. But a few days before I met him, he started getting messages—warnings that people were in danger. Somehow, he knew the details of what would happen to them and when it would happen—and he warned them. No matter where they were, he warned them of what was going to happen. Lives have been saved because of what he's done."

It feels strange to hear my situation being described to me, and in a tone of such respect, admiration, and reverence. Genevieve's face is beaming as she details the last two weeks of my life. She's not painting me in particularly heroic terms, but there's a quality to her voice as she relates my exploits at the museum and the airport and the home of the unfortunate, ill-fated Benton Tambril. Curiously, she chooses to omit the part about Ephraim and how he's managed to follow me time and time again. Maybe she doesn't want to worry her sister. In short order, she comes up to the present moment.

"The man in Plouton was part of a drug trial," she says, "for cancer patients. He was taking a very secret experimental medication. Tristan got a call from someone who said that this drug is at the heart of something very bad, something that could hurt a lot of people. And so he's going inside the facility that's administering this trial, to find out more and to stop them if they need stopping."

"And you're going with him?" Alison asks.

"Yes. I am."

"Will you be involved in this inside job?"

"Not unless he needs me to be. I'll coordinate things on the outside and be there with a safe place for him as he does his work."

Alison looks at her sister, a very serious expression on her face. "Gen, can we talk privately for a minute?"

"There's no need. What you need to say to me, you can say in front of Tristan."

I sit silently, hoping I won't regret that decision.

Alison takes a breath and begins. "I don't want you to go."

"Ali ..."

"No, let me finish. Genevieve, I know you're an adult, and I know you're capable of making your own decisions. I respect that, and I don't interfere. But this? This sounds like a fool's errand. And it sounds very dangerous. Nothing against you, Tristan. What you do sounds very noble and selfless. The part I can't figure out is why. You're not a cop, you're not with the government, you're not with the clergy. You're just a ... a man ... who travels around from place to place and tells people that their lives are in danger if they don't do what you tell them to do. How do people respond to that? Do they thank you? Do they treat you like an angel or a gift from God? Or do they doubt you, suspect you, question your motives? Do they think you've got some hidden ulterior motive and threaten to call the police if you don't leave?"

"Yes," I answer quietly. "To all of those questions. And in the spirit of full disclosure, I can't figure out why either. For reasons I'm not allowed to know, this is what I do now. Sometimes people listen; sometimes they don't. In Tuckahoe, right now, there's a woman, a mother of two young children. She heard my warning today, and she doubted me. She questioned my motives, my intentions. She wanted me to leave, and I did. If she listens to what I told her, the children will be fine. If she chooses to ignore it, those children will die in pain. A pain I can see in my head as if it already happened. Why do I do this? Because some greater power in this world knows what's going to happen, and sometimes it doesn't want those things to happen. And that's when it speaks to me. I'm not exactly sure what's going on in Washington, but I have reason to believe that a lot of innocent people are being hurt or killed. I have an opportunity to find out what's happening and maybe help stop whoever's doing this. I'm going, whether or not Genevieve goes with me. Without her there, it will be more difficult, but I'll do it. And if she does go, I will do everything in my power to keep her out of harm's way."

Long, tense seconds pass during which Alison says nothing. Finally, without any official word of acceptance, she asks Genevieve, "What day is trash pickup?"

"Wednesday," she replies. "Separate the recyclables."

"I will."

"Thank you, Ali."

"You come home safe, though. Both of you."

Genevieve spends the next hour packing things she thinks she'll need. Alison goes out to pick up something to eat, to give us privacy as we make our preparations. We don't say much to each other; what's unspoken feels much louder at the moment. With so much unknown, my promise to keep her safe feels hollow and without anything backing it. For all I know, we're walking into a situation where they know everything about us and they're just waiting for our arrival. Then what? I can't even imagine.

I'm going rogue on this. There was no pain, no message from above saying *stop these people*. It's just a feeling I have, a sense that I'm the only one who can do this—whatever *this* is. And that scares me a little.

When Genevieve emerges from her bedroom with a suitcase in hand, I ask her, "If Alison had insisted that you don't go, would you have stayed here?"

"I don't know. I guess it depends on how much she insisted. I wouldn't want to do anything to hurt her. But I wouldn't want to leave you all alone to face this."

"Thank you. I hope we don't regret that decision."

She nods and then checks her watch. "It's getting a bit late. Do you still want to make the drive to Ocean City tonight? We could still sleep here and start out in the morning."

"I think we should go. We can sleep at my house and then head to DC in the morning. I'm very aware of the loss of time today. If things are happening at that facility and lives are at stake, I want to get there as soon as I can."

"Can we at least wait until Alison comes back, so I can say good-bye to her?"

It's not an unreasonable request, but it introduces a lot of randomness to a day that's already slipped away from me. "She didn't say when she was coming back. She could be gone a couple of hours. I really think we should get on the road to Maryland. We have an early morning, and I want us to get some decent sleep tonight."

I can see in her eyes that my reasoning is sound, but I also see the conflict at leaving her sister without a chance to say good-bye. So I offer the best compromise I can. "How about if we phone her from the road?"

The drive north begins very quietly. Genevieve sits in the passenger seat, looking out the window as mile after mile of Virginia passes by. I contemplate putting on some music, but nothing sounds as fitting as silence at this moment. I search for the right words to offer any comfort, but there are none. More than anything I've done since this whole bizarre odyssey began, I am leading us into genuine peril. At least with the earlier assignments, I could mollify my own fears by thinking, *Well, someone must be looking out for me. After all, I'm on the side of goodness and light.* But I don't get that feeling this time. What got me into this, anyway?

Benton Tambril. The man in Plouton, Virginia, who took his own life right before my eyes; the man who led us to the study in Washington. Now I have to pretend to have cancer just to get inside. Inside where? Who are they, and what are they doing? Why cancer patients? Do they really want to help people? Are they doing medical experiments on individuals who are vulnerable? What did Benton Tambril know that was so terrible that he couldn't live anymore? It had to be something more than the physical pain. He'd lived with that for years, and this drug they had him on seemed to be combating that. *So what was it?* That's what I have to learn. It's too late for Benton, but who knows how many others are in the same situation?

"Are you angry at me?"

As I hear the words break the stillness of the car, I realize with slight surprise that it is I who have said them.

"No," she answers quietly, sounding confused by the question. "Why would I be?"

"For leaving without saying good-bye. For getting you into this. For disrupting your world with things that don't make sense."

"Tristan, don't. It's not like that. Yes, I wanted to say good-bye to Alison, but you're right—I can phone her. As for the rest of it …" She hesitates a moment, and in the dim light of the car, I see her shake her head a bit as she searches for the words. "When I chose to do psychic readings for my career, I closed the door on a lot of other, more mundane choices. You can imagine what my parents thought, what they said to me. And there were days, lots of days, when I wondered if I wasn't kidding myself about my abilities. If I wasn't scamming people into believing in something that doesn't exist."

"Are you?" I ask her point blank.

"A month ago, I would have to answer *I don't think so.* But now that I've met you, I can honestly say that I'm not. I know now that it's real, that there are things in this world that most people don't get to see and feel and experience. You're my gateway to those phenomena, and these two weeks have been the most exciting of my life. It's funny—most of my friends would give anything to meet a good-looking multimillionaire, but you know something? That doesn't matter to me. If you had ten dollars to your name and looked like Ernest Borgnine, I'd still be right here by your side."

"Borgnine, really?"

"Really."

"Those are pretty strong compliments. But I'm glad you told me. Because as I've been sitting here, driving us, I've been thinking a whole lot about how much I don't want to get us killed. Especially you."

"Listen to me. I wish I was the kind of psychic who could see her own future, but I'm not allowed that part. But I'll tell you this: I'm here because I want to be, and no matter what happens, even the worst, it won't be your fault. Deal?"

"I'd really, really like to change the subject," I say abruptly.

"Then change it."

"Okay, plans. It'll be pretty late when we get to Ocean City, so I'd like to propose that we go right to the house and go to bed."

"Ooh, I like the way you think."

"I was speaking of sleep, but I could be talked into other activities."

"Does it have a name?"

"What? The activities?"

"No, the house. I thought big East Coast houses have names."

"I never named it. Since it's just me there, and I get few guests, it never came up."

"We should name it," she says. "A proper, stately manor name."

"Umm, okay. What should we call it? Something foresty? Like Three Oaks or Birchwood Manor?"

"Mmmm, not digging the tree references. Something French, maybe?" She thinks a moment. "*Sans Souci,* perhaps. Or *Maison Hiver.*"

"Sounds a little snooty. I'm not sure it suits me."

She laughs, a laugh that accompanies the perfect answer. "I've got it. Easily House."

"Who's Easley?" I ask.

"No, no. Think adverb. A place where one can live and laugh and love quite easily."

"Ahh, Easily. Now I see."

"But it has to have only the two syllables. Eas'ly. Gives it an air of elegance."

I laugh a bit at this. "Easily House of Ocean City, Maryland. Tristan Shays, lord of the manor."

"And Genevieve Swan," she adds, pausing.

"Honored guest," I offer.

"I like that."

As conversation trails off, so does Genevieve, and soon she is asleep, her head resting against the side window. This is fine; I planned to do the driving anyway, and she needs her sleep. It also gives me a chance to be alone with my thoughts, something I'm finding very beneficial since this whole ordeal began. I reflect on Elaine Maxwell and her children, and I wonder if she took my warning seriously tonight. I deliberately avoided any news reports that might tell me the outcome; I have enough to think about without worrying whether those children are safe. I did my part, and the pain went away. That's all I can do.

One good thing about the task I'm about to undertake: because it isn't an assignment, I'm less likely to see Ephraim. His presence at recent assignments has made me uneasy, doubtful, uncertain of how to proceed. He was nowhere in sight this evening, but who's to say he wasn't driving the car that knocked down the utility pole? He's become a force of chaos, and as such, he's unpredictable. But if I can stay away from him …

Then it comes to me, the part of this grand plan I hadn't accounted for. *What if the assignments don't stop?* I'll need to be in Washington for several days or more to take part in the study and gather information. What do I do if I'm called to Virginia or Florida or California? I can't think about that now. If and when it happens, I'll decide what to do.

Mile follows mile, and just after 1:30 in the morning, I see the sign welcoming me to the city limits of Ocean City, Maryland. My home, though the nature of my life in recent days has kept me from seeing it as often as I'd like. A few minutes later, I pull into my driveway and shut off the engine. Somehow, Genevieve is still sleeping. She looks very peaceful, and I hate to wake her. If she were four years old, I'd pick her up, take her out of the car, and carry her up to bed. But she is considerably more grown up than that, and I'm not sure I could carry her out of the car, unlock the house, and bring her up the stairs without waking her, so I opt for the less romantic, more practical approach.

I touch her face gently, and she stirs a little. "We're here," I inform her quietly.

Amusingly, in her groggy state I see a hint of the four-year-old awakened from a nap prematurely. "What time is it?" she asks, the words somewhere near the sounds they should make.

"Bedtime," I answer simply.

"I fell asleep," she mumbles, doing her best to get out of the car.

"I saw that. We'll go upstairs, and you can fall asleep again."

"But I was planning to rock your world," she says drowsily, disappointment evident in her voice.

"Rock-a-bye for now. Rock my world later. I'm sleepy too."

"Okay."

I manage to get her and our bags into the house. She shuffles up the stairs, steps into my bedroom, and falls into bed. Exhausted as I am, so too must I. *Good night, moon. Good night, life as I once knew it.*

I awaken just after 9:30 in the morning, which is almost unheard of for me. Still, given the late night and the recent stress and activity level, it is understandable. I look over at where Genevieve should be and find only sheets and blankets; not turned down, not bundled, just flat, as if no one had been there. In my present state of consciousness, it engenders illogical questions about whether she had actually been there at all.

Of course she was there; this was no dream, and I have all my memories of what happened, not just last night, but all along the way.

Still, the strangeness of recent events gives me enough pause to doubt, and I get out of bed to look for her. A search of each room yields nothing, but as I glance out my kitchen window, I see that she is sitting in a chair on my back deck. I'm surprised to discover how relieved I am to find her there.

She turns to me as I step outside, but she doesn't speak. "Are you all right?" I ask.

"Yes. You were still sleeping when I got up, so I came out here to get some air before it gets too hot. It's going to be hot today, especially in DC."

"You slept?"

"I did," she says. "And you?"

"Some. Once I managed to turn most of my thoughts off. Do you want coffee or some breakfast?"

"In a few minutes. I imagine we have to be on our way soon?"

"Within an hour or so," I confirm. "Lots to do today." I leave room in the conversation for her to respond to this, but she just looks away, out at the ocean. "Anything we need to discuss before we go?"

She looks at me intently for several silent moments, and I feel like there are a hundred things she's not saying. Finally, she breaks the silence with, "Arrangements, actually. I don't know where we'll be staying or who's taking care of your house."

I hold up a hand with my phone in it to stop her from saying more. "Leave everything to me." A speed dial of a number from my address book, and I begin, "Sebastian, it's Tristan Shays. ... Fine, thank you. And yourself? ... That's great. I need to utilize the service. ... Today, please. ... I need custodial care for my home in Ocean City, and I need

12

a furnished apartment in Washington, DC. One-bedroom is fine. … Let's start with two weeks, with an option to extend. … Lovely. E-mail me the details, please. … You too, Sebastian. Thanks very much."

A smile and a gentle flourish signal my success. "If you're trying to impress me …" she says.

"Now, why would I want to do that? You wanted arrangements. We now have them. A fully furnished one-bedroom apartment in Washington, and people will come here every day to take care of the place."

"One bedroom? How will you stand the spartan arrangements?" she teases.

"Scoff all you like, but it's practical. If these people are watching me, I don't want them seeing me go to a luxury hotel every night."

"You don't think they've already done an extensive background check on you?"

"You think they have?"

She rises and steps over to me, placing a hand on my shoulder. "Tristan, I believe in you, and I'm with you in this, no matter what happens. But what you're seeing in my eyes—what you've seen for the past day is my need to tell you …"

"Tell me what?"

"You don't have the element of surprise, my love. You don't have the jump on them that you think you have. This stealth mission of ours, this covert operation—they know; they have to know. They have your name, and probably mine. If they don't know the cancer's not real, they can easily find out. They let you in because *they* stand to gain from it, not you. They're inviting you into a situation of their making, and they hold all the cards. So what you see in my eyes is a deep, overpowering fear for your safety."

For a long time, I say nothing. What can I say? She's given voice to a truth I've known from the very beginning, a truth I conveniently tucked away in the part of my mind that hides bad news. I've tidily covered it up with rationalizations about how I'm smarter, better-prepared, and more resourceful than they are—whoever they are. But all along, every word Genevieve said was still there, trying to be heard.

"Then why go?" I ask quietly. "Either of us? If we're walking into our own peril, why should we take this on? I can cancel the service, cancel the apartment. Take you back to Virginia, to your sister. And I can get on with figuring out what becomes of my life now."

She takes me firmly but delicately by the wrists and looks into my eyes again. "The answer, the one you already know, is that no matter how much danger we put ourselves in by doing this, a lot more people will be in a lot greater danger if we don't. These people running this drug trial, if they're the good guys, then we have nothing to fear, and if they're the bad guys, we might just be the only ones who can stop them. So go upstairs and get packed. I'll go into that medium-sized restaurant you call a kitchen and have your robot butler make us breakfast."

I laugh gently at this. "I don't have a robot butler."

"Guess I'll have to do it then, huh?"

I follow her back inside, and as she turns to go to the refrigerator, I call to her. "Thank you for understanding."

"Go pack. Busy day ahead."

Breakfast is good; brief, but good. Genevieve makes us each an iced coffee to take on the road, and soon we are underway. The drive is uneventful, and we arrive in the early afternoon. The first stop is at the apartment, which is in Georgetown, about two miles from the site of the medical facility. I park in front of the building, and we get our bags and go inside.

The apartment has only one bedroom and one bathroom, but it does not want for comfort one bit. It is designed for the business traveler, giving him or her a place of peace and respite during prolonged business trips. The furniture is elegant, the place is immaculately clean, and even the refrigerator is stocked. Tempting as it is to just sprawl out on the couch and relax, there's work to do.

"What's the plan?" Genevieve asks after we stow our bags in the bedroom.

"No time like the present. I'm heading in to do initial intake."

"All right, then. Let's go."

Exactly what I didn't want to hear. "No," I reply calmly, "you're staying here."

"You need me there ..."

"Maybe I do. I just don't know yet. This is the very first day, and for all I know, five guys with guns might be waiting for me the minute I walk through the door."

"Which is why ..." she begins.

"Which is why," I interrupt, "you'll be here, and I will place a call to you right before I enter the facility, leaving my phone on the whole time. I need you in a place of safety, in case something goes wrong. One of us has to stay mobile and at liberty, in case the other needs rescuing."

Her face tells me she sees the reason behind my plan. "Oh. I guess that makes sense then."

"Thank you."

"Just please tell me you're not going to protect me this whole time and keep me locked away in this apartment. Because if that's part of the plan, I want no part of it."

"I'll need you, and very soon. But let me do surveillance first. Then we'll figure out how you can be most effective in everything we do."

I hate to leave her there with things still unsaid, but I really have to go. Getting into the car, I pull the directions to the clinic out of my pocket and start the engine. It's time to put on just the right façade. I don't have to appear totally calm; after all, I'm a cancer patient signing up for a new treatment regimen, in a strange city for the first time. It's natural that I would be uneasy, even a bit frightened. What I can't look like is what I am: an imposter, their enemy, someone determined to shut them down at all costs.

Within five minutes, I arrive at the address. The building, from the outside, looks like a medical clinic, I suppose. There's a parking lot in front of a long, low facility. It has few windows, but I am surprised to see minimal security. No high fences, no guard house, no barbed wire. Just a single security guard at the front door, questioning each visitor as he or she enters the facility.

A sign above the front entrance informs me that I am at the Swift Medical Research and Testing Center. *Swift—not a word I'm used to associating with medical care. It'll make a nice change if they live up to their name.*

As promised, I place a call to Genevieve and leave the phone on in my pocket. I then give the guard at the door my name, which he checks against his master list. "Go through this main door," he instructs me, "turn right, and go down the hall to a sign that says *intake*. Give them your name, and they'll check you in."

"Thank you."

"Welcome to Swift Medical, Mr. Shays."

I can't help feeling like I'm getting away with something, having made it through the first security point. It's so distracting, I nearly forget that surveillance is an important part of my visit. Under the guise of curiosity, I look around, taking in as much as I can. On the surface, it looks like any urgent-care clinic I've ever seen. There are nursing stations, labs, patient rooms, doctors' offices, rooms for X-rays and myriad other tests.

I really don't know what it is I'm looking for; something sinister, I guess. But what does that look like? Doctors in capes and masks, twisting mustaches? Horror-movie nurses with sharpened instruments for inflicting pain? None of the above is present, or if they are, they're very well hidden. All I see are healthcare practitioners administering pain relief on a population that desperately needs it. And I'm here to shut it down.

By the time I reach the intake desk, I'm starting to wonder if I haven't made a colossal mistake.

Behind the desk is a pleasant-faced African American woman in her forties. She's reading a book called *French Quarter*—a bit of escapist fiction, it seems from the cover art. When she sees me standing there, she looks up and asks, "Checking in?"

"That's right."

"Okay, sir, I'll need to see a photo ID and the e-mail we sent you."

I produce both and present them to her. She compares my picture to my face and my face to my picture. Satisfied that they are a match, she smiles and hands me a manila folder. "Take this to room 16, down this hall. Someone will be with you in a few minutes."

Chapter 2

Room 16 is a nondescript exam room on the first floor of the facility. The walls are painted an inoffensive beige and decorated with the expected items: a calendar, a couple of framed prints of landscapes with birds flying across, charts of the various bodily systems, including a few detailing the ravages of cancer. There are no framed diplomas in the room; I don't know why this strikes me as odd, but it does. One thing strikes me as very odd, however: the presence of closed-circuit TV cameras, one in each corner of the room. I haven't been in too many doctors' offices over the years, but I'm certain I've never seen one with this kind of security. And courtesy of these very cameras, I can't even ask why they're here without arousing suspicion.

I'm very aware of the passage of time, checking my watch every minute or two that passes with no other human presence in the room. My anxiety is irrational, and I know it. In any other medical facility, it's common to spend an hour or more in the waiting room before even seeing an exam room; once inside, you can easily spend another half hour. Yet, here I am, ten minutes alone, and my mind is having a field day, imagining a squadron of armed guards amassing in preparation to storm this room and take me away. Is it regret? Second thoughts at the wisdom of this whole thing? Or is it just plain fear? Whatever the reason, I'm fairly convinced that this is my last opportunity to leave

17

here, tell them I made a mistake, and never look back. Where is a sign from above when *I* need one?

The door opens, and a woman enters carrying a small plastic tub of medical equipment. "Mr. ... Shays, is it?" she says, reading from a chart. "Tristan Shays?"

She appears to be in her early thirties, with a caring face and a gentle voice. If I were paying attention to such things, I could describe her as attractive, but I have far too much on my mind to assess her aesthetics beyond that.

"That's me," I answer, forcing a half-smile for some reason.

"My name is Cheryl. I'm the nurse practitioner who's gonna be taking care of you each time you come in."

"Hi," is all I can muster by way of response.

"It's okay if you're nervous. Lot of people are their first time. You can ask me any questions, and I'll tell you what I'm doing each stage of the way. As you may know, we're conducting a drug study on a new pain reliever for cancer patients. It's not a double-blind study; everybody gets the drug, and nobody gets a placebo. For the next seven days, you'll come in to the center three times a day to take your dose of the medicine, and I'll check your vital signs, ask you about your pain, answer any questions you might have. Now, I should stress that we're not here to *treat* your cancer, and while I wish we could cure it somehow, the best we can do is try to help you manage your pain.

"After the first week, if the pills are working, we'll send you home with a supply of them to keep taking. We'll check with you by phone to see how you're doing periodically, and if all goes well, we'll keep supplying you with the medication at no charge."

"That sounds great," I reply, playing the part. "What's the catch? I mean, I'm so used to nothing ever being for free. Why are they doing this?"

"Well, we need to see if the medication works on a volunteer test group. It's been tested safely on animals with no ill effects. Now we need to try it with the people it's intended for. If we have measurable success, we can get a patent and release the drug on the market."

"So it's not just altruism, then?"

"That's part of it, but not all of it."

"Sorry. I didn't mean to sound confrontational. I just … I'm nervous, and I want this to work. To help with the pain."

"We'll do what we can. Step one is …" She makes a grand gesture of displaying a form. "The paperwork. Fill this out for me, and I'll be back in a few minutes with the first dose."

"Should I be scared?" I ask a little playfully.

"If you're brave, I'll bring candy."

"You've inspired me."

She leaves the room, and I am alone with the form. I pause a moment to reflect on our interaction. Cheryl. She doesn't seem evil. Of course, if she came in here twisting a mustache—or some other gender-appropriate hair—the ruse would be over in a hurry. Is she one of "them," whoever "them" are? Or is she someone who comes to work each day thinking she's helping people, unaware of the sinister side of those who pay her? It wouldn't be the first time such a thing has happened. People do it every day, report to work for a corporation that does unscrupulous, even "evil" things. She strikes me as genuine, as caring—what a nurse should be.

I turn my attention back to the form. It looks pretty standard—personal information, medical history, details about the cancer and any treatment already sought for it. Fortunately, I studied the falsified medical report that got me into the program, so I can put down the details. At the bottom of the form is a space for an emergency contact's name and phone number; it gives me pause. Genevieve is the logical choice—hell, the *only* choice that comes to mind. But will I be putting her in danger if I list her? They'll have her name, her phone number. Easy access to her.

I take a moment and weigh the decision. If these people are legitimate, there's no danger in giving her information. If they're crooked, they probably already know everything about both of us. I decide to hedge my bet a bit. Under *name,* I write "Gen S." I include her cell phone for a contact number. Who knows? I may find myself in an emergency, and someone might have to get me out of here.

A few minutes later, Cheryl returns to the room. "All finished?" she asks pleasantly.

"I think so. I never know if I've completed everything on these things."

She looks it over briefly and tells me, "Looks fine. Now, on to the business of the day. Let's start with height and weight." She takes me over to the scale in the corner of the room and I stand on it. "Five-eleven," she says, and then slides the weights over on the balance bar. "Looks like 167. Is that about where you've been recently?"

"It was closer to 180 before my diagnosis," I reply, unsure where that little factoid comes from. I hope it sounds authentic.

"Some weight loss is normal. Have you done any radiation, any chemo?"

"No, not yet. My doctor says I'm a prime candidate, and I was considering it. Then I found out about this study, and if I can keep the pain in check, I want to delay the other stuff as long as I can. Sometimes I think the cure might be worse than the disease."

"I understand."

"I'm not being stupid, am I? I mean, should I forget about the pain and do the other treatments?"

"Every person is different," she says, a tone of genuine caring in her voice. "Some go for the radiation or the chemo right away, hoping to knock it back. Others rely on the body's natural healing mechanisms to fight off the invader. Will to live has a lot to do with it. You have a strong will to live, don't you, Tristan?"

"Oh, yes ma'am," I say, with an earnestness that could gain me a role on a remake of *The Waltons*. "Lots to live for, I hope."

"Then we'll do everything we can to make that pain-free. Open your mouth."

I do, and in goes a thermometer that appears from nowhere. She's good. Within a minute, I learn that my temperature is normal. Two minutes later, I know my blood pressure is too. *Well, hell, why wouldn't it be? Fake cancer is far less taxing on the body than real cancer.*

"Okay," she continues, "time for the pain scale." She pulls out a chart on a laminated sheet of paper. On it is a scale of numbers zero through ten. Along with each number is a slightly stylized stick figure in varying degrees of discomfort. For zero and one, he looks pretty mellow. Around four to five, the facial contortions indicate some displeasure. Long about eight, he's hating life. And for ten, I'm pretty sure his balls are in a threshing machine, from the look of agony on his face. "This is Mr. Payne," Cheryl says matter-of-factly.

"Mr. Payne?" I repeat, making no effort to mask my disbelief.

"I'm not saying it's subtle, but here it is. Mr. Payne represents the range of pain response, with zero being a total lack of pain and ten being the worst pain you've ever felt in your life. I want you to think about your present situation, right at this very moment, and tell me where on the scale you are."

I scan Mr. Payne's journey from left to right, his tragic decline from sublime comfort to the soul-shattering depths of stick-figure agony. My honest answer would be zero, as I don't even have a tiny headache, but zero doesn't get Daddy any candy, and today is all about the candy. So it's time for the land of make-believe.

"Well, I didn't want to make a fuss, but my insides have been burning all day. It's pretty intense. It's not the worst pain ever, but I think it's pretty safe to call it a ... seven? Does that sound normal?"

"Now, don't worry about 'normal.' Everyone's different, so everyone's pain is different. With the cancer you have, this type of pain is common. Let's get you the first dose of the medication."

She fills a small cup with water and puts a green, oblong tablet into a tiny paper ramekin, presenting both to me.

"So this is it," I say, absent anything actually intelligent to say.

"This is it."

"What's it called, this pill?"

"It doesn't have a brand name yet. For the moment, it's called CP117. Not terribly catchy, I know, but it's like a placeholder. If we bring it to market, I'm sure it'll get a long name that's difficult to spell, something with x's and z's in it. But for now, just say hello to CP117."

To my amazement, I actually greet the fucking pill. "Hello," I chirp in a voice so pathetic, I want to beat *myself* up on the playground after school.

"*Say hello* is actually a euphemism for 'down the hatch,'" she continues helpfully.

"Oh. Right." *Tragic little laugh denoting foolishness; check.* "Down the hatch."

I put the pill in my mouth and toss a swig of water down my throat, jerking my head back a little to help swallow.

"There," I say, handing her the cup, "that wasn't so ..." Unable to finish the sentence, I begin to screw up my face and inhale little breaths.

"Are you all right?" she asks, clearly not used to this reaction.

"I'b jus—" More facial contortion and little breaths. "I'b gudda—" Swiftly, I reach for a handkerchief in my pants pocket and bring it to my face just in time to intercept a mighty sneeze, which is followed by another, and another, and another. Three more follow, all caught by the hanky.

I offer my most embarrassed expression. "I am *so* sorry. I've had allergies since I was a kid, and sometimes they come out of nowhere. I hope I didn't get you."

"No, no, it's fine. Can I get you something for that?"

"I should be all right. I take something once a day. Sometimes it even works."

She laughs politely at this. "I want you to lie back on the exam table for about fifteen minutes. Close your eyes. You can sleep if you want to. I'll come back to check on you and see if there's any change to your level of pain."

"Sounds good, umm—what should I call you? Nurse? Nurse practitioner?"

"How about Cheryl?"

"Cheryl it is. I'll see you in a little bit."

She gathers her things and leaves the room as I put my handkerchief—and the tablet of CP117 it now contains—back into my pants pocket. I smile triumphantly to myself. *Gotcha.*

With that, I lay myself down on the exam table, which wins no awards for comfort by any stretch of the imagination. For some strange reason, I feel peaceful. There's no immediate threat at hand, though I have five hundred milligrams of Jesus-only-knows-what in my pocket. No one's bursting in to interrogate me, threaten me, torture me, or kill me, so that's a good start. And Cheryl has put me oddly at ease. So I allow myself the luxury of comfort, still aware of the cameras in the room, which will certainly detect any unusual activity on my part. I try to convince myself that they're there to alert medical personnel if a patient has an emergency while no one else is in the room, but I can't shake the belief that they have a more sinister purpose.

Flat on my back on the exam table, I close my eyes and work on my story. What should I tell Cheryl when she gets back? That the pill had no effect at all? No, that's no good; she might just give me another one, and two convenient sneezes in a row seems unlikely. That the pill works wonders and my pain is at zero now? Risky after just a few minutes, and hard to believe too. She may very well have given me a placebo for the first dose to test my reaction. Even if that's the case, the placebo effect would kick in. I can drop my pain level from a seven to a six believably. It shows positive results without instant miracles, and it's a credible reaction.

Six it shall be. Mr. Payne's face will go from a teary-eyed look of woe and misery to a doleful yet gently subdued look of resigned grief. Poor Mr. Payne. The worst shit happens to him.

When Cheryl returns, I am surprised to find that I have actually been dozing. I didn't think I would let myself fall asleep, but I awaken with a powerful sense of disorientation. I wonder for a moment if it's the effect of the medication but then quickly remember that it's still in my pocket, so probably not.

"I'm up," I say, unprovoked, and rather to my surprise as I return to a seated position.

"So I see," she says, looking gently amused at my reaction. "Did you rest?"

"I didn't think I would, but I guess I did."

She brings out the blood pressure cuff again. "Let's see how you're doing thirty minutes after your first dose."

"Thirty?" I repeat, amazed that it's been that long.

"Someone was tired."

"Well, it was a long drive from Virginia last night." *Oh, fuck.* It's out before I can stop it.

"Virginia? I thought you were from Ocean City, Maryland."

The recovery has to be swift and seamless. Humor. "Wow, a medical practitioner who actually reads the patient's form!" I laugh a bit, and she joins me. "You're correct. I was just visiting a friend in Virginia when I got the approval to join the study."

"Would that be 'Gen S.,' your I.C.E.?"

"Wow, you don't miss a thing, do you?"

"All part of the job. If I'm inattentive, people die." She tightens the cuff and inflates it with these portentous words. A few seconds later, she releases the pressure, announcing, "Looks good. How's the pain? Use the same scale."

I pretend to think about it for a moment and decide, "A six. It definitely feels a little better than it did before. I wish I could say I didn't hurt at all, but I can't."

"That's okay. Down one level in half an hour is good. It means your body took to the pill. Feeling any side effects? Anything unusual?"

I shake my head as I answer, "No, nothing out of the ordinary. Are there side effects I should know about?"

"Some people experience a few. I'll be back in a minute with a sheet of drug facts, including any known side effects. Sit tight."

She leaves again, and I'm struck by how very ordinary everything feels. The place, the people, it all rings true to what a drug research study should feel like. All of which makes me wonder if I've made a huge error in judgment. Maybe Benton Tambril was depressed or psychotic. Maybe his decision to kill himself was his only way out of the agony his life had become.

I came here based on my own intuition, with no assignment, no special knowledge of wrongdoing; just a strong suspicion that something was corrupt and dangerous. If these people wanted to hurt me, they had every opportunity to do so. For God's sake, I was asleep in their building for half an hour! *What if I'm just plain wrong and this company is trying to help cancer patients with their pain?*

Cheryl returns carrying a small stack of letter-size papers, three sheets stapled together in the upper left-hand corner. "All right, Tristan, I think we're good to go for now. You'll need to come in three times a day for the first seven days to take your dose, so we'll need to see you back here in four hours. In the meantime, read these instructions carefully. They'll tell you what you need to know about CP117 and the study."

She places the pages down on the basin next to the sink, and I step over to look at them. "This first page," she says, "contains a general description of the pills and the study itself, including frequently asked questions." Flipping the page, she continues, "The second page is a list of common side effects, and what to do if you experience any of them."

One more flip, and the third page is revealed. "And this page gives special instructions created for your circumstances."

I look at the typed instructions on the third page. At the bottom, handwritten in still-wet red ink, is a single word in large capital letters: RUN!

My heart skips a beat with the discovery. Cognizant of the cameras, I must keep my reactions subdued, but I have to know if this warning is for me. I look at her face, trying to hide the fear I'm feeling. She offers a small, inscrutable smile in response.

"So it looks like some vigorous exercise could be good for my health?" I ask.

"It's definitely recommended. Aerobics or swimming; a treadmill. Walking or even running is great for you, if you're feeling up to it."

"Well, I don't do it as much as I'd like to, but if it's nurse practitioner's orders, how can I refuse?"

"That's the spirit. We'll see you in about four hours, then."

"Thanks, Cheryl. You've been very helpful."

I fold the papers in half, careful to obscure the word from the watchful eye of the cameras. *I can't run out of here, not like this. It'll look strange, suspicious. I have to leave here in an orderly fashion, greeting anyone who makes eye contact and making my way to safety while drawing the least possible attention to myself.*

Trying to control my now-racing pulse, I exit the exam room and make my way back down the hallway toward the exit. If someone looks at me, I smile pleasantly. If they wish me a good morning, my one-word response is, "Morning." I can't look back to see if I am followed; can't look around to see if I am being watched. There's me and there's the steps remaining to the exit. And there's the all-important need to escape.

Mercifully, my egress is unimpeded, and I make my way to the parking lot, to the safety of my car. I pull out of the lot much more slowly than I would like to, still unwilling to draw attention to myself. During my brief ride back to the apartment, my mind is awash in nonstop thoughts, which I choose to verbalize to myself.

"I was right. I was right. I must be right. Run. It said *Run.* She wasn't talking about exercise; that was a warning. What else could it be? She knows who I am, or she knows I don't have cancer. I mean, she's a medical professional, and it's obvious that I don't have cancer, so she thinks I'm a fed or an investigative journalist or someone who's there but shouldn't be. And she wanted me to get out of there before something bad happened to me. Why? Why would she do that? Who am I to her? Nobody. She doesn't know me. Why would she care that much about someone she just met? Because she knows what they're up to. She knows what they're doing is wrong, and they're capable of hurting me. That has to be it."

Before I can fully work through my thoughts, I am back at the apartment. Grabbing the pages, I rush inside. As I fling the door open, I call out. "Genevieve? Gen!"

She hurries from the bedroom to see me, looking concerned at the urgency of my tone. "What is it? Are you all right? Is something wrong?"

I get a bottle of Perrier from the refrigerator and sit down with her at the dining room table, about to recount my tale of the morning's activities. She reminds me that my phone was on the entire time, and she was able to hear everything that transpired in the exam room and my entire conversation with myself on the way home. Finally, I display the instruction pages, with their written warning.

"Look at that," I tell her. "That's what she gave me at the end."

"What do you think it means?"

"I think it means she wants me to run from there and not look back. It means I was right to suspect them of wrongdoing. This nurse practitioner must believe that I'm not a cancer patient, and she's warning me to get out of there before bad things go down."

"So that's it then? You're not going back, right?"

"What?" I ask, surprised at the question.

"Well, if she says you're in danger, and if your cover is that easily compromised, I thought ..."

"I can't quit now. This proves that I'm on the right track."

"It also proves that they're on to you and you might be in immediate danger."

"We knew that was a possibility—we expected it. But I also thought we agreed that it was an acceptable risk."

She rises from the table and takes a few steps away, allowing a long silence to seep into the conversation. Quietly, and with her back to me, she continues, "It was. When we were in Virginia; when it was a plan, a discussion, a theory. But now that we're here—now that you have something so concrete telling you that it's dangerous … now I'm not so brave."

Needing to be near her, I rise and stand behind her. I begin by putting my hands on her shoulders and then gradually embrace her from behind, putting my face close enough to hers that my next words can be said in a whisper. "I respect your fear. I feel the love that motivates you to have this doubt. Believe me, I do. Two months ago, if someone suggested to me that I should come to this place and do this thing, I would've looked at them like they were out of their mind. Something's changed for me—something meaningful that speaks to me of a purpose beyond my own needs and my own wants, and if necessary, beyond my own personal safety. If it's too much for you, being here, being with me while I do this, I will arrange for safe, comfortable transportation home for you, and I will never exhale a single breath of blame or disappointment. Just say the word."

She looks at me in silence for a few moments before saying, "You dear, impossible man. How do you do this?"

"Don't ask too loud. I may realize that I don't actually have what it takes."

Genevieve turns to face me. "I'm staying. I will be here for you, ready to help you at a minute's notice. And I understand that you'll be putting yourself into dangerous situations. Promise me one thing; just one little thing—promise that you won't take unnecessary risks. I don't even know what the exact definition is, but promise me that."

"I promise. I have a lot to live for, and I don't want to throw that away."

"Thank you," she says, clearly fighting back tears. I hold her tightly, and a few of them flow onto my shoulder. "When do you have to go back there?"

"Three and a half hours."

"So soon. Can you—before then—would you hold me? Go to our room, lie down with me, and hold me?"

"Of course."

For the next two hours, we lie in each other's arms, saying very little, just feeling the warmth, hearing the other breathe, embracing the aliveness of someone so close. I try to turn off my thoughts, suppress my fears and self-doubts. Courtesy of my little nap at the clinic, I'm not sleepy, so I can't shut my thoughts out that way. And yet I feel like I'm close to knowing what I came here to learn. If Cheryl is willing to warn me, maybe she'll be willing to speak to me privately, away from the clinic, away from the cameras. They'd never allow it, of course, but they can't watch her every hour of every day. *Can they?* Even if she does agree to meet me, how do I ask her? I can't call her, e-mail her, text her. It'll have to be the same way she warned me—an old-fashioned handwritten note passed covertly to her.

I rise from the bed about an hour before I have to go back to the Swift facility. In the dining room, a computer is set up, complete with Internet connection. I sit down, open up a browser window and a search engine, and type in a single word: SODARCOM. It's time to see what the world knows.

The computer thinks a moment, and a screen appears, displaying the words *No results found for SODARCOM.*

Surprised by this, I try a second search engine and a third; a fourth and fifth follow. All return the same answer: *No results found.* A couple of them helpfully ask, *Did you mean SODA CAN?* Clearly, I did not. Something is up. Lots of hits equals court of public opinion. A few hits equals hush-hush but open forum for conspiracy theorists. No hits whatsoever speaks of something far more powerful—an organization so secretive that it has the power to black itself out of the greatest shared information network in the history of the world. I have to wonder who's watching the very fact that I've searched for their name just now. *Who are you, SODARCOM? What are you?*

My thoughts are interrupted by a hand on my shoulder, which startles me momentarily, until I realize that it belongs to Genevieve, who has walked up quietly behind me. "Couldn't sleep?" she asks.

"Didn't really want to. I wanted to be awake and aware of holding you close. What about you? How are you doing?"

"As well as can be expected, I guess. This has been a lot to take in."

"Of course."

"It's strange, not being at work," she remarks.

"For now, consider it a vacation. My NP said I have to be at the facility for seven days. Then they can send me home with the pills."

"Where's the one you didn't swallow?" she asks.

"In my pocket. Thank you for reminding me." I abandon my search and bring up a page for a company called Murray Laboratories.

Looking over my shoulder, Genevieve asks, "Who are they?"

"People I work with. They do all the lab-related work for my company. They're in Annapolis, not far from here. I need their help. And yours." I use the land line phone in the bedroom to call the number I find on the computer screen. "Hello, may I speak to Wayne Prescott, please? Tristan Shays calling. … Thank you." In less than a minute, my business associate is on the line with me. "Hello, Wayne. How have you been? … Glad to hear it. Listen, I have a business-related request to make. I'm going to send an associate of mine over to see you. She's going to bring you a pill; I need it analyzed up, down, and sideways. What it is, what's in it, what it does, possible side effects. Can you do that for me? … Great. There's a degree of secrecy about this, so I'd be grateful if you keep the team to one or two of your most trusted people, and have them sign confidentiality agreements. … Thank you. Her name is Genevieve Swan, and she'll be by to see you within the next hour or two. How long do you think it'll be before I get the results? … Three or four days? Ooh. Any chance it could happen quicker than that? … I see. Well, please do the best you can. Money's no object. … Thank you, Wayne. Bye, now."

I end the call and remove the pill from my pocket, handing it to Genevieve. "In the kitchen are zip-top sandwich bags. Please put it in one of them for protection. I'll print out the address of the lab. Best if you go in the next few minutes."

"How will you get to the clinic if I have the car?"

"I can take a cab; that's no problem."

"Yes, but if I'm on my way to Annapolis, you'll be on your own for this afternoon's visit. What if something goes wrong?"

"Just added incentive for me to be careful. If I sense that things are going badly, I'll call your cell phone and leave the message, 'I need a taxi, please.' If you hear that, come rescue me."

"And if I'm an hour away?"

"Then come rescue me eventually."

"All right, but please try not to do anything overly heroic this time around. I'd rather be much closer if a situation arises and you need me."

"That's reasonable. Oh, say, I need your help on something. I was able to avoid swallowing this pill via a faked sneeze. I can't count on doing that every time. What can I do for future doses? I won't need to keep them each time, just not take them, that's all."

"Hmm. Does she hand you the pill?"

"In a manner of speaking. She puts it in a tiny paper cup—you know, the kind you put ketchup in at the burger joint."

"Piece of cake, then. You just need a little sleight of hand. The secret is exaggerated movements. You take the pill cup in one hand and the water cup in another. Hold the pill against the side of the cup with one finger. Make a good showing of pouring the pill into your mouth, all the while holding it in the cup. Then drink the water and do the head tilt and shake to wash it down. Crumple the pill cup, put it into the water cup, and crumple that around it. Put it in your pocket, and it's done."

"You're brilliant, do you know that?"

"Yeah, I kinda do. But it's good to hear."

"I have to go soon," I remind her quietly.

"I know. I guess I do too."

"I'll come back to you."

"You'd better."

Chapter 3

Twenty minutes later, Genevieve is on her way to Annapolis, and I am in the back seat of a taxi, heading back to the Swift Medical Research and Testing Center. Fortunately, my driver is more interested in driving than in talking, so I can be alone with my thoughts as we return to the facility.

Run. That's what the note said. Not "Be careful" or "Things aren't what they seem." But "Run." A single, unambiguous word as an unquestionable warning. Who is she? And who does she think I am that I need to be warned thus? An Internet search for me would yield hundreds of results relating to my work with my company, but nothing to suggest that I was investigating this or anything. For all they know, I'm a rich businessman who fell ill and is looking for a way to alleviate his pain.

And yet this nurse practitioner knew better. Suddenly, the suspicion that I was willing to put aside about this place is back in the forefront. Once again they are suspect in Benton Tambril's death. But how did they do it? Hypnosis? Brainwashing? Mind control of some sort? I have to find out without falling victim to the same forces myself.

Arriving at the facility, I am ushered inside and sent to the same exam room I was in this morning. Coincidence? Maybe. Or maybe it's the one with the cameras. I'd like to see some others, to see if they all

31

share this level of security. If not, it supports my theory that they're on to me and keeping a close eye.

Within the first couple of minutes, Cheryl enters the room. When she makes eye contact, I swear I see something visit her expression, just for an instant: surprise. As if she didn't expect me to return after her warning. She can't press the issue, of course, and I can't ask her about it, so the expected interchange follows.

"Good to see you again," she says pleasantly. "Any difficulties since you've been away?"

"No. Just went and got some rest. Wanted to make sure I was back in time for my next appointment."

"Well, you did just fine. Let's get a quick listen to your heart and your breathing."

She takes the stethoscope and listens to my heartbeat and then instructs me to take some deep breaths. "Any difficulty breathing?" she asks.

"Not that I'm aware of."

"Have you given some thought to the exercise that I recommended?"

Interesting. I didn't think she'd press the point here. "It sounds like a good idea," I reply, "but I need to look into it first, see what's the best plan for someone in my situation."

"Well, that's good. Just don't put it off. The health benefits begin the sooner you start."

"Thank you. I'll do that."

"I need to get your pain level," she says. "Need me to bring the chart out again?"

"No, I think I've got the visuals down. At the moment, I'm going to say the pain is a six."

"So, about what it was after the last dose took effect. No better, no worse?"

"Yeah. A six."

She gets a cup of water and a smaller cup with a pill in it. "Let's see what this dose can do then."

She hands them to me and watches as I tip the pill cup into my mouth. Seconds later, I drink the contents of the water cup and make pronounced movements with my head to indicate the act of washing the pill down. I then crumple the pill cup, put it inside the water cup, crumple that, and put both in my pants pocket—with the pill safely inside. The action is smooth—I think—but I watch Cheryl as she watches me, and there's something hidden deep behind her eyes that tells me she suspects the ruse. She doesn't even ask for the empty cups; this alone strikes me as odd. But if she's not going to ask, I'm not going to offer.

"Let's have you lie down for a bit while that takes effect."

"I've been lying down most of the afternoon," I reply. "I'd rather … well, I'd rather see some more of the facility if I can. I've barely seen any of it, and I think it's so great what you're doing here."

Now she's looking at me intently; this is clearly way out of the ordinary, and it's probably a bad idea. Still, I trust her not to let me do anything that'll put me in immediate danger. "Well," she says, "it works faster if you rest, but I suppose we can bend the rules this once. I can't let you wander around by yourself, but I have a few minutes before another patient arrives, so I can show you around."

Cheryl opens the door to the exam room and steps out into the corridor, inviting me to follow. I try to take it all in, as white-coated medical professionals go from place to place, some carrying clipboards, others carrying trays of equipment, still others carrying laptop computers. Ashen-faced patients sit in waiting rooms. Phones ring, but not many. Also absent are the expected announcements over the public address system. I guess I expect it from years of hospital shows; but this is no ordinary hospital. There is a prevailing quietness here, born perhaps of solemnity, perhaps of secrecy.

"This is the main patient area," Cheryl says, and I am aware of the hush in her voice as well. "Here we have the exam rooms and the waiting rooms, a few labs for running tests. Because of the nature of the trial, we do all our lab work in house."

A bit further down the corridor, I see an open exam room—just what I've been looking for. "What's this?" I ask, already knowing the answer. But it gives me a chance to get ahead of her and enter the room first. A glance upward tells me what I need to know: there are cameras in here too.

"Just another exam room," she replies, following me inside. "I don't think it's any more interesting than the one you were in."

Satisfied with what I've found, I venture back into the corridor. Cheryl shows me conference rooms and even a staff room. But there's more, and I know it. "This is a two-story building," I point out. "What's on the second floor? Can we go up there?"

"I'm sorry, but we can't. It's not allowed. The second floor is the inpatient rooms. Some members of the study are quite ill, and they're in residence here, receiving their medication in a hospice-like environment. For their privacy, no visitors are allowed. They get round-the-clock care and intensive pain management to help ease their passing."

A thought occurs to me. The phone call I received the other day; the mysterious caller who knew details about this place but wouldn't leave his name. I wonder if he could be on the second floor. "The patients up there," I say to her, "do they have phones?"

"Phones?" she repeats, sounding surprised at the question.

"Either land lines provided by the facility or access to their own mobile phones?"

"No. There are no phones in the rooms, and besides, most of them are far too ill to talk to anyone anyway. Why do you ask?"

Why do I ask? That's an unusual question, certainly. "Well, the fact of the matter is, if I get worse, if I end up there, I'd like to be able to talk to people."

She offers me a kind smile and a gentle hand on my shoulder. "Tristan, I understand the fear and the uncertainty, but I don't want you to worry. You're young, in good health, and taking a proactive response to your illness. Most of the people on the second floor are quite elderly and suffering from very aggressive, late-stage cancers. I really don't think you'll end up there." At this moment, the hand on my shoulder gives a gentle but very noticeable squeeze. "Especially if you follow the exercise regimen I suggested."

I greet her words with surprised silence. Once again she is reaching out to warn me, to tell me that this second level is the place I could end up if I'm not careful. The place people go to die.

"Time to send you home again," she says pleasantly. "Where would you say you are on that pain scale this time?"

"Let's go crazy and say five."

"That's good. A little bit of progress each time. Just in case you're not sick of seeing this place yet, I want you back here in four hours for your third dose of the day, okay?"

"Okay." She's such a comfort; there's so much I want to say to her, but I don't dare. "Thank you, Cheryl. Really. You're making this so much easier for me."

"That's my job. Now go out and enjoy this day. We got a little break in the heat."

I bid her good-bye for now and exit the building. Outside, as she said, the heat has eased up a bit, making it a warm but pleasant afternoon. With the raising of a single hand, I hail a taxi, which pulls to a stop at the curb in front of me.

I open the back door and climb in, glancing up at the driver. He's an older man, looking more like a professor than a cab driver. "Where would you like to go?" he asks.

"Can you take me somewhere I can just sit and think?"

"We can do that," he says pleasantly. "Get comfortable."

He starts the meter and pulls away from the curb. "What brings you to Washington?" he asks.

"I'm on business. Something I have to do."

"Sounds serious."

"It is."

"Something you have to do, but maybe not something you want to do?" he asks.

"Lately, what I want to do and what I have to do are two very different things. I have a responsibility—things I'm entrusted to perform. It's dangerous, and it's difficult, but I have to do it."

"How do you know you're on the right path?"

"I'm guided," I reply, unsure why I'm engaging in this discussion but unable to stop.

"Are you guided today? To this place? To Swift?"

"What are you talking about?" I ask him, a feeling of uneasiness starting to creep over me.

"The medical facility. The reason you came to DC. I'm just wondering if you're here for the right reasons. Or have you gone rogue?"

"What is this?" I reach for the door handle, but I can see that the door is locked, and we're traveling at thirty-five miles per hour anyway.

Even if I knew how to do something heroic like tuck and roll or some shit, I'd be a pavement pastry.

The cabbie continues in his calm, fatherly way. "You have a gift, Tristan, but with it comes certain rules and responsibilities."

"Who sent you?" I pause to marvel at the observation that I've just used the words *Who sent you?* and it felt less weird than I thought.

"We've been trying to reach out to you. Trying to help you."

"Are you with the people at the facility? Or did Ephraim send you?"

"You don't even know who your friends are, Tristan. Doesn't that trouble you?"

"Of course it troubles me!" *Composure being so overrated, and all.* "Why are you saying this?"

"Because you're about to go somewhere to sit and think. I just want to give you something to think about. You receive information, you act on it, and you save lives. Where is the information that sent you *here?* Who said to come to this place and open yourself up to such risk? To risk the life of someone you care about deeply?"

"Who are you?" I ask, afraid of the answer.

"The answer won't mean anything to you yet. One day it will, but not yet. For now, you just have to make the wise decision to leave here. Don't go back to that place. It's not safe."

"But if it's not safe for me, it's not safe for others. *That's* why I'm here; with or without specific instructions, I know that what they're doing in that facility is wrong. And I think you know it too. What can you tell me about SODARCOM?"

"Shh, shhhh. The less you know, the better. Knowledge isn't always a good thing. We're watching you the best we can, but we can't always be there to protect you."

The cab pulls to a stop at the curb. "I want to get out," I tell him. "Please let me out."

The doors unlock, and in that same pleasant tone, he says, "It's okay. We're here. No charge for the ride. Just be safe and follow the path you're meant to follow."

Without another word, I bolt from the cab, and he pulls away. It takes me a few seconds to realize that he's let me out at the National Mall, right by the reflecting pool that separates the Lincoln Memorial and the World War II Memorial. My head is spinning, overwhelmed by what this stranger said; a stranger to me, but not the other way around. What have I gotten myself into?

I half-walk, half-stagger to a bench, looking—I'm quite sure—like the victim of some really bad drugs ... or some really good ones. As I find a place of inner calm, I allow myself to sit and breathe, relax and think.

The ringing of my cell phone startles me, to the point where it actually takes me a moment to remember exactly where I am. I pull it out of my pocket and read the screen, which says *Genevieve calling*. To my surprise, it also says 4:25 p.m. Somehow, I have been sitting here for almost two hours. *She must be worried.* I answer quickly. "Hello?"

"Where are you?" she asks, dispensing with pleasantries. "Are you safe?"

"I'm safe. I'm fine. After my second dose, I took a cab. I'm at the National Mall."

"The National Mall? What are you doing there?"

"Losing all track of time, apparently. Where are you?"

"At the apartment."

"Can you come pick me up? We have time to get dinner somewhere before I have to go back to the facility."

"All right. I can be there in a little bit. Where will you be, exactly?"

"On a bench by the reflecting pool, by the end closer to the Lincoln Memorial."

"Okay, thanks. Sit tight. I'll be there. I'm just ... I'm glad you're okay."

"I'm fine."

Within twenty minutes, Genevieve joins me on the bench. At first, she simply sits quietly, and for a few seconds, neither of us knows what to say. She turns and puts her arms around my neck and shoulders.

"Something's going on," I tell her quietly.

"Tristan, it's you. Something's been going on since the day I met you."

"No, this is different. Well, not really different, but kind of the same. A different kind of same. The cab driver who brought me here knew my name."

"As in remembered it after you told him?"

"As in knew it without my telling him. He told me that I have a gift, but there are rules, and I have to follow the right path. He told me that I'm not supposed to be here."

She lets out a little sigh. "That's a relief."

"Why is it a relief?"

"You've been unsure if this is the right course of action, whether you should be here, doing this. Now you've met someone who obviously knows you, knows where you're supposed to be and what you're supposed to be doing, and he told you that this isn't the right path. I think that's the sign you've been waiting for."

"You're just going to believe him?" I ask, surprised.

"I ... I guess. Shouldn't I?"

She's not seeing what I'm seeing. "Let me ask you this: who would want the good guys to stop going after the bad guys, the good guys or the bad guys?"

"The ... bad guys?"

"Yes. And if the bad guys want the good guys to stop going after the bad guys, wouldn't it make sense for them to make the good guys think *they* were the good guys too?"

"Probably."

"So you see?"

She looks confused. "Not really."

"They waited for me to leave the facility, and they sent someone to pick me up and pretend to be on my side. Someone who would warn me about the dangers of being here and suggest that this isn't where I'm supposed to be. They want me gone before I figure out what they're up to."

"That means you're going to stay, doesn't it?"

"You sound disappointed."

"I was so worried," she says. "The whole way there and the whole way back. I kept thinking, what if something went wrong? I don't know if I can keep doing this. Living in fear this way."

"I understand. And I'm sorry. It's a lot to ask. Much too much to ask. Let's go get some dinner, and we can talk about the day. After dinner, if this is too much, I'll get you home."

"Tristan, I—"

"It's okay. We'll figure it out."

We drive to a French seafood restaurant that touts "fine dining in a casual atmosphere." Works for me, as neither of us is particularly dressed for formal. We ask for and are shown to a table in a corner of the restaurant, away from other diners. For appetizers, I order escargot, while she opts for the crab cake. She chooses monkfish for the entrée, and I go for eel.

Before the first course arrives, we compare notes. "How did today go?" I ask.

"Fine, I guess. I found the place, saw the person you talked about, and delivered the pill to them. Like they said, it'll be a few days before they know anything, but they'll call you once they find out."

"Did they ask a lot of questions?"

"None. Apparently, the fact that it's you asking for this was good enough for them. What about you? How did the second visit of the day go?"

I tell her about my afternoon visit, including the impromptu tour around the facility. The conversation doesn't return to the cab driver and his warning; it doesn't have to. She knows how I feel. Now more than ever, I know that I'm on to something, and it's making them nervous. They're trying to throw me off the trail. Inventing allies to protect me? Nice try. I know I'm in this alone. Yes, Genevieve's on my side, and she'd do anything I asked her to do, but when it comes down to it, I'm on my own. *Going rogue,* the cab driver said. If that's what it takes, yes. I may be on the side of goodness and light, but if they push me, they'll see a side of me so dark they won't know what they're up against.

Dinner is good; quiet, but good. I've upset her, I know that. Something tells me she didn't know the full extent of what she was getting herself into, even after the time we'd spent together previously. I could try to reason with her, but I'm afraid I'll end up upsetting her even more. She's got enough on her mind, what with her sister's warning to come back safely. At this point, the best I can do is to cut my losses, finish this mission as quickly as possible, and if it's not too much trouble, try not to get us both killed while doing so.

I take Genevieve back to the apartment so she can rest, as I make my way back to Swift for my final non-dose of the day. As they have each time, they check my identity and show me to the same waiting room. To my surprise, it is Cheryl who enters the room for the third time today. "Not possible," I say to her with a little smile. "You do go home sometimes, right?"

"Frequently," she says. "Every day, in fact. I chose to work overtime today so I could be here for your final dose of the day, so you'd have some continuity. Don't get used to it, though. I can't put in these kind of hours every day."

"That's fine. I'm kind of glad you're here. This whole thing is a little scary, and it's good to have a familiar face to see me through it today."

"Any problems since the last time I saw you?" she asks.

"No. Some anxiety, but that might have nothing to do with the medication. It's just this whole thing."

"It's a big change. I understand. Am I right that you were just diagnosed within the past year?"

I truly hope that my answer supports the fiction I've created when I say, "Yes."

"That comes with a lot of information. You have all kinds of choices to make, paths to follow, treatments to consider. Then something like this study comes along, and you wonder if it's legitimate. You wonder if they're really looking out for the patients. And are the patients here because they really want help, or are they just drug-seeking? There's bound to be some anxiety. After a few more days here, that should pass, and you'll start to feel at ease again."

"Thank you, Cheryl."

"You bet. I'm gonna go get your final pill for the day. In the meantime, I've got a task for you." She hands me a piece of paper and a pen. "On here, I want you to write down everything you've eaten today. We need to keep track of it. I'll be back in a minute or two."

With that, she leaves me alone—or as alone as closed-circuit cameras allow me to be. I think back over the day's meals and write down the components of each. As I finish, just as I am about to put the pen down, a thought hits me, a stupid, very dangerous thought that should not be acted upon under any circumstances. Which is why it takes me five whole seconds to decide to act upon it.

At the bottom of the page, far from the words above it, I write five additional words, words meant for Cheryl's eyes alone: *Have lunch with me tomorrow.* They are words I dare not speak in this well-monitored room. Writing them down is bad enough. I have to count on her seeing them and finding a way to separate that part of the page from the rest of it without it being conspicuous to her employers.

And what do I expect in response? For her to read it and say, "Sure, lunch tomorrow would be great! What should we talk about?" How could she even reply without everyone knowing? It's a fool's maneuver, and I briefly contemplate crossing it out or crumpling up the page and starting over. But then she walks in with the pill in a cup, and I do nothing about it.

"All done with that?" she asks. I reply simply by handing it to her. "Let's have a look." As she reads, she says, "That's good. Good. Fine. That's—" At that moment, I see her come to the words at the bottom, and they stop her in mid-sentence. She's quick enough to realize what a hesitation would look like, and she promptly finishes. "That's a little high in fat, that last one. You'll want to limit your intake." She slides the page into my file in one rapid movement.

High in fat? Is it code? Some sort of clandestine reply that I need to interpret? Does high in fat mean yes, while high in cholesterol means no? Or did I just catch her off guard and she had to say something? Her eyes are inscrutable, not inviting or scolding.

"Time for the tip and swish," she says, offering the cups.

Dutifully, I pantomime the swallowing of my third time bomb of the day. Once again, the offender goes into a crumpled heap in my pocket. And once again, her expression betrays nothing—not complicity, not detection, not disappointment, not relief. I hope I never have to play poker against this woman. She will kick my ass.

"Go home," she says.

Though the words lack ambiguity, I am nonetheless confused. "Excuse me?"

"Go home for the evening. I've got enough information for the day. We can get detailed notes in the morning. It's important that you sleep well tonight. If you have any side effects or extreme symptoms between now and morning, call this number." She hands me a business card with a local number on it. "Don't go to an emergency room or another facility. They won't know how to treat you in light of the medication; we will."

As I prepare to make my way out of the room, I watch her face for any sign of a reply to my invitation—a smile, a wink, a nod, a facial tic, anything. But she just maintains her composure. She must know better than I how watchful those cameras are and how risky it would be to be caught fraternizing with a patient—particularly if they know the real reason I'm here.

Out in the parking lot, I get into my car and start the engine. My first day at the Swift Medical Research and Testing Center is done. For reasons still unclear to me, I have not been captured, questioned, tortured, experimented upon, molested, damaged, or otherwise killed. I think that makes it a good day. I may even get a milkshake on the way back to the apartment.

Fifteen minutes later, milkshake blissfully consumed—chocolate-banana, by the way; I found a place that would mix flavors—I park the car in the lot behind the apartment building that currently serves as home. As I enter the apartment, I see Genevieve in the living room, sitting in a chair; not reading, not watching TV, not doing anything, just sitting. Were it not for her eyes being so obviously open, I would swear she was asleep.

No words pass between us as I stand there in the room. I look at her and she at me. Her expression is impenetrable, and it's unsettling me terribly. I search for something to say, any words that will break through this barrier that stands between us. Mercifully, it is she who finds the first foray into conversation. "You have chocolate on your nose," she says quietly.

She is correct. I rectify the problem. "Thank you."

"Are you all right?"

"Yes."

"You didn't take the pills?"

"No."

"I thought I could do this."

"This?" I repeat, seeking clarity.

"Be here. Stand vigil. Hold down the fort. It should be easy."

"But it's not?"

"No. I think it may be the hardest thing I've ever had to do. I can't focus or concentrate enough to do anything meaningful. All I can do is wait here and think far too much."

"What do you think about?"

"About you, and whether you're the person I'm supposed to spend my life with."

"That's a big question," I remind her.

"Of course it is. You'd be surprised how much thinking you can do in hours of silence and solitude. I get the little questions out of the way early. What will I wear? What's for breakfast tomorrow?"

"Ooh, and …?"

"Scrambled eggs with goat cheese and tomato, toasted sourdough bread, and corn muffins."

"I like those things."

"I like them too," she says, standing up. Finally, her face gives up an expression, and it is one of barely contained emotional turmoil. "And if we were here, having these things, playing house for a week, I'd be so stupidly happy, I could barely stand it. But we're not just playing house. We're playing something else, too, and I don't even know what to call it. Cops and robbers? Angels and demons? I don't know. All I can do is sit and hope that the phone doesn't ring and tell me that you're never coming back to me."

If I don't put my arms around her at this point, then I am the most heartless creature ever to draw breath. Fortunately, that's not what I am. She allows me to hold her, as her tears dampen my shoulder with the release she's needed for many hours.

"What should we do?" I ask her. "Do you want to go home?"

"Yes. But not without you."

"I can't. Not yet. Today was successful, and there was no show of force on their part. I asked my nurse practitioner if she'd meet with me tomorrow to tell me what she knows. I'm hoping she'll take me up on it."

"So you're staying?"

"Five days. Give me five days here to learn what I can. When that's over, I'll take us both out of here, and then we can contemplate those big questions together."

"Five days? You promise?"

"I promise."

"Okay."

Chapter 4

All things considered, I get a restful night's sleep. I fully expected to toss and turn, anxious about this mission and about the way I know Genevieve is feeling. But when I see her able to sleep, it gives me an unspoken permission to do likewise, and I do. The feeling is a great relief; I was tired and stressed when I went to bed, but upon awakening, I feel more at peace with myself and with what I have to do. A glance at the bedside clock tells me that it's just after 7:00 in the morning; a glance in the other direction shows me that Genevieve is still asleep. Not wanting to wake her, I quietly slip out of bed to start my day.

Remembering what Genevieve had told me she was making for breakfast today, I decide to take the initiative to make it for her—for us. I owe her that, and a lot more, I'm sure. The fact is, I haven't been romantically attentive to her, despite her clear signals of interest. It's not that I'm uninterested; far from it. She's lovely, desirable, sexy. And it's not performance anxiety on my part, thank you very much. If called into action, certain parts would be ready for service. Instead there's something distressing about the concept of bonding this way, letting her get this close when I know how very real and immediate the danger is. I'm already falling in love with her; with the level of intimacy we both want, things will change. I know myself; I know what will happen. I'll get all protective of her, keeping her out of harm's way. And we just don't have that luxury this week.

Within half an hour, coffee is on, muffins are in the oven, and breakfast is in progress on the stove top. Gen walks—shuffles a bit, really—out of the bedroom and into the kitchen. She looks at me in the middle of my culinary duties and asks, "What's this?"

"It's obvious—you can see the future. Everything that you said would be for breakfast is here."

"I was fully ready to make it. You didn't have to go to any trouble."

"It isn't trouble when I enjoy it, and I do, so there."

"Well, thank you," she says, moving toward the coffee with clear intent.

"You're welcome. Did you sleep?"

"I did. Did you?"

"Yeah, I did, thanks. It's a relief. I wasn't sure I would, but I guess I was really tired."

"What time are you going in to Swift today?"

"I'll go in for the first dose at 10:00. I'm still hoping that Cheryl, the nurse practitioner, will have lunch with me, so 10:00 would give us both time in between."

"Do you really think she'll be able to tell you what you need to know?"

"I don't know. If she's part of the clandestine shit that's going on, probably not. Either that or she'll deliberately mislead me, to throw me off. But if what I suspect is true, and she's a good person who took a job without knowing what she was getting into, then maybe she'll see me as someone who can help her and everyone else at that place."

"I hope you're right."

"So do I. I took a big risk, inviting her to meet me the way I did."

"Don't let her trick you. She may pretend to be your ally but secretly be working for them."

She's right, and I know it, but I don't have words to admit it. Fortunately, the timer gives a very convenient ding at this moment, allowing me a graceful exit from the discussion with the words, "Muffins are ready."

The morning passes too quickly and with too many important things left unsaid. But today is a turning point; I can feel it. Today I will find out if my mission is justified, if my cause is right, and if I can help the people I came here to help. As I enter the facility, I'm struck by how oddly familiar it feels already. After just one day, I know where to go, who to talk to, what to present to them. I call staff members by their first names, and they me by mine. They make me feel welcome, cared about, appreciated. And I don't know what to do with that.

My morning appointment with Cheryl is entirely uneventful. She asks about my night's sleep and my meals, she checks my vital signs, she asks me to rate the level of my pain. When she's satisfied with my fabricated information, she gives me the morning dose of the drug, I pretend to take it, I thank her for her time, and I prepare to make my way out of the exam room. And that would have been the end of it, if it weren't for the little slip of paper she very discreetly slides into my hand while taking me by the wrist to help me stand up from the exam table where I'd been sitting.

It takes me a moment to realize what's happening, and when I do, I have very little opportunity to react. Instead, I hide the paper with my fingers and exit the room, trying to look like everything is perfectly normal. Out of the building, out of the parking lot, a full mile away from the facility before I even dare to look. At a red light, I unfold the little slip, which simply says: *Finn's. Emerald and 14th Street. 12:30 p.m.*

It's on.

I hurry home and excitedly announce upon entering, "I did it! I got the meeting!"

Genevieve comes out of the bathroom and asks, "What meeting?"

"The meeting. The one I've wanted. The private meeting with Cheryl!"

"The nurse?"

"Yes. Well, nurse practitioner, but yes. She agreed to meet me for lunch today."

"That's good," she says. "Can I come too?"

I'm unprepared for that question. "Umm ... I— I don't think it's a good idea."

"Why not?" she inquires calmly.

"Well, because it's not really about lunch."

"And just what is it about?"

"Gen, it's nothing like that. I just need an opportunity to drill her ..."

"What?"

"Not drill her. I mean pump her—"

"That's not better."

"For information. Interrogate her completely non-sexually. Please tell me that's not jealousy I'm hearing from you."

"Maybe it is. I don't know."

"Jesus, Genevieve, what the hell is going on? You were so keen on being here with me to help me and support me during this mission, but ever since we got here, you've been unhappy, suspicious, quiet. Exactly what have I done to earn all this?"

I brace myself for a shouting match, for accusations, for well-deserved barbs about my lack of attentiveness, my singleness of focus, my callous disregard for my safety as well as hers. But none of that comes my way. Instead, her eyes get wide for a second and then snap shut, her face screws up, and tears begin to flow, accompanied by the most doleful sobs I've ever heard.

Fuck me. I hate making people cry.

"Gen, I ... I'm sorry. Don't cry. Please don't cry." *In front of me.*

"You're right," she sobs.

I am? I thought I was being a dick.

"I'm being selfish and unfair to you, and- and- and ..."

I'm trying very hard not to smile or laugh; she's doing that hitching stutter thing that little kids do when they try to talk while crying. It's making me picture her as a little girl, which must have been adorable, and it's reminding me all over again that I'm falling in love with her. Before she can even finish the sentence, I take her in my arms and hold her close.

"Shhhhh. It's okay. You're not being selfish or unfair. If anybody is, it's me. I put this mission ahead of everything else, including you, and that's very unkind. And I'm very sorry. As soon as we're done here, we'll go somewhere together; wherever you want to go. The Caribbean, Europe, South Pacific. You name it, and it's on me. No missions, either. I'll bring a bottle of Extra-Extra-Extra-Strength Tylenol and tell God he's on his own for two weeks."

"Thank you," she says, starting to subdue the tears. "I'll try very hard not to be unreasonable while we're here. It's just—"

A long pause suggests to me that she's unable to finish that sentence on her own, so I prod her a bit. "Just?"

"This is going to sound stupid or crazy."

"This is me you're talking to," I remind her. "Continue."

"It's just that I have a voice in my head that guides me. It shows me the path I should take, and ever since we got to Washington, I can't hear that voice. That scares me, and I don't know what to do about it."

I don't know what to say to that, but my silence must be reading as criticism, as she continues, "I told you that sounds crazy."

"No," I reply quickly, "no no. Nothing like that. Of all the people in the world, I'm the last one to doubt you when you tell me you're guided by voices. Do you have any idea what's happened to yours?"

She shakes her head. "It's like it's being blocked. Like something is using that channel."

"Today, when I get back, let's open that channel again—together. Like we did in Virginia Beach. Focus your energy and open yourself up to the voices. I'll be here to keep you safe."

"You would do that?"

"That and more. Anything you need to feel safe, grounded, and at peace."

"Thank you," she says, barely above a whisper.

The emotional crisis successfully averted, Genevieve decides to go for a walk to clear her head. This is fine, because it gives me the chance to strategize for my upcoming meeting. I know this is a one-time-only opportunity, so I can't waste it and I can't blow it. There are so many things I want to ask, but will she be able to tell me, even away from the watchful eyes of the Swift facility? It's possible that she doesn't even have all the answers I seek. I just need *something*, some sense of who's behind this, of what they're doing and why. It's too much to hope that she can lead me to the heart of SODARCOM, but if she can even tell me who they are, I'll be much further ahead than I was yesterday.

About twenty minutes before the appointed meeting time, I get into my car and head to the restaurant. I can barely focus, so it's a good thing that I'm relying on maps rather than a GPS to get me there; it gives my poor brain something to do as each block passes, rather than think about the thousand different ways this could go down.

I somehow manage to catch good traffic—which I didn't think existed in big cities, least of all during midday—so I arrive at the address at 12:25, a full five minutes early. I luck into a parking spot right out front, which does nothing to eat up the extra minutes. Too fidgety to stall any longer, I get out of the car and enter the restaurant.

The hostess greets me. "Welcome to Finn's. One today?"

My *voce* gets all *sotto,* and I'm not sure why. "Umm, no, actually. I'm meeting one other person. I'm wondering if you could put us at a table for two in a corner somewhere, someplace quiet where other patrons won't hear us, and the staff won't hear us either, if possible."

She gives me a knowing look, and I realize that I'm describing the ideal circumstances for an illicit romantic encounter. But it's too late now, so I let the request stand.

"Follow me," she says.

The hostess leads me through the dining room to a corner of the restaurant, as requested. Upon arriving, I am surprised to see Cheryl already sitting there, with two drinks on the table and a plate in the middle, covered with tan-colored oval objects. "Is this him?" the hostess asks her.

"Yes, thank you."

"Enjoy your lunch."

The hostess walks away, and I sit, mildly confused. "How long have you …?"

"About ten minutes. I didn't want to risk not getting a private table, so I came early. I ordered sweetened iced tea for both of us; I hope you like it."

"I do. And these things?" I ask, pointing to the objects on the plate.

"Scotch eggs. I figured as important as this conversation is, we shouldn't eat anything more than finger food, so I ordered Scotch eggs."

"And what are Scotch eggs?"

"You've never had them?" I shake my head. "They're hard-boiled eggs wrapped in a thin layer of sausage and deep-fried, served with ranch dressing."

"That sounds amazing and deadly. I thought I was supposed to be watching what I eat."

"Those were the instructions for Tristan Shays the cancer patient. But I don't think that's who's here with me."

Her words leave me silent for a few very uncomfortable seconds. She's fired the first salvo, and it's an icebreaker. The silence hangs between us for several more seconds. When I decide it's time to speak, she and I actually utter the same words at the same moment: "So who are you really?"

"Okay," I say quietly, "that was weird."

"Wait a minute," she says, "are you saying you're here to question me?"

"Are you saying you're here to question *me?*" I retort.

"Of course. Why else would I have come?"

"Because you trusted me and you wanted to tell me about what's really going on at Swift."

She looks confused by this. "What's really going on? You've seen what's really going on."

"I have?"

"Yes."

"So there's nothing sinister, maybe lurking beneath the surface, where the patients and the public can't see?"

"No," she replies. "We're a research-and-development facility for a government agency developing a narcotic designed for cancer patients, to alleviate their pain as they seek treatment."

"So if there's nothing going on, why did you hand me *this?*" I produce the piece of paper that contains her handwritten note: Run. "And please don't tell me it's an exercise plan. I think we both know better."

A guilty look visits her features. "I know you don't have cancer. I see hundreds of people a week who do, and I know that you're healthy. I also know you're not a drug addict seeking free narcotics. We've had our share of those, and they're easy to spot. That leaves one of three possibilities: journalist, corporate spy, or law enforcement. They know you're here; they know you're not a legitimate patient."

"Who's *they?*"

"The people who are conducting the study," she answers.

"You mean SODAR—"

"Shhhh!" Curiously, she stops me in mid-word, yet another person who can't even let this organization's name be spoken. "Yes. They know you're not a real patient, but they don't know why you're here. They wanted me to question you, but not at the facility, where other people could hear. So when you asked me to lunch today, they allowed me to go, knowing this would be my opportunity."

"So they know you're meeting with me."

"Of course."

"Are any of them here?"

"No, I looked. They trust me to get the information they need. If you cooperate and give it to me, they're more likely to let you leave unharmed."

"Unharmed? Listen to what you just said. Are those the words that describe a benevolent organization?"

"They're very protective of their research and their product. If you're a journalist, they can't risk you printing the details of what they're doing until the pills go on the market. If you're in law enforcement, there's nothing illegal to see, so they want you to go peacefully and let them conduct their study without alarming any of the patients. And if you're a corporate spy from another pharmaceutical company ... well, that would be the worst option. They have no patience and no mercy for them. I couldn't guarantee your safety if you were here to steal the drug."

"Cheryl, what if I tell you I'm not any of the three?"

"What does that leave?"

"The answer's a bit complicated, but if you'll hear me out and trust me, I'll tell you." I pick up one of the eggs, dip it in ranch dressing, and take a bite. "I'm here because—holy shit, that's delicious! Why have I never eaten these before?"

With one hand, she conceals a laugh at my reaction. "Would you like to finish that egg before launching into your story?"

"Yes. And maybe three or four more." I finish the egg with amazed delight, clean my fingers with a napkin, and begin again. "I'm here because I have reason to believe that this study isn't what they say it is."

"What is it, then?"

"That's the part I don't know. The part I'm here to find out, and I thought the only way to do that was to take part in the study as a patient."

"But you're not a cop or a fed?"

"No. I'm the CEO of a company that manufactures LED lights." She stares at me for a moment, trying to find the connection. I take the opportunity to snarf another half of a Scotch egg. "That part's unrelated to why I'm here. For the past couple of months, I've started getting … messages, I guess you could call them; warnings about people who are in imminent danger. I know what's going to happen to them, and when and where. I'm given time to warn them, and a couple of weeks ago, I stepped down from my job as CEO so I could devote my time to doing this."

I pause for a moment, awaiting the almost inevitable disdain and disbelief. Strangely, it does not come. Instead she says, "And that's why you're here? You got some kind of message that one of our patients is in danger? You came to warn them, and the only way you could gain access was by pretending to be in the study too?"

"A very good and reasonable assumption, but not quite. This is where it gets strange."

"*This* is where it gets strange?" she says, clearly alluding to the prior revelation.

"Strang*er*. I didn't get a warning this time. I'm not here to save one specific person."

"Then why—?"

"Last week, I did get a message, a warning to go to Virginia and save a man from killing his wife, his two children, and himself." She audibly gasps at this announcement. "When I got there, I found the man and his family, and the warning was right. He was prepared to kill them all."

"What happened?" she asks. "What did you do?"

"I got his wife and kids out of the house, and I talked to him. And I listened to him. Listened to his frustrations and his fears. Listened to him express all his despair and self-loathing. Cheryl, this man was a cancer patient in your study."

"Oh my God …"

"Yeah. He showed me the bottle of pills, the same pills that were given to me yesterday."

"Is it ... can you tell me his name, or are there confidentiality issues?"

"His name was Benton Tambril."

Her face goes ashen at this revelation, and I see the birth of a tear in one eye. "Benton? Did you say *was?*"

"Yes. Despite my best efforts, he took a handgun and ended his life right in front of me."

The first tear is followed by many others. "I thought he ..." She trails off, unable to finish the sentence.

"So you see now why I'm here. I need to know if Benton's suicide—which very nearly included the massacre of his whole family—is connected to the drug trial somehow. While I was still there at the house, a man came in disguised as the police. Cheryl, he took the bottle of pills with him, and then he disappeared from town."

"Who was he?"

"A dangerous individual. Someone who's been trailing my steps, actively working to thwart what I do. His only interest was getting those pills out of there. That's the main reason I suspect a connection. You knew Benton Tambril, didn't you?"

"Yes. I worked with him in the first days of his participation in the trial. I know he was upset, depressed even, but I didn't think he was suicidal."

"He never gave you any indication that he was capable of such a thing? None of the warning signs—talking about death, casually mentioning a desire to die?"

"No," she says, "nothing like that. He was angry about the cancer, but he seemed willing to believe in the pill's ability to help him with the pain."

"What's in those pills?"

"I don't know."

"Cheryl, this is no time to protect a patent. I watched a man put a bullet through his head. I've put my life on hold and myself in jeopardy to come here and see if there's a connection. If you know something that might explain why Benton Tambril killed himself, I need you to tell me."

"It might …"

"Yes?"

"There could be …"

"Cheryl, please! There's more to those sentences. Things they don't want you to tell anyone. Things I need to know."

Fighting back tears, she takes a deep breath, lets it out in one puff of air, and says quietly, "There are possible side effects to the drug."

"Go on."

"Things they told the medical staff about but not the patients. I was concerned about that, but they said that it's common practice in a blind drug trial. If you reveal possible side effects to the testing population, it creates false positives; people believe they have these symptoms. Instead, we ask them if they're experiencing any side effects, and we keep careful track of what they report."

"Have there been any reports of suicidal thoughts or actions?"

"A few. But it's possible that some people don't report them. They think the thoughts are part of the trauma of being diagnosed with cancer, or they're ashamed of having these thoughts, so they say nothing."

"So they're creating a drug that could be persuading people to kill themselves?"

"Please keep your voice down. All drugs have potential side effects. There are several antidepressants that have this exact side effect. It's unfortunate, but it's part of the biochemistry."

"Yes, but with the other drugs, the public is aware of these side effects, and they can watch for them. You have to let the patients know."

"I can't, Tristan. It's not up to me. If they knew that I even told you this, I could lose my job."

"Then I'll tell them I found out on my own. Tell me who they are. Who signs the checks? Who pulls the strings? Cheryl, who or what is SODARCOM?"

"I swear to you, I don't know. If I did, I would tell you, after what I've heard today. But I don't. There are firewalls, layers of secrecy between the Swift staff and the group. I don't know if it's a brand name or an acronym or some other abbreviation. I've tried to research it, but I always come up empty."

"Yeah, so do I. It's maddening. If they're legitimate, why the secrecy? And if they're not, what's the purpose of the drug study?"

"I'm sorry; I wish I could give you more information, but they're very private."

"Are you going to keep working there?" I ask her point blank.

"I don't know. An hour ago, I would have said yes without hesitation, but you've given me a lot to think about. I can stay for now, maybe try to learn more to help you."

"Don't put yourself in danger," I warn.

"I won't. I've never done anything to upset them, so I don't think they consider me a troublemaker."

"Tell me something," I begin. "What would have happened if I'd taken those pills yesterday?"

"Any pain you were feeling would have gone away, but I don't think anything else would have happened. I think you would have been fine."

"The side effects wouldn't have hit me?"

"No. I don't think so, anyway. Some patients reported mood swings or depressed thoughts, but nothing life-threatening."

"Benton Tambril was still in the study, yet you didn't know he had died. Doesn't the group make weekly calls to patients after they leave Swift?"

"Yes."

"And you don't get reports if patients die?"

"Not exactly. Every week, we get what's called a DCP report. It stands for discontinuing participants. Those who drop out of the study. The version the staff gets doesn't include the reason for discontinuing; just the names. It's possible that some of them each week have died or even committed suicide."

"About how many people are on the list each week?" I ask.

"Usually seventy-five to a hundred."

"A hundred who drop out each week? Cheryl, how many people are in this drug trial?"

"I don't know the exact figures, but I think the number is close to sixty thousand."

The statistic hits me like a pie tin filled with rocks. Sixty thousand people, and they're able to keep things this quiet? How can that even be possible? I consider asking her this question, but a quick look at her face tells me that I've already disrupted her inner peace and seriously dislocated her world view. *How the fuck are they doing this?* is clearly a second-date question. Instead, I pose another. "How can I get a hold of the files of patients who have left the facility and are continuing the study at home?"

"That's not possible," she says quickly. "After patients leave Swift, the files get transferred to the SODARCOM central office. I think it's here in Washington, but I don't know where it is. I don't know if anyone at the facility knows where it is. I'm sorry."

"Cheryl, what are they going to do to me?"

"I'm not sure. They know you're not a cancer patient, but they've told me to treat you as if you were. To play along with you and give you the regular doses. I know you weren't taking the pills, but I don't know if they know that."

"I can't imagine they'd be too happy if they knew I was taking the pills out of the facility."

"You did?"

"Yes."

"What did you do with them?"

"Three are in the apartment I'm renting. I sent one to a lab for analysis."

She looks very troubled by this. "Tristan, you shouldn't have! Which lab was it?"

"I'm not saying. This time, the less *you* know, the better. I'm not going to share the results with any other pharmaceutical company. I just want to know what's in these pills. Especially now that I know about the side effects."

"Be careful. Please be careful. They're interested in you, and they want to keep you alive, but I've seen what they've done to investigative journalists and one undercover cop who came through Swift. I don't want that to happen to you; that's why I told you to run."

"I'll be okay. But what about you?"

"I should be fine. After all, I'm here with their permission, and I can tell them that you're not a threat—or whatever they need to hear to keep you safe. But I need you to stop trying to communicate covertly with me. If you're going to stay in the program, you have to play the part of the dutiful patient. Don't snoop around, don't ask questions, and only go where you're told."

"I can't promise that," I answer honestly.

"Then I can't protect you."

Many seconds of tense silence pass between us before she says, "I have to get back. We should leave separately."

"I'll get the check," I reply. "Thank you for trusting me with this information."

"Thank you for lunch. Don't be late for your appointment this afternoon."

Without another word, she gets up, leaves the table, and hurries out of the restaurant, leaving me alone with a hundred more questions, half a glass of iced tea, and three Scotch eggs that are sure as hell not going to waste.

I return to the apartment with just as many new questions as answers I've received. Genevieve looks calmer, better rested than she did when I left. I fill her in as best I can, given the incomplete information I now possess. She's intrigued and just as curious as I am.

"What do you think it means?" she asks.

"I have some possible ideas, but I don't like the implications of any of them. The possibility exists that this is a legitimate drug trial, and they're using human lab animals to work through the dangerous side effects. After all, they're cancer patients; they're gonna die anyway, whether it's from the disease or by their own hand."

"That sounds so callous."

"Yeah, and it's the less sinister possibility."

She blanches at this. "Do I want to hear the *more* sinister?"

"What if it's a testing ground for some kind of new bio-weapon? Maybe the government is working on a drug they can test on our enemies, something that makes them turn violent toward their families and themselves. They test it on cancer patients to see if the narcotic effects and the side effects work. Then, once they find that it works, it mysteriously never makes it to the US market, but it turns up on the streets of places like Iraq, Afghanistan, Saudi Arabia. We make a big show of providing medical aid to our former enemies, and then, after the initial good feelings calm down, people there start mysteriously dying. Will anyone there think to tie it to the drug? Maybe, but maybe not. Overseas, domestic violence is prevalent, and suicide? Probably the same story."

"I don't want to believe that our government is capable of that," she replies softly.

"They've done worse, and they'll do it again. But if we can stop this, or at least expose it, maybe they won't be quite so quick to try something like this next time. Gen, I know this trip has been an ordeal for you already, but do you see the need for me to be here, to try this?"

"Yes. How can I help, though?"

I think a moment, and an idea I'd been percolating on the drive back to the apartment stirs inside me. "You remember on the day we met, in your hotel room, how you opened yourself up?"

"I hardly think *that* will help our cause!"

"No no, not like that. How you opened yourself up to channel voices from somewhere else?"

"Yes."

"What if we do that again here? Only this time, instead of being open to just anyone who's listening, we adjust the dial a little. I guide the session, and we invite anyone who has additional knowledge about these people and their operation."

"Tristan, I don't know. Channeling always comes with risks. There's always a chance that something less than pleasant can come through me."

"I'll watch for that, and if it happens, I'll bring you out. That should be the end of it, right?"

"In theory," she says. "There have been reports of cases where it wasn't."

Unpleasant as that possibility is, I still think we should try. "Are you willing to attempt it?" I ask her.

She hesitates a moment before answering, "Yes."

We go to the bedroom and she sits cross-legged on the bed, closing her eyes and breathing deeply for a few minutes. I opt to keep silent, as my voice would only be a distraction to her as she prepares for this process. I stand there, watching her prepare to use her mind and body as a gateway to entities unknown, and I realize that six months ago, if someone were to tell me about this—let alone show me the process—I would have thought them to be out of their mind. Six months ago, the world made sense. There was science and nature, and there were laws that govern things. There was no such thing as channeling or psychic ability or precognitive warnings from unknown realms. How blind I was, I realize now.

I think back on all the people who believe in such things, and how I considered them to be gullible, uneducated dreamers. But of course they believe. A world in which such things are possible is a fascinating world, a world of boundless possibility, where God-or-someone-like-him really *is* watching out for us, and death might not be the end of everything that we so desperately fear it is.

A glance back at Genevieve tells me that she is there—wherever *there* is. No fear this time, and no hesitation. I stand before her and announce, "I seek audience with one who will speak with me."

Genevieve's eyes snap open, but it's clear to me that it is not she who is looking at me. There is someone or something present behind her eyes, calling the shots. "Approach," it says.

I take a step forward. "Who speaks with me now?" I ask, in a speech pattern I don't think I've ever used before.

"Ethrais-en-Uhen-Ra, sentinel," comes the response, in a baritone I wouldn't have thought Genevieve Swan's vocal cords capable of producing. "Put out your hand that we may know you."

I extend my hand slowly, and like a shot, the entity borrowing Genevieve takes it in its grasp. Her touch is cold, but at the same time I feel a latent electricity through her fingertips. I am making a very diligent effort not to lose my shit and start babbling. *Focus on what you know.* "I am Tristan Shays."

"Yes," it responds coolly, "at present." *Curious answer. God, I wish I was videotaping this.* "Why have you come?"

"This woman and I seek answers that we can't find on our own. We seek the knowledge of one who will speak truth, for the sake of good in the world."

Silence is my reply for several seconds, as the sentinel's eyes bore into my face. "Ask."

"What is SODARCOM, and what are their intentions?"

The grip on my hand tightens and the eyes close. Did my question offend, or is the sentinel seeking others who might know? Seconds pass, I don't know how many, and then Genevieve opens her eyes again—opens *someone's* eyes, at least.

From her lips, a voice not hers asks, "Why am I here?"

"I summoned you," I answer, figuring it's as good an explanation as any. "What's your name?"

"I am ... I *was* ... Michael Saunders." The voice sounds almost fearful.

"Michael, I'm Tristan. I need your help. I think you're here because you know about something I need to know. What can you tell me about SODARCOM?"

The word evokes a reaction of shock and fear on Genevieve's face. I watch in wonder as she starts to cry his tears. "I'm sorry," the bodiless spirit sobs, "I'm sorry. I did as I was told. They said it was for the greater good. Those were the words: for the greater good."

"Michael, listen to me. Please listen. No one's here to blame you or condemn you. I just need to know what SODARCOM is. Anything you can tell me. Who they are, where they're located, what they do. What is it they did for the greater good?"

"Can't speak of it. Signed a promise not to speak of it."

"You're free from that promise now. You can tell me. Who are they, and what is it they're doing?"

"Many ... people," he says timidly, now in control of his emotions, "one cause. Many people. One cause. Many people. One cause."

"Yes, yes, that's good," I reply, trying to keep my patience. "Who are the people, and what is the cause?"

"Tell them you're strong. It's safe if you're strong."

"Strong? What—?"

Without another word, Genevieve's eyes close, and I feel that Michael Saunders is gone. Before too much else happens, I write his name down on a pad of paper on the bedside table. When my back is turned, I hear a voice, a woman's voice, but not Genevieve's, though it comes from her.

"Well, what's *this?*"

I hurry back to stand in front of her again and see a strange expression on her face, something playful and maybe even a little dangerous.

"Did the sentinel send you?" I ask, unsure of what I'm facing.

"No, I just kind of turned up," she says.

"Are you here because you can help me?"

"Oh, I can help you. I can help you with a lot of things."

"What can you tell me about SODARCOM?"

"So dark? Is that what your world is? So dark? So dreary? I can help that too."

Something's not right. "Who are you?"

"A new friend," she says.

"Spirit, I command you to tell me who you are!"

Genevieve's face shows surprised amusement, and she lets out a little laugh. "Spirit? Oh, my. You're new at this, aren't you? Somebody read too much Dickens in high school? I'm very much alive, muffin. Question is: are you?"

"Yeah. I'm alive. And I don't have time to waste with you."

Her tone pretends hurt feelings. "Ohhhh, that's not nice. We'll have time later. I didn't expect to find you here, but thank you for making it so convenient."

The next few seconds are a blur, an unexpected, rather horrible blur. I feel myself extend my right hand and deliver a firm slap to Genevieve's face with an open palm. The force of it knocks her backward on her back onto the bed. At the same time, it breaks the connection, closing the doorway she had opened. A shriek of pain and surprise escapes her lips—her own pain and surprise—and in that same moment, I grasp with stunned realization what I have done. Mortified, I rush to her side. "Honey, I'm so sorry. I'm so, so sorry!"

"You … hit me," she says, astonished.

"I did, but it wasn't me. Well, no, it was me. But it wasn't you."

With a hand to her injured face, she says in an angry voice, "It was me. Trust me."

"Someone else was here. A woman … a living woman. She was speaking through you, trying to manipulate me. I lashed out. I don't know if I was trying to break the trance or just hurt her, but— Here, wait here. I'll get some ice."

I quickly grab some ice and put it in a wet washcloth, holding it to her cheek. "I'm sorry. I would never deliberately hurt you."

"What happened here?" she asks.

I recount the discussion with the three visitors, with particular interest in the words of Michael Saunders, the one who came closest to telling me what I needed to know.

"I could try to go under again," Genevieve says, the concern evident in her voice.

"No. Thank you, but no. I don't know who that was who showed up at the end, but she was trouble. I know that much. I don't want her to have access to you again." A difficult question is lurking beneath the surface, and I have to ask. "There's no easy way to ask this, but … do you feel like you're … alone again? Are you sure they're not still with you?"

"I'm alone. If they were still here, I'd know."

"Is there anything I can get you? Anything I can do for you?"

"Not hitting me ever again would be a really good start," she says.

"I'm sorry. It was a terrible thing to do."

"I think I need to be alone for a while."

"Okay. I have to go in for my afternoon appointment anyway. If you need me, or if anything happens, please call me."

I don't know what came over me. In the minutes spent alone in the car between the apartment and the medical facility, I go over it again and again in my head. The sentinel; the crying man; the dark woman. Why did they show up in particular? I think back to the first channeling session with Genevieve in Virginia, how a single voice appeared and spoke to me as if it knew me. *Find the singularity,* it told me. But what is a singularity? It's the quality of being unique or even peculiar, but I don't think that's what it meant. I think it was referring to a singularity in the astronomical sense; a black hole. A force so powerful that it draws everything to itself, even light. But where is it, and how do I find it?

I try to put these thoughts out of my mind as I arrive at the facility. Cheryl needs me to play the role of patient. I can do this—for now. It's important for my safety and hers. So I park in the lot, and I greet the guard at the door and the nurse at the registration desk. And just like every other time, I wait for a few minutes until I'm sent to the same exam room. I make myself comfortable for about five minutes, until the door opens and in walks—

A short woman of about fifty I've never seen before. *What?*

"Mr. Shays, is it?"

"Yes, that's right." *What?*

"I'm Greta. I'll be your nurse practitioner for the duration of the study."

"I ... I don't understand. Where's Cheryl?"

"Cheryl doesn't work here anymore."

"What!"

Chapter 5

"What do you mean she doesn't work here anymore?" I ask in astonishment. "She worked here this morning. She treated me this morning."

"Mr. Shays, you need to stay calm. I know that it's very easy to become attached to your healthcare provider, but I assure you that I can and will deliver the very best care to you. I have all of Cheryl's notes and your medical records. You'll only be here a few more days, and I'll make sure that anything you need, you'll get, and any questions you have, I'll answer to the best of my ability."

I'm relatively certain that these are the words she uttered, though in my current state of distraction, my mind picked up something more along the lines of, "Mr. Shays, blah blah woof woof calm. Blah woof woof care, blah blah notes, flurftygoob blahty-blah best of my abiliblah."

"Can I talk to her?"

She looks surprised at my question. "Talk to who?"

"Cheryl." I'm starting to surprise myself with this line of thinking.

"Why?"

"To ... um ... thank her and say ... good-bye. And, um, wish her well."

"That's very thoughtful of you, Mr. Shays, but I'm afraid she's already left the facility. Let's focus on you now. We'll start with your temperature." She shoves a digital thermometer under my tongue. I'm vaguely aware that I'm looking around the room—for what, I don't know, as I'm relatively certain that Cheryl isn't hiding in the drawer where they keep the paper liners for the exam table.

Helga ... Greta ... shit, what was her name, anyway? Not-Cheryl pulls the thermometer out and announces, "Ninety-nine point five. Slightly elevated. Let's check your blood pressure."

Like a child with the world's worst case of abandonment issues, I struggle not to fidget as she wraps the cuff around my upper arm and inflates it enough that my head could pop off and ring the bell, were my head positioned somewhere below a bell. *Cheryl was more delicate with my blood pressure.*

"Hmm," she says after my deflation, "170 over 110. That's quite a bit higher than it's been so far. Are you feeling poorly?"

"No, I feel fine," I toss off far too casually, two seconds before the part of my brain responsible for telling me *no you don't, dumb fuck* tells me, *no you don't, dumb fuck.* And thus, it is time to back pedal. "I mean to say, I don't usually have high blood pressure. I feel as well as can be expected under the circumstances. You know, the usual troubles. But with moments of ... feeling ... less bad."

If the Olympics had a bullshit competition, I can safely say that I would come nowhere near qualifying with that performance. At this moment, I can only hope that Not-Cheryl also knows that I don't actually have cancer, and she just lets it go.

"How about your pain level?" she asks, choosing to disregard the baffling string of sentences that have just fled my mouth without the benefit of my brain. "Where would you say you are on the scale today?"

"Four," I answer, hoping that a low enough score will allow me to skip this dose, just in case she's one of the open-up-and-show-me-you-made-all-gone crowd.

"That's good," she says. "That's lower than your previous visits. It sounds like you're responding well to the medication. We'll see how this afternoon's dose works for you."

Crap.

She gets the very familiar cup-with-pill and cup-with-water and presents them to me. Now it's a brand-new game. With Cheryl—

particularly after our meeting—I knew where I stood. She was aware that I was pretending to take the meds, and as long as it looked good for the cameras, I could pantomime the whole thing. Now there's no telling what this one will do.

I suppose I could take the pill. After all, Cheryl said that a single dose wouldn't be harmful. Thinking back, Benton didn't display any signs of danger until well after he'd been home. I'm pretty sure that once she leaves the room, I can make myself vomit it back up somehow. This isn't the best choice, but under the circumstances, it may be all I have.

I look up at this moment and realize that as I've been having this little debate with myself, time has been passing, and this woman has been patiently standing there holding the two cups out to me, waiting for me to take them. I'm not sure how many seconds have passed, but I suspect it's enough that I've earned the strange look on her face.

"Did we go away for a minute?" she asks pleasantly yet still condescendingly.

"Guess so," I offer with a little self-deprecating laugh.

She shakes the pill cup to remind me that it truly is time. I take one cup in each hand and tip the smaller one into my open mouth. The chalky oval contents tumble onto my tongue. If there's a taste, I'm unaware of it. The overpowering awareness of having the weapon of the enemy inside of me is all I can focus on. I'm just glad she's not taking my blood pressure at the moment. My mind races for any option to avoid swallowing this pill, but nothing comes to mind. I'm too tense to try the sneeze trick; ditto with hiding it under my tongue.

It's time; I have to do this. I take in some water, tip my head back, and in seconds, the pill is down.

She smiles. "There we go. That wasn't so bad, was it?"

With that, Nurse Not-Cheryl turns around, prepared to leave the room. *Excuse me?*

"Don't you want to make sure I took it?" I open my mouth wide to show her.

"Why would I need to do that?" she asks. "You're an adult, and there's no reason *not* to take it, is there?"

"No," I reply in quiet disbelief, "I guess there isn't."

"I want you to lie down for twenty minutes, and then I'll come back and check your pain level." Without another word, she leaves me alone in the room.

Well, fuck me.

Alone in the room, resting comfortably is the last thing on my mind. I feel like I've just swallowed poison or a time bomb, and I have to get rid of it. I rush to the sink, ready to do the distasteful act of sticking my finger down my throat, but then I look up at the cameras. I can't induce vomiting with them watching. Not deliberately anyway. So I put my imagination to work, trying desperately to conjure up the most nauseating images I've ever beheld, from every horror movie, crime scene, or atrocity. I focus on the body of Benton Tambril after he fired his fatal shot. That did the trick back then, when I was with him, but will the memory alone be enough? I visualize his lifeless form, the destroyed mess that once was his head. I recollect the smell—the overpowering odor of his insides come out. I feel myself cough and even gag. But the best I can muster in my current state are dry heaves, which do nothing to dislodge the offender and simply hurt like a bitch.

It's in me, and it's going to stay in me. I'm afraid, but there's something else going on. Oddly enough, it's a feeling of pain, actual physical pain. It's centered in the back of my head, traveling down my neck and into my spine. Initially, I'm ready to believe that somehow, this pill designed to relieve pain has caused it. But then the visions come. I see a man in a bed; he's very sick, maybe dying. Suddenly I know his name, and I know that he is quite sick and he plans to take his own life. And I realize that this is my next assignment.

Two suicides in a row. This is not a specialty I want to be known for.

Then it gets weird. As more details filter in, I receive his location, which is in the very building I'm in right now. This man is a terminal patient on the second floor.

Impossible. And yet it makes sense in its own bizarre way. Had I not come here of my own accord, my next assignment would have sent me here anyway. This is it; this is all the proof I need that my cause is just.

Whoever or whatever is sending me must have some sort of GPS-like knowledge of my location, as I have less than thirty minutes to get to this man. Not enough time if I were anywhere else but right here.

But how do I get to him? My new best friend, Whatserface, will be back in less than twenty minutes. On top of that, he's in a restricted area; the stairways and elevators to the second floor all require a key card, something I lack. I'm going to have to steal one, but how?

One thing's for certain: I can't do it from inside this room. Cautiously, I open the door and look out into the corridor. People are milling about, doing their business, coming and going. I quickly realize that my efforts at caution only serve to make me look suspicious. Rule number one of being where you're not supposed to: look like you belong there. So I drop any attempt at stealth and pose as what I am: a patient stepping out of the room after his dosage of the medication.

A quick survey of my surroundings shows that the key cards are actually the workers' ID badges. There's no retinal scanner or any kind of spy nonsense like that. Just a simple swipe of the key card against the scanner. Now all I have to do is get one.

I enter the men's room, looking for a quiet place to strategize. At the moment, there is only one other person in there, a custodian, cleaning the place. He's in one of the stalls at the moment, but his cart is out by the sinks. On it, in plain sight, is his ID card—my ticket to where I need to go.

I look around again, making sure that no one else is here; we are indeed alone. Moving as quietly as I can, I approach the cart, silent step by silent step. I'm close to the card now, just beyond arm's reach. I extend my right hand, slowly, gently, working up some plausible explanation about something else on the cart that I could be reaching for—soap or a towel or tissues. Finally, my fingers touch the card, and I very gingerly unhook it from the side of the cart.

"What are you doing?"

I actually jump a little at the sound of the custodian's voice, startled at being discovered. In so doing, I succeed in unhooking the key card, which ends up in my hand. I am caught, plain and simple. It's time to put the best of my intellect to work in the speedy concoction of a brilliant explanation.

"I'll give you a hundred bucks if I can borrow this card for twenty minutes."

Masterful.

"What do you need it for?"

"Did I say one hundred? I mean two hundred. And I promise, it's not for anything bad. I have a friend upstairs on the second floor. He doesn't have much time left. I'm in the treatment program too, and I asked the doctors if I could visit him one last time before he passes. They told me I couldn't. It's not allowed. But if I can borrow that card, I can go up there, pay my final respects, come back down, and nobody needs to know."

He looks me over, probably checking to see if I give off a terrorist vibe. "You can keep your money," he says. "I'll take you up there by the stairs. You can go see your friend, but please don't interact with anyone else."

"I won't."

"And if anyone sees you up there, you took a wrong turn. Understand?"

"Yes, I do. Thank you."

As he leads me to a back stairwell, I notice that the pain in my head and neck are subsiding. Whether this is the work of the medication or the acceptance of the assignment, I don't know, but I'll take it; I'll definitely take it.

The custodian does not accompany me upstairs. Before he departs, he cautions me one more time. "Go quietly, and don't stay long."

"Thank you again. For everything."

The door to the stairwell closes with a hollow metallic sound. For the moment, I am alone. I haven't thought about what I'll say to any staff members I encounter upstairs, but I'll work out that story as I need it. Time is short, so I have to move quickly. I take the stairs as fast as I can without making too much noise. At the top is a door identical to the one below; there's no window in it, so I can't see who or what is on the other side. I just have to hope for the best. Pushing the door open, I notice immediately that the ambient light on this floor is about half what it is on the main level. Not far from the stairwell entrance is a nurses' station, which is initially a cause for alarm, but I soon discover that it is unmanned. Each patient's vital signs are being monitored on a computer screen, but there is no one at the desk. In fact, there is no one in sight at all. No doctors making rounds, no nurses seeing to patients' needs, no orderlies transporting food or medication to the rooms.

The silence that engulfs me is chilling, interrupted only by the faintest sounds of heart monitors and respirators. Patient rooms line the walls, their doors open. From each room comes the tiny spill of a dim table lamp. No pervasive wash of fluorescents; no flickering color of television screens entertaining those in residence. Just muted light and muted sound, telling me that this may be the most awful place I've ever been.

I realize that I've been standing still as I take in these troubling details, and I don't have the luxury of time. As I make my way down the corridor, I look into a few patient rooms. In each one, I see the same thing: human beings, unconscious and hooked up to tubes, shells of their former selves. Some tubes introduce fluids, drugs, and nutrients into their bodies, while others remove waste. The figures range in age, but all share one characteristic: they are alive only in the strictest definition of the word.

Courtesy of my assignment, I know where to find the man I'm looking for. I hurry down the corridor to a room in a corner of the building. Unlike some of the other rooms on this floor that house three, four, or even six people, this one houses just one—the man from my vision; the man I am here to help. But how can I begin to help a man who's unconscious and barely alive to begin with?

"You ... came."

The voice startles me as it reaches me from the bed several feet away. It is the first human sound I've heard since arriving on the horror that is the second level, and though the voice is weak and faint, it gives me a fright nonetheless.

Cautiously, I approach the bed. "You were expecting me?"

In the dim light, I can make out the gaunt features of a man of about fifty, his body wasting away. He smells like what he is: a person not long for this world. He manages something that could be taken for a smile. "Hoping ... you would ... come."

Something surprising occurs to me. "I know your voice." It's true; though I've heard it only once before, there's a cadence to it and a trace of a European accent that's distinctive, despite the weakness.

"I'm f- flattered ... you ... remember."

"It was you who called me. Three days ago, after Benton Tambril's suicide. You told me to follow the pills; that's why I came here. It's because of you. Now I got a warning to come and save you, because you were going to kill yourself."

"I guess … someone's … looking out … for me."

"I don't understand. Who are you? What's your part in all this?"

"So much … to tell you. But … hard to talk. Come closer. Sit … on the bed."

I sit down next to the frail figure, and seconds later, he reaches out with one emaciated hand and grasps me firmly by the forearm. It's disturbing, and I'm about to ask him to remove his hand, but then I hear his voice—not the weak, halting words that had escaped his lips seconds ago, but a stronger, healthier voice—as healthy as it was on the phone three days ago. And I hear it directly in my head.

That's better. Thank you. I'm sorry to do this, but it's so difficult to talk, and it's important that you know the reason why you're here.

"How are you doing this?" I ask, using spoken words, as that's the way I know how to communicate.

He, however, persists in option B. *I think you're learning, Tristan, that there are forces at work in the world beyond what people know and understand.*

"So, when you called me the other day, you weren't even using a telephone, were you?"

No. I have no phone.

"How did you find me? How did you know to bring me here?"

I saw you try to help Benton, and I became aware of what you're capable of. I saw in you the rare kind of man who would take on this task because he knows it's the right thing to do. And I helped you to find this place. I couldn't say too much, in case they were listening. I'm glad you knew what to do. Do you see now the extent of this? The importance of what you need to do?

"I'm starting to, but there's still so much I don't understand. I spoke with my nurse practitioner earlier today, and she told me what she knew, which wasn't much. But now, I'm told she doesn't work here anymore."

Who was it?

"Cheryl. I don't know her last name."

I know her. She's a good person; she's not involved with the worst of what they do here. They must have heard what she told you somehow, and they've let her go.

"It's my fault."

You did her a favor. If she knew the darkest parts, she wouldn't be able to live with herself.

"What's happening here? And what's your relation to it?"

I was one of them once. Not all that long ago. I worked in the inner circle, privy to their plans, their goals, their secrets. But I asked too many questions, had too many problems with their answers. Shortly after that, I was diagnosed with cancer, after almost fifty years of extremely good health. I was placed on medical leave and put here. For the last six months, this bed has been my world. Fed through a tube. Cut off from human contact with anyone except the people they allow.

"I don't understand. If you're that big of a problem for them, why didn't they just kill you outright? Why imprison you here in this weakened state for the rest of your life?"

Because I'm still useful to them. In my head are facts and figures they need, strategies that they extract from me through the careful administration of all the right drugs. I help them now without the benefit of my free will. And because I'm still technically on their payroll, they've found a loophole that even makes it all legal—as if anyone could even find me here to question it. Soon, very soon, information I possess is going to help them begin the most comprehensive aspect of their plan, and I don't want to be responsible for that.

"Plan? What plan? What is it they're trying to do?"

In your memory are the words of a man, someone who spoke to you recently. He gave you a figure—30 million—but he didn't explain what it was. Am I right?

I don't know how he knows this, but he's right. "Yes. I assumed at the time it was a sum of money he was willing to give me, to keep me from pursuing this."

Not at all. The 30 million is their goal. It's the number of people in this country today who will die by their hand if they succeed.

"What? That's … that's an inconceivable possibility. That's one out of every ten people in America."

Yes, it is.

"Why would they do that? *How* would they do that?"

Time is short. In just a few minutes, you will be missed downstairs. Now that you know this, it's crucial that you help me. I'm unable to get out of this bed. I don't have the ability to end my own life, but it's the only way to stop them from getting information they need to carry out this plan. I need your help.

"But I was sent here to stop you from killing yourself."

There's no time to debate the merits of saving me. I just need you to bring me what I need. At the nurses' station, there are IV bags filled with potassium chloride. It will be a painful ending for me, but it should be relatively quick. Get one of the bags, and replace the saline drip with it. Go now.

My head is practically spinning as he releases his grip on me. I venture back into the hallway, toward the nurses' station, but can I really do as he asks? I was sent here to prevent this man's suicide, and now, to honor his wishes, I have to assist him with it. For now, we'll skip over the part where he spoke his thoughts directly into my mind; I'll schedule a panic attack on that part later. But it did do one thing: it showed me the truth of his words in a way that a spoken voice couldn't. There was an honesty present that convinced me without a doubt that everything he shared with me is absolutely true.

But how is that possible? SODARCOM plans to kill 30 million Americans? The scale of it is staggering, the implications even more so. I've heard of government agencies covertly targeting civilians in enemy nations, but to literally decimate the population of their own country? I can't even begin to conjure a reason to do so or a way of making it happen. I think of the circle of people I know, and I try to imagine who among them would be in the doomed 10 percent. The exercise is pointless and disturbing, so I quickly abandon it in favor of finding the IV bag.

In a drug cart behind the desk, I find numerous IVs filled with fluids. Some are saline, others bear the identification code of the trial's pain reliever. One is marked *potassium chloride,* just as he said it would be. I grab it and hurry back to his room, holding it up to show him I've succeeded.

He grasps my forearm, and once again I am privy to his thoughts. *You found it. That's good. On my IV stand there's a wheel that cuts off the flow of whatever is dripping. Move that wheel until the dripping stops. Then take out the bag of saline and replace it with the potassium chloride.*

"I- I don't know if I can do this. I'll be killing you, when I was sent to save you."

Tristan, do you feel any overpowering forces trying to stop you from doing this?

"No, I guess I don't."

You were sent as a last chance to stop me, but I actually needed you here to facilitate what I have to do. I absolve you of any guilt or any responsibility in this. Do this as an act of mercy, and know that by doing so, you may have helped stop these people from taking millions of lives.

I nod and release his grip long enough to switch out the bags. It's done. I've released the poison that will kill this man. He takes my arm again.

This is what has to be. I'm guilty of things I can't even think of in your presence, out of shame. You are innocent in all of this, but your presence here may be the most important thing you ever experience in your life.

"I have so many questions. So much I don't understand yet."

There's no time now. They're already looking for you downstairs. You have to go back. Follow the pills. Find a way to stop them. Now go.

Quickly I make my way out of his room, down the stairs, and back to the first-floor hallway. Fortunately, no one sees me exit the stairwell, as I don't have a good excuse handy. I head back to my exam room at a brisk pace, in time to find Nurse I'll-Remember-Her-Name-One-of-These-Days standing in the doorway, looking for me.

"I'm back," I say from behind her, as cheerfully as possible.

"You were supposed to be resting," she says. "Where did you go?"

"Had to use the men's room. Sorry."

"You're out of breath."

"It was an urgent visit. I'm okay, really."

"What about your pain level? Where would you say it is on the scale?"

Here's hoping a good report earns me a pass to get out of here. "I really think it's down to a two."

"That's very good," she says. "You're free to go. Come back in the next four to five hours for the third dose of the day."

I thank her and make a hasty but not overly suspicious retreat to the exit. Gently proud of myself for keeping my shit together, I leave the parking lot and find a quiet side street two miles away where I can park safely before I lose it.

And lose it I do. Seconds after parking the car, I find myself sobbing loudly and openly, and the worst part is, I'm not even sure why. Is it because I helped a stranger take his own life today? Is it because I now know that I may be the only thing stopping the wholesale slaughter of a tenth of America's population? Is it because I'm in so far over my head that I can't even see daylight below the surface anymore? Yes to all of those, plus a few more I haven't let myself reason out yet. So I sob and I wail and I tremble a little, and I wish someone was here to hold me.

Genevieve. She'll be at the apartment, and she'll hold me. I have to focus long enough to get home safely.

The rest of the drive to the apartment is shaky at best. I manage to control the trembling, but my eyes refuse to dry up completely, making me look to neighboring drivers like the world's biggest basket case as I navigate the streets of Washington, DC. Somehow, by the grace of God—or whoever's calling the fucking shots these days—I make it home safely and weepily stagger inside.

Within seconds, Genevieve intercepts me and rushes to my side to hold me up. "Tristan! My God, what have they done to you?"

"Nothing, nothing," I answer in a none-too-reassuring voice. "Help me to the bed. I need to lie down."

She does the bulk of the work in getting me to the bedroom and placing me comfortably on my back, while I continue to take hitching breaths like a small child who's almost all cried out after a long tantrum. "What do you need?" she asks. "Do you want some water or something?"

"No, I just ... need to rest."

She climbs in next to me and holds me, just as I hoped she would. "When you're able to talk, tell me what's happened. For now, just be still, and know that you're safe."

Safe. Will that ever be possible again?

For many minutes, I lie quietly and allow her to hold me. I know that because of my silence, I'm making her wait and wonder what could be wrong. Ordinarily, I would be concerned that what she imagined would be worse than the reality of the situation, but this time, I don't think that's possible. So I rest and I wait, letting my mind and my soul recover from the onslaught they've just been through. True to her word, Genevieve stays right by my side, breathing in rhythm with me.

Finally, when I feel able to recount my story without breaking down again, I take a deep breath and tell her everything. I start with the meeting with the new nurse practitioner and the news that Cheryl was no longer there. I tell her that I had no choice but to swallow the pill this time. She receives this news with fear and alarm, rightly concerned for my well-being, but I try to assure her that I'm feeling no ill effects of the medication.

This seems to put her mind at ease, but only briefly, as the strangest, most disturbing part of the story is imminent. I share the details of my assignment and my covert excursion to the facility's upper level. She listens intently to the details of the darkened rooms, the absence of staff members, and finally, the strange patient who spoke to me inside my head. She shudders a bit when I tell her of his final request and my willingness to assist. She shudders more when I reveal the news about SODARCOM and the 30 million.

When my narrative is done, she remains silent for a minute, her eyes telling me that she's working things out. "I have a question," she finally says calmly. "Are you sure the meeting with the man in the room really happened?"

"What?" My response reflects my confusion; the possibility never occurred to me. "You don't think I imagined the whole thing, do you?"

"Wait, hear me out. You took a dose of the drug, a drug you still don't know the contents of. This was your first time taking it, and within a few minutes after you took it, you experienced the kind of pain you get when you get an assignment. Then you went to a place whose sights and sounds were the opposite of what you expected. You met a man who you say spoke to you in your thoughts and provided you with answers to questions you've had since you got here. And more than that, it was the same man who called you to let you know about this in the first place. I believe that you experienced these things, but for a moment, entertain the possibility that the drug they gave you was some kind of hallucinogen. Maybe you're part of an experiment they're doing, to see how you'd react to a given situation. I mean, think of it: what are the odds of getting an assignment to be carried out in the same building where you were? I'm wondering if physically you didn't leave that room, but mentally, these things happened to you."

Her words make a great deal of sense—probably more than I want them to. The implications are disturbing, to say the least. With one pill, they can manipulate not only my thoughts but my actions. *Is it even possible?* Everything felt so real, looked and sounded so real. Well, *surreal* is a better word, but never for a second did I doubt that this was happening to me. Finally I have to admit to her and to myself, "I don't know."

"It's okay," she says gently. "It's not your fault. If you were drugged, you couldn't help what you saw and heard."

"But what do I do if I can't trust what I see and hear? How do I finish this assignment if my own senses are working against me?"

"I'm not sure."

I sit up in frustration, feeling that tears could once again start. In anticipation, I reach into my pocket to pull out a handkerchief. In doing so, a piece of clear plastic, looking like a shred of a sandwich bag, flutters out of my pocket and onto the bed. Genevieve picks it up and examines it carefully; as she does, a smile returns to her face.

"What?" I ask. "What is it?"

"Proof," she says, holding it up for me to see.

It is indeed a circle of thin plastic about three inches in diameter— the sterility seal for an IV bag. On it are printed the words: "Solution of potassium chloride for intravenous drip. Danger: Dosage of 10 or more mEq/hr. can be fatal. Use with extreme caution."

"You didn't imagine it," she says. "And this proves it."

"Honestly, I don't know if that's better or worse. Because it means that what this man told me about SODARCOM's plans is true."

"So what do we do?" she asks. "Go to the police? The FBI?"

"And tell them what? That a government agency nobody's heard of is planning to kill millions of Americans for reasons we don't know, using a method we can't describe? I think you know how they treat those kinds of calls. No wonder nobody's talking about SODARCOM; the absurdity of the situation is a built-in firewall."

"Then do we give up?" she asks.

"No. Especially not now. This man suggested that my efforts might be able to stop them. I have to keep trying."

"Do you know his name? It would help if we knew who he was."

"He didn't give me his name, and with everything that was going on, I didn't ask."

She stands up abruptly. "Wait a minute. When you get assignments, isn't the first piece of information you get the person's name? Otherwise, how else would you find them?"

She's right. I always get the name, and in the recesses of my memory, I dimly recall a name for this man being included in what I received. "I did, but I can't remember what it was. I'm searching and searching, but it's just not coming to me."

Now she's smiling broadly, appearing very proud of herself. "I can help you."

"How can you help me?"

"I can help you extract that name."

"What devil magic is this?" I ask playfully.

"Let me hypnotize you."

"Oh no you don't. I've already been somebody's plaything today. I'm not going to cluck for you while you videotape me!"

"The chicken bit? Really? Oh, Tristan, that went out of style in the eighties. You give me two minutes and I'll have the name, with no videotaping and no clucking, I promise."

"All right," I reply, "I'll try this. As long as it doesn't hurt or anything."

What follows is the sum total of my memories of the hypnosis session.

"When I count to three," Genevieve says, "you'll awaken relaxed and refreshed. One, two, three."

Upon opening my eyes, I blink several times to orient myself, and I look up to see her standing over me in my seated position on the bed. "Don't tell me it's already done," I say.

"All finished."

"I didn't cluck, did I?"

"No clucking, but you sang beautifully. I have the name of the person you were sent to help today."

"Please tell me it's not something like John Smith or Bob Jones."

"How about Stanislaw Kolodziej?" she says, reading it off a slip of paper.

"Seriously? How the hell did I manage to forget *that?*"

"I suspect you had a lot on your mind. But the good news is, when we look him up online, I don't suspect there will be too many people with the same name. Shall we?"

I rise from the bed and look at her curiously. "What's that I'm hearing in your voice?"

"The thrill of the chase," she replies. "We're on the trail, and I'm helping. Now let's go to the computer and see if Stanislaw is a bit more present than his employers."

We move over to the PC and open up a search engine. I type in "Stanislaw Kolodziej," and I am quickly amazed to see over five thousand matches. "Clearly," I say, "not popular here does not equal not popular elsewhere in the world."

"Now what do we do?" she asks.

"Narrow it down." I return to the search bar and add "+ Washington" to his name. This time, the results come back with twenty-three matches. "That's a little better."

I find a page on a site called Professional Profiles and click on it. It brings up a profile page for Mr. Stanislaw Kolodziej of Washington, DC. The photo included is barely recognizable as the man I saw today. It shows a smiling, healthy, middle-aged man in an expensive suit and designer tie, rather than the haggard specter in a dirty hospital gown who lay waiting for someone to show death to his doorstep.

His profile paints a picture of an expert in his field. A PhD from Yale, followed by twenty years of experience in his chosen area of study: socio-anthropology. He has extensive field experience in African and Mayan cultures. The professional network displayed on screen is vast, with contacts in six continents.

"Impressive," Genevieve comments.

"Come on," I say to the computer, "come on, where is it?"

"What are you looking for?"

I click through to the next screen. "There. E-mail address. Get ready to be impressed." I get out my cell phone and dial a number. "Jeff, it's Tristan Shays. ... Good, thanks. Listen, time is tight. I need the Terrier."

"Terrier?" Genevieve repeats as I wait to be transferred.

"Trust me." My contact comes on the line. "Terry, it's Tristan. I need a favor, and I can pay double your usual rate if you can get this information to me today. I need you to hack an e-mail account and transfer all e-mails, coming and going for the past six months, to my personal account. This guy's highly placed, and there's probably firewalls out the ass, so I need your best work. And, Terry, this is not a place you want to be caught snooping, so if you even think you've been detected, get out fast. You can go in through the IP gateway in Norway and reroute through the server in Iceland. The account name is s-k-o-l-o-d-z at stats dot gov. … Yeah, I know a dot-gov is going to be trickier. But if I wanted to hack a Yahoo account, I'd hire an eighteen-year-old who needs fifty bucks. The big jobs need the big dog, and that's you, Terrier. So, if you would be so kind, dig for me. I need these by 5:00 Eastern today. … In fairness, you've never met my mother, but thank you for thinking of me. Good luck, Terry. This is probably the most important thing I've ever had you do. And when you do get hold of these, don't read them. Trust me: the less you know about this stuff, the better."

I end the call and notice that Genevieve actually does look a bit impressed. "He's called the Terrier?" she asks.

"Only to his close friends."

"One of whom is you, obviously. Should I ask why the CEO of a respectable corporation is on a nickname basis with a high-level information hacker?"

"For the same reason you keep the electrician's number in your Rolodex: sometimes shit needs to be fixed."

"Do you think he can do it?" she asks.

"I'll tell you this: if it can be done, Terrier can do it. If I'd been thinking when I was at Swift, I would've gotten Kolodziej's name and password from him, but I wasn't doing much in the way of thinking. Besides, I'm not sure he would've wanted his communications examined. Hence the need for secrecy. And I suspect that once SODARCOM knows he's dead, they're going to purge his files within twenty-four hours. Hence the need for speed. Did you notice the domain? Stats dot gov. No SODARCOM dot gov, nothing to track him back to the organization he worked for. Their employees are probably housed in other benign departments for the sake of recordkeeping."

"This is awfully secret-agency of you. Should I be worried?"

"No more than usual."

"That's good," she says with a smile.

"So what should we do while we wait?" I wonder aloud.

"Well, when I was channeling, you spoke to someone, a man, you said. He might have had something to do with SODARCOM. Do you remember his name?"

"Yes. Saunders. Michael Saunders. Hardly as distinctive a name as our friend Stanislaw, and there were five thousand matches for him."

"Let's try him," she suggests.

I type it into the search bar, and sure enough, more than a million matches appear. "I don't know if we'll be able to find him based on this."

"Step aside, lad," she says confidently, trading seats with me. "Part of finding something in this life is knowing where to look." She closes the search engine I have open and chooses another, one I've never heard of. In the main search bar, she enters "Michael Saunders." Below it, several other bars appear. "You said he told you he was dead?"

"That's right."

She clicks a button marked "and"; into the next search bar she types "deceased." Another button marked "or"; a search bar now says "died."

"What else do you have?" she asks. "How can we narrow it?"

"He sounded American," I suggest.

She clicks another "and" and types "United States."

"Try it. See how many it gets us."

She hits *enter*, and it returns just over seventy-two thousand matches. "Down from a million," she says, "but not exactly pointing us right to him."

There's something else, something I'm not seeing. Something I heard in his voice. It's a long shot, but it's worth a try. "Go back to the search. Keep the other terms, but add *suicide*."

"You think?" she asks, typing it in. "Did he say as much?"

"No, but there was a deep feeling of guilt that I heard in everything he said. It was like an apology or even a suicide note. I don't know for sure, but if it narrows the search, it's worth a try."

Genevieve adds the limiter and hits *enter* again. This time, only nineteen matches come up. "That's few enough that we could check them all," she says.

"If I'm right about the suicide."

"One way to find out."

Together we read through the links and start to rule out the unlikely suspects. A Michael Saunders killed himself in his garage a year ago, after battling drug and alcohol addiction. Another was part of a murder-suicide with his girlfriend in Nevada. Still another fell to his death from the top of a parking garage, and the police ruled out suicide. Twelve links in, I am beginning to fear I'm on the wrong path, but the thirteenth time is different.

"Tristan, look at this," Genevieve says as the page opens.

After a quick glance, I am initially skeptical, as the page is part of a website called Xpoz'd TruthZ—a deliberate misspelling, I hope, but not the sort that leaps up, gives you a big kiss, and says, "Hi, I'm dripping with credibility!"

"A conspiracy theory site?" I ask, reeking of dubious.

"When the legitimate press fails, it's time to see what the extremists are saying."

She may have a point. So we read, a page headed "The Empty Death of Michael Saunders." With it is a photograph, an old black-and-white photograph of a man apparently in his forties. He's starting to lose his hair, and his face shows no humor, no mirth, just the image of a man trapped by his life. The caption reads, "Michael Saunders, six months before his death in 1931."

"He died in 1931?" I ask aloud. "Why would he still be able to talk to us now?"

"If it's true, if that was him you talked to, then his spirit is trapped here for more than seventy years. It's unusual but not unheard of. He'd be in considerable pain and suffering, wanting to cross over. That poor man."

Whoever keeps the irritatingly spelled Xpoz'd TruthZ site prefaced the historical article with a bit of editorial commentary: "The SDC is not new. Read the shocking true story of how one of their agents engineered the United States stock market crash of 1929, and learn the terrible truth about why!"

"SDC," Genevieve points out. "Short for SODARCOM, maybe? The new name may be for internal purposes only. But what does it stand for?"

"No clue. C could stand for committee, council, corporation, croutons."

"Croutons?"

"Less likely, but it illustrates the challenge."

"Shocking true story," she says. "Why is it always a shocking true story?"

"More interesting that way. Let's see what the real article says."

Though the article's source is not shown, the material presented is a scan of a newspaper that appears to be decades old. It says:

MAN FOUND DEAD IN MANHATTAN APT.
RULED SUICIDE

(New York, N.Y.: Jan. 1, 1931) The body of 42-year-old Michael C. Saunders was discovered in his New York City apartment this morning by his landlady, Elsbeth Nye, after Saunders had not been seen or heard from by family members and neighbors for more than a week. Police found a stark scene when they entered the flat on West 48th Street that Saunders had occupied for the past four years. The windows were blacked out, covered with newspaper clippings about the Wall Street crash of Oct. 1929. Police initially surmised that Saunders had lost his fortune in the economic downturn, but two shocking discoveries within the apartment brought an even more curious and terrible truth to light.

The first discovery was Michael Saunders' bank book, which contained more than $30,000 in liquid assets. He had left it in plain sight, with instructions that the money be given to his mother. This level of stability ruled out the likelihood of financial ruin being the motivation for suicide. Questions were soon answered—and others raised—when police found Saunders' suicide note.

The exact text of the three-page handwritten note was not released to the press, but sources at the scene have shared details from the document that suggest it is a confession. The note details Saunders' participation in events that directly caused the stock market to crash on Oct. 29, 1929. He alluded to a shadow organization (not named) by which he was employed that allegedly orchestrated the upheaval on Wall Street that has devastated the global economy.

Sources further say that the final part of Saunders' suicide note featured a prolonged apology to everyone he had harmed by his actions. The note ended with the words "I'm so sorry. I did as I was told. It was for the greater good."

I stop reading at this point. "Those were the exact words he said to me," I tell Genevieve. "For the greater good. This has to be him. Holy shit, are we to believe that this man triggered the Great Depression?"

"And more than that," she adds, "that SODARCOM has been around for seventy years or more, causing chaos quote-unquote *for the greater good?*"

"Yeah, I'm stumped on exactly how that works. Millions unemployed, global economies crushed, thousands taking their own lives in despair, businesses failing ..."

"Say that again," she says, her eyes telling me she's on to something.

"What? Businesses failing?"

"No, before that."

"Thousands taking their own lives in despair."

"Suicide," she says. "Manipulating people to take their own lives."

"You think there's a connection?"

"It's the only common thread we've got. Saunders and company caused an event that led to mass suicide. Now we have a study affecting thousands of people nationwide, giving them a drug that might cause them to do likewise. What if that's SODARCOM's mission? Some kind of league of chaos and evil that tries to see if it can commit mass murder by inducing mass suicide."

"That's almost too horrible to contemplate," I reflect.

"There have been mass suicide events in human history. What if this group, whoever they are, had a hand in this? How deep does this go, and how far back in time?"

I start to feel sick inside. "Do you get the feeling that we've jumped into a pool that's much deeper than we bargained for?"

Chapter 6

For several minutes, we just sit there, trying to make sense of what we're learning, this flood of unspeakably horrifying information. Where do you even begin to get a handle on such a level of power and influence? And the thought of being the only ones capable of standing against them is more frightening than anything I've ever known.

"What if the website's bullshit?" Genevieve asks quietly. "Like you said, it's the work of conspiracy nuts. Isn't it possible that they're making something out of nothing?"

"I'd be ready to believe that if it weren't for two things. One: the scan of the 1931 article. This looks genuine; it looks like a clipping from an actual newspaper from that period—though I wish I knew which one. And two: the words at the end of Michael's suicide note are exactly the same as the words that came out of his mouth ... er, *your* mouth ... in this very room. I'm ready to believe that a man named Michael Saunders who died in New York City by his own hand in 1931 was an employee or free agent of SODARCOM or an earlier incarnation of it. I also believe that somehow, he manipulated the New York Stock Exchange in October 1929, causing the greatest economic disaster in American history."

"I could try to channel him again ..."

"It's risky. He was scared and upset, and he might not come back. Besides, I don't want to risk encountering *her* again, whoever she is."

"Not a fan of threesomes, are you?" she asks with a little smile.

"No, thanks."

"Wait a minute—the website uses SDC, rather than SODARCOM. Let's search the site for other articles about them."

"Good idea," I reply, moving to the site's search function. I type "SDC" into the field, and it returns with more than seventy articles from this site alone. Curiously, though, every single one of them is followed by the words: *This article has been removed by the site administrator. Error 404: File not found.*

"Damn it," she says. "All gone."

"And not by choice, I suspect. But why would this one be allowed to stay when it mentions the SDC?" I scroll back up to the mention of them at the top of the page and find my answer. What I had read as *The SDC is not new* actually said *The S\DC is not new.* "So, whoever was searching for references to them didn't take stray characters into account. A typo is the only reason why we got to see this page at all."

"Somebody's responsible for maintaining this site," Genevieve postulates quite reasonably. "You can delete an article, but it's more difficult to delete a person. If we can find an owner, a webmaster, somebody—maybe we can find the answers to what was on those deleted pages."

We search page after page of the site, looking everywhere for any sign of who's creating Xpoz'd TruthZ. Unfortunately, that particular truth is not so easily "Xpoz'd." I suppose if I were generating volumes of potentially libelous accusations against everybody and their grandma, I wouldn't be so quick to slap on the "Howdy, my name is …" tag either.

A quick trip to *whois.com* also fails to produce a name. The owner information comes up as "in review," which doesn't bode well. "I think we're headed to a dead end," I tell her. "We should probably count ourselves lucky to have found what we found."

"So what do we do?"

"I say we map out what we've already got and hope that the Terrier does his thing and gets us those e-mails. Until then, we wait. And we eat. All I had at lunch was a few Scotch eggs. Would you be interested in ordering a pizza?"

"Totally."

Forty minutes later, the hot little pizza is in our hot little hands. Italian sausage, Portobello mushrooms, fresh basil, banana peppers, and goat cheese. In short, heaven on a crust. Together we sit at the dining room table and assemble our notes on letter-size paper. It's a very orderly map of a very incomplete set of facts. Conspicuously unfinished is the page labeled "What We Know." The one we most need. Another page is labeled "Theories," and on it is every possible explanation we can come up with, plausible and implausible. "Alien invasion" isn't on there … yet. But the evening is young.

"I'm really stuck on the mass suicide angle," Genevieve says in between bites. "I can't for the life of me figure out why they would want to do it, but it feels like the one commonality we've found between Saunders in 1929 and Swift in 2007."

"Okay, let's start with that. Say SODARCOM has the resources and the ability to cause thousands of people at a time to commit suicide. Why do it? And more, why do it to American citizens, people who seem to have done nothing to harm them? Crime is about means, motive, and opportunity. I'll give you means and opportunity in both cases, but motive? I'm scratching my head. If you can come up with one, that's the piece of the puzzle we need. Why these people? And why make them do it themselves? They're a wealthy, powerful government body. Why not just quietly send death squads out to do it? I doubt they'd be too squeamish about getting their hands dirty."

"Maybe they need to keep a good public image …"

"I'd buy that if they *had* a public image, but this group is so invisible, they could do what they want, where and when they want, and nobody but the most hardcore conspiracy theorists would even know it was happening. So why do it? I feel like the answer, if we ever find it, will be so obvious, we'll be kicking ourselves that we didn't see it."

"Okay then," she says, "let's do this. Instinctive dialogue."

"Come again?"

"Maybe the reason we can't think of it is because we're thinking too much of it. The brain is a remarkable thing. You know how test-takers and game-show contestants do so well when they give the first answer that comes to mind? There's something hard-wired into our mental processes that gives us the answers we need. When we overthink, we cloud things, we muddy up the process. We doubt the reptile brain within."

"Reptile brain?"

"The primitive part, the part before all that pesky evolution. The instinct."

"You'll forgive me if I'm feeling a little reptile dysfunction."

"Then let's wake the lizard, baby. Sit in that chair and face me."

I do so, still a bit unclear on the concept.

"I'm going to say some things. Basic statements, questions, ideas. All I need you to do is respond. First thing that comes into your mind. No more than a single second to give your answer. Don't think of what's the right thing or wrong thing to say. Just say it. Clear?"

"Kind of."

"Now banish your rational self and focus. Ready … begin. I want you dead."

"I don't want to die," I reply without thinking.

"I'm stronger than you, and I want you dead."

"Now that I know this, I'll protect myself."

"There's no protection."

"Then I'll tell someone. The police."

"I own the police," she says.

"Then I'll run away, hide from you."

"If I can't kill you myself, I'll make *you* do it."

"I'll resist you," I reply, not even sure where these words are coming from.

"Why resist?"

"Because I'm happy and I want to live."

"What if you're not happy?" she queries.

"I know it's only temporary, and things will get better."

"Then we'll make it so things won't get better. We'll destroy your business. We'll take your home. We'll find you when you have a deadly disease. You'll thank us for the chance to be free of your misery."

"But why do you hate me enough to want me dead?" I ask.

"Because you're weak."

A terrible silence suddenly passes between us at those three words. *Because you're weak.* The connection is broken, and we stare at each other, wide-eyed.

"How did you do that?" I ask her in disbelief. "Were you channeling? Was that someone else?"

"No, I swear. I did what you did. I turned off the reasoning side of my mind and just let the first thought enter my head each time. And that was what it said."

"You—you were them. You were SODARCOM, the SDC, whoever they are. You were talking like you were them."

"Tristan, I had to get you to speak for their victims, so I could understand the motive. At the end, what we both said … do you think that could be it? *Because you're weak?*"

"I don't know. It sounds too much like Nazi Germany. Building the master race. Only this time, people volunteer to go to the camps. They annihilate themselves. Holy God, Gen … a government agency whole sole purpose is to convince the weak in society that their lives are worthless and then help them to commit suicide? I don't know what to do with this information. It scares the hell out of me."

"Who can we even report this to?" she asks. "We don't know who's in on this. I'm new at this government conspiracy stuff. Honestly, I thought it just existed in movies."

"So did I. Really, I don't know if there's anyone we can report it to. For all we know, this is a sanctioned, funded, above-board government project held in the strictest secrecy. Until we know more, we're on our own."

Before she can respond to that, a sound from the computer tells us that I have a new e-mail. I only hope it's the one I've been waiting for. We move back over there quickly, and sure enough, it's a message from the Terrier. "Yes. Come on, Terry, tell me you found what I needed."

I open the message and find thirty-nine attachments, all of which are archived e-mails. The body of Terry's message says:

> T.S. [which I hope are my initials, and not short for *tough shit.*]
>
> Did what I could in the time I had. NEVER seen such firewalls before. What are they keeping in there? As I was working, I saw large chunks of this guy's archived stuff disappear. I don't know if that's because of me or what, but I got almost 40. I hope they help. Be careful

w/these people. That much security means they've got a lot to hide.

Paymt. to me by standard method w/in one day, please.

—Terrier

"Only forty e-mails," I mutter in disappointment. "Damn it."

"It's forty more than we had. At this point, any piece of information is valuable. We should start reading through them." She hesitates a moment. "Just out of sheer curiosity, how much did this online fact-finding mission cost you?"

"That's not important."

"Of course it's not. But I'm still curious."

Begrudgingly, I reply, "Three thousand dollars."

"Oh my God!"

"Thirty million people, Gen. That's a hundredth of a cent per person. Well worth it to me, believe me."

"I do. And I'm sorry for the reaction. I'm just … not used to dealing in such large numbers, that's all."

"Welcome to my world. Sometimes I don't even flinch under five digits. Sorry if that sounds arrogant."

"From anyone else, it might."

With that, I click on the first attachment, ready to delve into the private communications of Stanislaw Kolodziej. I brace myself for some kind of electronic booby trap that wipes out my hard drive or sets my PC on fire, but no such thing happens. That's a good start, anyway. The first message is just over seven months old:

To: S. Kolodziej

From: SDC Actual

"Actual?" Genevieve asks.

"It's a military term. It refers to the person in charge. This one comes from the boss."

Stan,

So very sorry to hear of your diagnosis. Always a shame when the disease strikes someone so young. You are, of course, welcome to work for as long as you're able. If that becomes too much of a burden, you are entitled to up to a year's medical leave at ¾ pay. Additionally, at no cost to you or your family, you have at your disposal the medical staff, facilities, and treatments at Swift, if they can help in any way to ease the effects of your illness. Anything you need, simply ask, my friend.

Sincerely,

PK

"Jesus, he gave him a warm invitation to the prison cell where he'd spend the rest of his life."

"You think this 'Actual' person knew that he was locking Kolodziej away?" Genevieve asks.

"I do. Now I just want to see the e-mails where we find out why he had to."

One by one, we open the others. Six in a row are completely mundane. An order for office supplies. Birthday wishes to a friend. A request for a staff meeting. Reminder to get all expense reports and receipts in by the end of the month. Nothing of value. But then, message by message, things start to change. We begin to see pieces that are illuminating.

All systems are on track for mortgage situation in FY07, Q3. Anticipating a 43% jump in foreclosures, leaving an estimated 525,000 homeless by end of FY. Blame will be placed on banks and lending organizations. Govt. to bail out, but will try to prevent.

And another:

Excellent news. We've found a way to gain access to the tobacco after state and federal inspections but before processing. We should have no trouble implementing the process.

Still another says:

> Making inroads on infant formula. Having more of a challenge with the birth control angle. Lots of oversight and intervention there. May have to scrap that, but not ready to give up on it yet. Will apprise by week's end.

One from a year and a half ago says:

> Project Glass hit a snag. Legislation went into effect limiting the sale of pseudoephedrine in OTC meds. I thought we had someone working to get around that? Anyway, now there are extra hoops to jump through, so we'll have to rethink this aspect or at least diversify. Possibly get it from overseas? Maybe the Caribbean. Things are looser down there. At any rate, we can't risk losing the momentum we've built up. This stuff is like a dream. It practically sells itself, and the people who buy it are squarely in our target demographic. It's doing our work for us.

Three in a row provide answers I wish I hadn't seen:

> To maximize the effectiveness, we've placed an agent at the distribution center for the food stamp debit cards. Casual contact with the card, by supermarket cashiers and such, will have no effect, but prolonged possession of it by the cardholders themselves will increase sterilization rates by almost 60%.

> Yes, sir, your instructions were clear, and I did check with our operatives. Only the prenatal vitamins in the lowest 25% of the range of prices will be affected. Women who take the more expensive vitamins will see no increase in miscarriages. Sorry for any confusion, but all is well.

> As of next week, we will have 900 additional men patrolling the border in southern Texas, Arizona, New Mexico, and California. All are well armed and ready to do what's necessary.

Still another provides what looks like something valuable, only I can't make sense of what it's saying:

> Current efforts are good, and projects in development have potential for success. In order to meet the goal of PY12, we're going to have to go for the last-ditch scenario, the one we talked about at the conference in Colorado. The tricky part is, the whole premise stems from inaccurate information. The calendar thing. It's just not true, not correct, and one or two very credible experts standing up and debunking it could have a very detrimental effect on what we want to do.

> The good news is, it plays on some very scary superstition, and it's just believable enough that it could have a chain reaction. Actually, when I think about it, the presence of credible evidence to the contrary is a good thing. Looking at our target demographic, we want those who are credulous, under-educated, easily manipulated. I'll do what I can to spread the word in the media that these people would seek out, and I'll avoid the more reputable channels.

> I'm not going to sugar-coat it: this is a huge undertaking. To get the kind of results we need, it will take something resembling a nationwide panic. I've never done anything on this scale before, but I'll do everything I can.

"What do you suppose he's talking about?" Genevieve asks.

"I don't know. The calendar thing? What's that about? They want to start a panic among under-educated people, and ... what? Inspire another round of mass suicide? But how? And why would they want to do that?"

"The more we read, the more it seems like that's their goal—suicide and self-destructive behavior among weak or undesirable subsets of American society. The poor, cancer patients, smokers, meth addicts. You remember years ago when people were whispering that AIDS was created by the government to get rid of people they didn't like? At the time, I shook my head and thought it was ridiculous. Looking at these e-mails, I don't know what to think now."

I open the next one, which is dated shortly before Kolodziej was admitted to Swift. It appears to be a message from him to his boss, and the tone is one of remorse:

> I don't know whether it is my illness or something passing for a conscience or simply self-doubt, but I'm not sure if I can continue with my role in the project, at least not now. Logistically, I'm equal to any challenge, but once each challenge is met, I look at it from an intellectual level and an emotional level, and I find myself sick with worry over what I have done. I wonder, each time, if our cause is truly just.
>
> Please forgive the seemingly insubordinate nature of those words. It's not my intention to question you or undermine your work. But this world of ours—it's such a self-correcting system that I have to wonder. If we were to step back and simply let nature find a way, could we avoid the task that's upcoming? In all the years I've worked for you, I've never known such a feeling of uncertainty. Perhaps facing my own mortality has given me insight into the premature mortality of others, and I've developed a sense of empathy that I've lacked before.

His words are heartbreaking, particularly knowing that my actions have almost certainly ended his life today. After God knows how many unspeakable acts this man his overseen, at the end, he found contrition, remorse, maybe even redemption. Isn't that the goal of the justice system? How, then, do I find justice for Stanislaw Kolodziej?

Genevieve snaps me out of my thoughts. "Tristan, I think you need to get back there for your evening dose."

"Hmm?" I look at my watch, and she's right; it's close to 7:00, and I do need to get back. "Oh, thank you. I won't be gone long."

"Please, whatever you do, *don't* take the pill this time."

"Trust me, now that I know she's not watching carefully, it's not going anywhere near me."

I make the trip back in to Swift, but my mind is a million miles away. As I'd hoped, Kolodziej's e-mails—few though they were—contained a wealth of information, confirming what I suspected. SODARCOM is responsible for crimes against humanity, attacks on the most vulnerable segments of society. Message after message detailed what they've done; still missing is the all-important *why*. A group this big, this powerful doesn't kill for fun or for sport of for practice. There's a goal, a purpose. Something that motivates them to take 30 million American lives. Usually, money is the motivating factor in anything, but I can't for the life of me see how it would be profitable for anyone but the funeral industry to lose that many people.

My evening dosage is uneventful. A less-than-watchful eye from my nurse practitioner allows me to slide the pill straight up my shirt sleeve and carry it out with me. A brief waiting period later, I am released to return to the apartment.

Tempting as it is to return to the computer and finish going through the e-mails, I just can't do it. I'm afraid of opening the next one and learning that they're responsible for the Holocaust or the extinction of the dinosaurs. Hell, I don't even know anymore. The part I do know is already more than my little brain can process. Maybe Jack Nicholson was right in that old movie—I can't handle the truth.

I realize that I am standing in front of the computer, staring at it as if I could move it with the power of my mind. After the couple of weeks I've had, it wouldn't completely surprise me. Genevieve's voice from behind me startles me a bit. "You look tired."

"Do I? I guess I am."

"Should I skip the part where I ask if you had a rough day?"

"Probably for the best."

"I know it's only 8:00, but we could go to bed."

I smile at the suggestion. "I haven't had an 8:00 bedtime since I was six."

"I didn't say we had to go to sleep," she says with no subtlety to her invitation.

The sheets are soft and welcoming, and the bed is like an old friend I haven't visited in far too long. As I crawl under the blankets, I realize that I could be asleep in mere minutes; but then I feel Genevieve crawl next to me and press her body next to mine. I hold her close, and she kisses me. But then I engage in that very male behavior of doing something wrong without knowing I'm doing something wrong, and she pulls away and gives me a very serious look.

"What?" I ask, afraid of the answer.

"Am I ugly?"

"Ugly?"

"Am I hideous or physically repulsive in some way I'm not aware of?"

"No, of course not!"

"Then please explain to me why you've been unwilling to touch me for days. I thought we had something special. I thought things were good. But since we've left Virginia, I feel like your very chaste chaperone, and I really don't want to be your very chaste chaperone. If it's something I've said or done, please tell me, so I can make it right again. Because right now, I want to do you like long division."

Curious metaphor. It makes me wonder if she'll leave a remainder and show her work.

"It's not you, it's me. And before you tell me you hate that statement, I hate it too. But it's true. You are lovely and desirable and hot, and any reasonable man in his right mind would want to do delightfully filthy things with you. I just don't know if I'm in my right mind at the moment. The stress of this trip is taking its toll, and I don't want to start something I can't finish. I don't want to disappoint you that way."

"Tristan Shays, the only way you could disappoint me is not to try at all. I want you to clear your mind, banish any stress you feel, any fear or anxiety, and just open yourself up to feel. Let me take us where we want to be. You just come along for the ride, and I promise to take you places that will take away any troubles you're feeling."

I do—and she does.

SATURDAY, AUGUST 18, 2007

Screaming. I'm awakened hours later by, of all things, a man screaming in pain. It's been awhile since I've had to deal with the lack of privacy that comes with apartment life, but all I can think as this poor bastard screams me awake is *It's a little early for this, don't you think?*

God's truth, it takes me almost a full minute of this sonic intrusion before I'm aware that the poor bastard screaming in pain is me. A combination of weariness and the sheer impossibility of this level of pain actually dissociate me from the moment long enough to make me believe that someone else is enduring the agony. If only it were. Because, in actuality, as the present circumstances become clear, I realize that my eyes are burning as if someone has diced a bowl of jalapenos in there.

Further lucidity grants me even worse news—I can't see through the four-alarm fire that is my eyes. I feel Genevieve sitting next to me in bed, holding on to my shoulders, desperate to know what's wrong. Among the screams, all I can say is, "My eyes! Burning! I can't see!"

She leaps out of bed and returns seconds later with a wet washcloth and a small bowl full of cold water. Quickly she assists me in dunking my eyes into the water. The relief is extremely fleeting. The pain returns in a few seconds, as strong as before, and my vision is still gone. I can hear the fear and confusion in her voice as she wonders aloud what I wonder silently—how could this happen, particularly during sleep?

My answer comes moments later, as I begin to see. For a moment, I am relieved, thinking I have my eyesight back, but then I realize the images are in my head—a building marked Hart Senate Office Building, a door, a man at his desk. "Oh, shit," I manage to say, "it's an assignment!"

"Your eyes?" she asks. "The pain? It's an assignment?"

"Yes. Yes." I try to stay focused as the details come in, and when I have enough information to what I need to do, I cry out, "I'll do it! I promise, I'll go there! I'll go today, I'll go now. Just make it stop!"

And like that, the pain subsides. It is not gone completely, but it ebbs enough that I can open my eyes. To my supreme relief, I am able to see what's happening around me. "What is it?" she asks. "Where do you have to go?"

"It's here," I reply, not believing my luck. "It's in Washington. But I have to go this morning. A senator is in danger, the senator from Florida. He's planning to visit his home tomorrow, and if he does, there are people there waiting for him who plan to kill him."

"But why?"

"I'm not sure. I didn't get that information. But it's not just some private citizen with a gun and a grudge. This is professional—like organized-crime level professional."

"What are you going to do?" she asks.

"I have to go there, to his office, and warn him. A phone call or an e-mail won't do it. He has to see my face, see that I'm serious, that the threat is credible."

"What if he thinks that you're behind it somehow?"

"I have to take that chance. For one thing, if I don't do this, I may never be able to see again."

"Just be careful, please."

"I will. But I don't know how long this is going to take, so I have to take care of some business." I get up and find my phone, followed by the business card for the Swift facility. I dial the number and warm up a voice I haven't had to use since the day I didn't want to go to school. "Hello, this is Tristan Shays," I say in a pained moan. "I'm in the study, and I'm supposed to come in this morning. I'm having stomach issues, and I don't think I'll be in for the morning dose. ... Yes, I understand, but I literally can't be away from my bathroom for more than five minutes at a time. I'll be back in as soon as I can, but please let my nurse practitioner know that I can't come in this morning. ... Thank you."

As I end the call, I am aware of a dull residual pain in my eyes. At the moment, I'll take it. Honestly, I can't remember anything ever hurting as much as my eyes did just minutes ago. Mercifully, because the pain had no physical cause, it subsided just as quickly as it came. Now all that remains is a hint of its former fury, just to remind me that it could return if I'm not diligent.

A thought occurs to me. "Would a senator be in his office on a Saturday?"

"I don't know," she says. "I imagine it's the kind of job that calls for long hours. How are you going to get in to see him? Can you just show up, or do you have to make an appointment?"

"Good question. Let's go see if our guy has a Web page."

A quick check online shows that Hector Marquez, Democratic senator from Florida, does indeed have a Web page, as well as an office in the Hart Building. It is no surprise to see that he is currently in Washington and will be in his office from 9:00 a.m. to 3:00 p.m. today.

On his page, he welcomes his constituents to have coffee with him in his office when he's there. I've found my in.

It's still pretty early, but it's worth a chance. I call the number for the Washington office, and I'm surprised to get an answer after two rings. "Senator Marquez's office, can I help you?"

"Yes, thank you. I'm glad you're in. I'm one of the senator's constituents, and I'm only in Washington for the weekend. I know it's very short notice, but I was hoping that I could do a quick fifteen-minute coffee with the senator this morning. I'd like to talk to him about volunteering for the initiative he's planning. I also have some discretionary income from a recent inheritance, and I'd like to discuss donating to the fund he's established."

I know I've said a lot rapid fire, and I hope it's not too much, but I'm definitely stacking the deck. Maybe it'll be enough.

There is a pause, and then the woman on the line says, "The senator has a pretty full schedule today, but I'm showing fifteen minutes available right at 9:00. Can you be here at that time?"

"Yes, I can. Thank you very much."

"And can I have your name, please?"

I'm not sure why, but I think an alias is a good idea here. "It's Alan White."

"All right, Mr. White. We'll see you at 9:00."

"Thank you again. I'll see you soon."

The appointment means I don't have much time to prepare. A shower is definitely in order, particularly in light of my surrender to Genevieve's seduction of last night. Good clothes; don't want to look shabby when I spout wild prophecies of doom. Sad to think that my outfit could be the barometer of my sanity. *Listen to that man and his ravings! Yes, but look how nice his slacks are.*

"Showering," I announce.

"Want some company?"

"Tempting as that is, I'm on a tight schedule." I put my arms around her. "But you've shown me the true path, and I promise not to leave you hungry for affection from now on."

"Thank you. Now go get clean. You've got a senator to save."

I feel good about this assignment. The fact that it's in Washington and I'm in Washington make me believe that even though my current task at Swift isn't an official assignment, whoever's pulling the strings doesn't want me to leave here until I succeed. That's a positive reinforcement, definitely. On top of that are the details of this situation. I'm not supposed to leap in front of a bullet or defuse a bomb. I just have to tell the man that he's in danger if he goes home tomorrow. He thanks me, I go back to the apartment, and all is well. No fuss, no danger. *Just this once, please?*

I follow the directions to the Hart Senate Office Building. I was hoping to go to the Capitol Building itself, but no such luck. Just as well, anyway; I'm not here to sightsee. Safely parked in visitor parking, I check the directory and find that Senator Marquez's office is on the third floor. It's 8:58 when I enter the office, very glad not to be late.

As I enter, a woman behind the reception desk says, "You must be Mister …" She hesitates a moment, and then, in a less certain voice, finishes, "White." She looks up at me, her face a combination of puzzlement and familiarity. "Wait here just a moment."

With that, she disappears into the senator's inner office. But who is she? She looked at me like she knows me, but I don't recognize her face. Her voice did sound familiar, but I couldn't say from where. And why did she say my name like that? Does she doubt my alias? She has every reason to, and now that I think about it, if she asks for ID, I'm done.

After a couple of minutes of waiting, I begin to wonder if coming here was such a good idea. Just as I start toying with the idea of making a quick and discreet exit, the office door opens again, and the woman steps out. "You can go in now, Mr. White."

"Thank you."

She returns to her desk as I enter the inner office and close the door behind me. Inside, the senator is seated at his desk, with coffee service for two in front of him. No one else is in the room, which I find strange. I don't know if I was expecting Secret Service or a private security guard or something, but I didn't expect alone time with a United States senator, that's for sure.

He stands as I enter, offering his hand. "Thanks for coming in this morning, Mr. White. It's good to meet you."

I give him my hand in return. "Thank you for seeing me, Senator."

He offers me a seat and pours coffee for us both. "I'm told you wanted to see me because you were interested in volunteering to help with the Florida Wildlife Initiative."

"Actually, sir, that was a pretext. I'm sorry, but I had to get in to see you today."

He looks concerned at this; no doubt the risk of having an open-door policy when you're an important elected official. I need to set his mind at ease.

"I assure you, I mean you no harm, but there are people out there who do. That's why I came to see you, to warn you about a threat to your safety. If you want to call security personnel or anyone you like in here while I'm telling you about this, that's fine. I don't want you to feel uncomfortable around me. But the threat I've learned about pertains to tomorrow, so I had to see you today."

"I'm going to assume that your name isn't actually Alan White, then."

"No, sir. It's Tristan."

"Of course," he says. "Tristan Shays, isn't that it?"

My turn to be surprised. "Do you know me?"

"We've only met once, when your company put in the LED lighting system for the Florida state capitol building, but I remembered your name and your face. And now, here you are, to warn me of danger. How did that come about?"

"Very recently, I've become aware of a gift I possess, a foreknowledge of dangerous situations. I have the ability to warn people about those situations, to prevent them from happening. Today I got a warning about you."

"That's extraordinary. Well, Mr. Shays, I can't say I understand how this is possible, or even say for certain if I believe it. But I think, given the circumstances, I'd be a fool not to listen to you. So please tell me what you came here to say."

"Thank you, sir. As I understand it, you're planning on going home to Tampa tomorrow, is that correct?"

"That was the plan, yes."

"From what I was able to see, there is a group of people there who are opposed to legislation you're working on. It would harm their business activities, and they plan to stop you by using violent means. I'm sorry; I know that can't be easy to hear."

"Consolidated," he says, a frustrated familiarity in his voice.

"I'm sorry?"

"Consolidated Offshore. They're an oil interest that's been looking for drilling rights off the coast of Florida. Trouble is, the area they want is protected, and I've been working on legislation to keep it protected. They have lobbyists who've been trying to sway me, win my favor, but I've rejected everything they've offered. They hadn't turned to violence yet, but now it looks like they're changing gears. I had hoped that they would be reasonable and enter into discussions on the subject, but it seems they want to make an example of me."

"Now that you know, I hope you'll cancel your trip tomorrow."

"I appreciate your concern, but I have to go."

"But why?" I ask, feeling like my trip was wasted.

"Because backing down would be a show of weakness, a message to those who want to control me that they're in charge. I need to be there, surrounded by security and surrounded by the media. Consolidated's people hide in shadows and strike without being seen. Tomorrow, if they plan to be there, I'll make sure that they are seen."

"Everything I know about tomorrow tells me that the only way you'll be safe is if you're not in Tampa."

He nods. "Understood. Just as you understand why I have to be there. Consider your endeavor a success. You delivered your warning, and because of it, I'll have an advantage. I know they'll be there, and I know what they're planning. Maybe they'll get lucky and injure me or even kill me. But they'll do so in front of the eyes of the world, and the act will be shown as one of violence and cowardice."

"What if they don't mind that? What if a public spectacle of taking down their enemies is just the shot in the arm that Consolidated needs to display how dangerous they are?"

He smiles a bit at my words. "You've given this some thought. If they were an organization devoted exclusively to criminal activity, that might have some appeal, but this is, by all appearances, a respectable business, one that wants to do what's right for America. Killing senators would tarnish that image."

"You're a brave man, Senator. Knowing what I know, I don't think I could still be at that place and time, standing tall like nothing's wrong."

"There's some fear there, Mr. Shays. Don't doubt it. I don't know if there's a man alive who could remain unflinching at a foretelling of his own murder. All I can do, all any of us can do, is make the best decisions based on the information we have."

"I hope to hear many good things you've done in your long and healthy future," I tell him, rising from my chair.

"I hope to do those things," he replies, rising from his. "Thank you for coming here today. Some people would have ignored such a warning or left things to fate."

"Believe me, I had a burning need to share this warning with you."

He shakes my hand. "Enjoy the rest of your stay in Washington. And be safe in wherever the world sends you."

I step out of Hector Marquez's office feeling like I've failed, even though my rational mind (and my unburning eyes) tell me that I've done everything I can do. Still, despite my best efforts, this good man might be killed tomorrow. So distracted am I by this thought that I almost exit the outer office without acknowledging the woman who showed me in. Before I can complete this breach of courtesy, she stops me by asking, "Everything go well in there?"

Huh? Oh, right—you.

"Yes, thank you. The senator is a good and thoughtful man. Thank you for helping me to meet with him today."

And that would have been the end of it. A moment of polite conversation to end this social interaction. I would never have even thought about her again, except she chooses to say, "Maybe we'll see each other again."

Without a reply, I leave the office, my face almost certainly reflecting the puzzlement at that statement. It isn't so much *what* she said but *how* she said it that leaves me wondering. *Who is she? Why does she sound familiar but not look familiar? And why say that? Is that how she sends everyone off who comes to visit? Damn it, who is she? When she saw my face, she hesitated over my alias, suggesting that she knows me from somewhere. I would call that too great of a coincidence, but the last few weeks have shown me an interconnectitude of events beyond anything I would have thought possible. So maybe the forces that use me have put me in the path of someone I know—or someone I should know. One way to find out: do nothing and see if she appears in my path again. If so, I'll know something's at work here beyond what's normal.*

By the time I get back to the apartment, it's a bit late to go in to Swift for my morning dose, but more importantly, I really don't want to. Missing a dose isn't going to hurt me, because—let's face it—the plan is to miss all the doses. Nurse Whoever doesn't even check to see if I've taken it—which I know shouldn't bother me, because my goal is to fake swallowing the pills anyway—but there's a certain feeling of inattentiveness that just annoys me about her. A rational person could point out that I'm probably just pouting over Cheryl's dismissal, which is, I'm 160 percent sure, my fault. Ergo, anyone who follows her will fail by comparison. Florence goddamn Nightingale herself could have walked into my room, and I would've sulked because she's no Cheryl. I am clearly undergoing the wrong kind of therapy.

"You're back so soon," Genevieve observes upon my return. "Did it work? Did you convince him?"

"Yes and no," I reply, proceeding to explain the relative ease with which the senator accepted my words, followed by his brave and potentially foolhardy decision to go ahead with his trip tomorrow. "But at least he goes in knowing what's waiting for him. Maybe he can catch someone in the act, before the act gets too dangerous."

The day continues, and I do go in for my afternoon and early evening doses, both of which I conveniently pantomime. I could go into detail about the appointments, but they are both dull—that's right, frightfully mundane. No chase scenes, no mysterious substances in syringes, no evil henchmen, not even a dramatic pause as a door opens slowly. My appointments today have all the narrative appeal of a prostate exam, without the dramatic tension.

This uneventfulness eats at my thoughts on my way back to the apartment. I'm surprised upon arriving to find Genevieve outside, waiting for me. "What's up?" I ask.

"I'm hungry," she says. "Trust my judgment?"

"Uhh, sure."

She gets in the passenger side. "Good. Then turn left at the stop sign. I feel like chili dogs tonight."

We head to a venerable Washington establishment world famous for the entrée in question and get a booth. While I don't normally seek out chili dogs in my daily travels, I have to admit that the one in front of me, along with its accompanying french fries, looks pretty damn good. My companion, be it through means psychic or just observant, sees my current state of mind. "You look troubled."

"Ironically," I reply, "I'm troubled because I'm *not* troubled."

She takes a bite of her chili dog, pausing to make a face of complete ecstasy, before saying, "Explain."

I take a bite of my own, making a similar face. "Today's appointments were completely uneventful, and I don't know why. They know I'm here; they even know I'm not part of their study. Why is nothing happening?"

"So you want them to … what … kill you to prove a point?"

"No, of course not. But why has nobody confronted me? Why was I not manhandled by two big goons and dropped before the desk of the man in charge, so he can explain his nefarious plans before he kills me?"

She takes another bite and a couple fries. "Sweetheart, you watch too many movies."

"Perhaps."

"Okay, let's turn things around. You're the bad guys, and you're in your lair. The police show up outside, shouting, 'Open up! Let us in!' Do you start shooting, or do you open the door, show them around, and let them believe everything's on the up and up?"

"B, I suppose."

"B if you're smart. You came here for a showdown. You wanted to collect enough evidence to prove they're crooked and then have a final standoff where you take them down, exposing their nefarious plans, thwarting them, and getting the girl. Stop me if I'm off track."

"Well … I'm doing okay on the getting-the-girl part."

"Granted. The rest of it, though? I don't mean to burst your hero bubble, but if you're expecting that kind of confrontation, it's not going to start with them. They don't have to beat you, Tristan. They just have to outlast you. The study calls for patients to spend seven days at Swift. All they have to do is lay low for those seven days, do nothing suspicious, and then send you on your merry way. Bye-bye, thanks for visiting. Tell your friends!"

"But, with Cheryl …"

"Cheryl said too much, and odds are, they showed her the door. They couldn't risk letting you talk to her again after that, so they quietly sent her home and didn't make a big deal about it with you. Strategically speaking, they're playing things perfectly. I don't think they know about the level of evidence that you've collected. Somehow, and I don't know how, they don't even know about what you did with Kolodziej. I suspect if they did, you wouldn't be quite so unmolested."

"As tight as security is at that place, how could they let me be alone up there, give me access to those drugs, and give me time alone with him? There's a piece missing that I just don't know, and it's frustrating."

"Whatever happens, don't feel like you have to do everything while you're here this week. You can gather evidence while you're here and then strategize from home, where it's safer."

"I suppose you're right." My attention is diverted by a familiar-looking restaurant patron getting up from his table behind Genevieve. "Huh."

"What?" she asks.

"This must be meet-your-legislators day. Coming up behind you is Senator Obama from Illinois."

"Isn't he running for president next year?" she says.

"Yep." The senator passes our table, and I figure, why not greet the man? "Evening, Senator. Good luck next year."

I offer my hand, and he shakes it. "Thank you. I hope I can count on your support."

"I think that can be arranged," I reply, "just as long as you can give the country some change we can believe in."

The senator pauses at these words. "Change we can believe in. You know something? I like the sound of that."

Chapter 7

It's been a good night's sleep. This realization strikes me as I awaken Sunday morning, feeling refreshed for the first time in a week. I feel like I can face whatever the day brings. At this precise moment, I decide to roll over onto my left arm, and I realize how very wrong I am.

"Ow!"

The sound wakes Genevieve, who groggily asks, "What's wrong? Are you all right?"

"I think so. I just rolled over, and I got a real twinge in my arm."

"Try to sit up. Let me take a look at it."

I try to move into a sitting position, but in so doing, I have to put weight on that arm, and it simply won't accept it. The result is a flash of pain so strong, it feels like a knife is being thrust into my shoulder. "Ahhhhhhh! Ow, damn it. I can't. What's going on?"

She helps me to sit up and begins working her hands up and down my arm, looking for anything out of the ordinary. When she gets up to my shoulder, every place she touches radiates pain up and down my arm. "Did you strain it somehow, injure it maybe?"

"No. I don't think so, at least. But it hurts so much."

"Can you lift it?" she asks.

I make an attempt to lift my arm straight out at the shoulder, but I quickly realize this isn't going to be possible. The best I can muster is

109

to raise my forearm at the elbow, while my upper arm remains tucked to my body. Even this causes more pain than I'm comfortable with.

"I hate to mention the subject," she says, "but is it possible that this is part of an assignment?"

"No, if this were an assignment, I'd also be getting—" Before I can even finish the sentence, my senses are assaulted with the sights, sounds, and smells of a house on fire. The sensation is so real, I can feel the smoke and the heat of the fire. I am dimly aware of Genevieve saying my name, but my entire thought process is absorbed with the details of this fire. An old house, made of wood; a Victorian. One person inside, asleep; but outside it's daylight, late afternoon. She's unaware of the fire and has to be warned. A name comes to me—Editha Sayre—followed by an address, 1894 North Kellogg Street, Galesburg, Illinois.

No, no, not Illinois. How can I possibly get there? How can I leave Washington now, with everything else that's going on?

As if in answer, I get to watch her fate, as the flames and smoke fill her bedroom. The smoke is so thick, I can barely see her; she is just an outline of a form as the fire steals her life. The sight of it jars me from the vision and back to the present moment.

My lungs are burning as I look into Genevieve's face, a look of panic starting to creep over me. "What did you see?" she asks.

"Someone's going to die this afternoon."

"Where? In Washington again?"

"No, in a small town in Illinois."

"That's so far away ..." she says.

"How could I possibly go? I already missed a session yesterday. I'd have to miss all three today. I can't risk getting kicked out of the study."

"Send me," she offers.

"It's a house fire. It's too dangerous."

"Another fire. Like the church in Georgia. You warned *them* by phone. You could warn this person."

"And you remember how well that worked *last* time."

"Yes, you scared the receptionist, but she did what you told her to do, and by doing that, you spared that church from burning to the ground. Come with me." She helps me to stand, and we go to the computer. "Do you have a phone number for this person?"

"No, just a name. Editha Sayre, and an address in Galesburg, Illinois."

She opens a web browser and inputs the name and address. No listing comes up. "So we can't contact her directly. But Galesburg has to have a police department and a fire department. Let's start with them."

We get the number for the Galesburg Police Department, and I place the call as best I can, one-handed.

After two rings, a man's voice says, "Galesburg Police, Sergeant Waggoner speaking."

"Sergeant, good morning. I'm calling from Washington, DC. I have information that I need to share with you. I know this is going to sound strange, and I can't even fully explain how I know this, but there's going to be a fire, a house fire, later today, just after 4:00 in the afternoon."

"You mean to tell me someone's going to set fire to a house?" he asks.

"That's right. They're arsonists, and they're going to burn the house at 1894 North Kellogg Street." I don't actually know this for sure, but I'm much more likely to get their cooperation if they think so.

"Who are they? Who's going to do this, and why?"

"I don't know who they are," I reply, disturbed by how much my arm still hurts, despite my efforts to prevent this fire. "I don't have that information. But I think they're trying to kill the person who lives there and make it look like an accident."

"Sir, you said you're in Washington. How did you learn about this plan?"

I don't like where this is going. "I'm part of a citizens' security team that monitors criminal activity and shares its findings with local law enforcement."

"I see. What's the name of the group, please?"

Words come out of my mouth, loosely strung together. "Citizens … Organized … for Urban Protection."

"Ah, you're a member of COUP. I'm familiar with them."

How the fuck did that happen? I could just as easily have said Fornicating Wombats in Grape Jelly, in my current state of mind. But somehow, my brain put together the name of an actual citizens' group?

"Yes. Yes, I am."

"And what's your name?" he asks.

"I'd rather not say. It's part of the ... the code of how we conduct our business."

"Sir, I appreciate this information, but it's department policy not to act on anonymous tips. I assure you, I'll keep your identity safe from these people, but in order for me to get my officers on this, I'll need your first and last name."

So close now; so close to having them take me seriously. They want a name? Fine, I'll give them a name. "My name is Tristan Shays."

For a moment, there is silence on the line before he speaks again. "Tristan Shays. That's what you said your name is?"

"Yes."

"Well, that's a strange coincidence, sir. I happen to have the current issue of *Business Week* magazine on my desk, and I just read an article about a Mr. Tristan Shays, who stepped down as CEO of a major manufacturing company."

"Yes, that's me."

"You wouldn't happen to have that same magazine, and that was a name you saw and chose to give me?"

"No, honestly, I'm Tristan Shays. I'm not making this up."

"Tell me again what the name of your group was?"

Crap, what was it again? "Citizens United for Urban Protection."

I screwed it up; I know I did. He knows it too.

"Sir, I'm not sure what it is you're trying to do, but there's such a thing as false reporting, and it's against the law."

"Okay, you got me. I'm not in Washington; I'm in Galesburg. My name is Pete Johnson, and I'm the arsonist. Send your people to 1894 North Kellogg at 4:00 this afternoon, and I'll turn myself in. I'm crazy, and I'm a little dangerous, and boy, do I love burning stuff. Meet me at that house today, and I'll go quietly."

"Have a good day, sir. Please don't call us again."

He hangs up, and I realize—courtesy of a fresh flare-up of pain in my arm—just how colossally I have wrecked things.

"That didn't sound so good," Genevieve observes. "They didn't believe you?"

"Yeah, imagine that! With my watertight story and all. It figures that when I finally decide to use my own name, I find the one person who's heard of me, and he doesn't really believe it's me."

"So they're not sending the police?"

"I'm not sure. They might, but there's no guarantee. But I'm not done yet." I do a new Web search, this time for the Galesburg Fire Department.

Seeing this, Genevieve says, "Good thinking."

I find the number, but instead of calling it, I write it down. "It's the foreknowledge that always gets me in trouble. But if I call them just before this fire is set to start, they can get there in time to prevent any loss of life. Fire's supposed to happen just after 4:00, so I'll call at 3:45."

"Wait, 3:45 or 2:45? Does the warning give you the time zone you're in or the time zone the other person is in?"

"I … I really don't know. I've never warned anyone in any time zone besides my own. I have to believe that it's the time zone of the person I'm sent to warn."

"Given that you don't know," she says, "maybe you should go with the earlier time, just in case."

"So 2:45 today. I'll remember."

"And I'll remind you."

"Thank you. But I'm still not done. I can't leave this to chance." I open my phone again and go to the directory, looking for a specific name. Finding it, I call that number, and I listen as the phone rings once, twice, and then a third and a fourth time.

At the moment I'm certain I'll be talking to a machine, a familiar voice says, "It's pretty early in the morning for my phone to be ringing. This better be good."

Harry Cohen. My friend of fifteen years and the best private investigator I've ever known. Over the years, he's been a tremendous help to me in personal and professional matters. His chosen location of Chicago has occasionally been an inconvenience, but today it puts him right where I want him.

Despite the stern words, the voice makes me smile. "Harry, it's Tristan. Forgive the early hour, but I need your services, and it's kind of an emergency."

"Tristan Shays," he says, sounding glad to hear from me. "What's this shit I hear about you stepping down from your position? You get some secretary pregnant?"

"Nothing so scandalous or romantic. I just found a calling that needs my time and attention."

"Please don't tell me you found Jesus, or I may just puke."

"Don't worry," I reply, "you're safe. But the truth of the matter is relevant to my call today. You ever work with psychics?"

"I've met a couple. Never put much stock in 'em, though. Most of the time, they're full of shit. The ones who get the job done are either exceptionally observant or lucky guessers. Why? What are you trying to tell me?"

"Awhile back, you told me that when you work, you get hunches. Really strong intuition about a person or a place, and it directs you. Harry, I've got something like that going on too now. But it's beyond hunches. It's like … visions. Dates, times, names. I know ahead of time when something's going to happen to somebody."

"Jesus. Do you know tomorrow's lottery numbers, too? Of course, with you, y'don't even need it, do you?"

"Harry, please. I know that world-weary skepticism is like a fashion statement for a P.I., but I need you to believe me. A woman's going to burn to death in her home today if I don't find a way to stop it. I can't reach her by phone, and I've already screwed things up with the local PD. I'm going to try the fire department closer to the time it's supposed to happen, but I need a backup, a failsafe. I need you there, Harry."

"Where exactly are we talking about?"

"Galesburg, Illinois."

"Galesburg? Shit, Tristan, that's almost five hours from here by car."

"You're my only hope."

"I charge more for only hope, you know."

"I'll give you a thousand plus mileage. I need you to be in Galesburg, at this house, no later than 3:45 this afternoon. Harry, I think this might be a case of arson, and if it is, I'm hoping you can stop them and find out who they are. I don't know if you can get the police to come out there. I already told them the address and the time, and they didn't believe me."

"Piece of cake. You'd be amazed how quickly three shots in the air bring the police."

"So you'll do it?"

"Shays, if this was anyone else calling me before 7:00 in the morning with this kind of thing, I'd tell them to go fuck themself. But because it's you, I'll do it."

"Thank you, Harry."

"I would tell you it's on the house, but I'm not *that* nice."

"You'll be compensated. Don't worry. I may have quit my job, but I have a little money saved up."

"Yeah, like the same way Singapore's got a little money saved up. Gimme the details—name, address, exact time, anything I should know."

"The address is 1894 North Kellogg Street, Galesburg. Resident's name is Editha Sayre."

"Editha? Sounds like a beauty."

"Be nice, *Harold*. We're not recruiting her for a swimsuit calendar. When you get there, if you determine that it's arson, talk to her. See if she knows who might want to kill her. The fire is going to start at 4:03 this afternoon."

There is a moment or two of silence before he quietly asks, "This is really what you do now?"

"Yeah. It's what I do now."

"Why? I mean, for me, it's the money, the thrill of the hunt, that sort of thing. But you? To give up running your own company so you can chase around warning people they're in danger. Why do you do it?"

"You want the honest answer or the noble answer?" I ask.

"Give me both."

"I do it because it's the right thing to do. Because for some reason, I have advance knowledge that can save people's lives, and when I do, it feels incredible. Better than anything I've ever felt in my life."

"And the honest answer?"

"If I try to refuse, I'm hit with pain somewhere in my body. Right now, it feels like I have about five swords going through my left shoulder. I'm hoping like hell that sending you will make that pain go away. I would go myself, but I'm on another assignment now, tracking down what might be some really bad people. That's why I need you."

"Well, that's very touching, Tristan, but I'd better go hit the showers. I think I've got a bit of a drive ahead of me."

"Call me on this number if you need anything. Thank you, Harry. I really appreciate this."

"Thank me when I save her."

I put the phone down with my good arm, and Genevieve quickly steps behind me to put her arms around my shoulders, being careful not to hurt me. "So he'll do it?" she says.

"Yeah. He'll do it."

"That's a relief."

"It is. What troubles me is that my arm still hurts. This much effort on my part should have done something to take the pain away, even a little. What if it's not good enough for them? What if it has to be me?"

"It's okay, it's okay. Come back to bed. I'll make up an ice pack for your shoulder. That should help with the pain."

With considerable effort, I return to our bed and lie down on my back, struggling to get into a comfortable position without relying on my left arm. As I do so, I think about my day ahead and how beneficial it might be to have two arms. But if that's not going to be the case, I'll have to get by with one. Lots of people do it every day. It's not like I have any paper-hanging to do today. Three trips in to Swift, that's all. The rest of the day can be spent in this bed, covered by blankets and soothed by ice packs.

Genevieve enters the room carrying a small towel wrapped around a considerable number of ice cubes from the freezer. She's even moistened the towel to allow the cold to conduct through it faster. Gingerly she sits next to me on the bed, slowly lowering the makeshift ice pack to my afflicted shoulder. I brace myself in the manliest way I know how, trying hard not to look as if I'm about to shriek like a little girl. As the ice meets my skin, I feel a subtle sensation of relief; numbing would be a better description, as the feeling of cold temporarily overwhelms the burning, stabbing, shooting pain that ruled only seconds ago.

The relief is fleeting, though, as the pain surges again, throbbing with each heartbeat. She runs her fingers through my hair as I utter subdued cries of discomfort. Then, to my surprise, she begins to sing.

"Through darkest night and steepest road,
When winds are harsh and bleak and cold,
When sunlight's dimmed and gone away,
And clouds have stolen warmth of day.

"Just rest your head and ease your pain,
And let me hold you once again.
Just close your eyes and feel my touch,
And know I'll love you, oh so much."

"That was beautiful," I say quietly. "Who wrote the song?"
Tears come to her eyes as she answers simply, "I did. Right now."
My next words follow without doubt or hesitation. "I love you."
She continues to cry, tears without sorrow. "And I love you."

I awaken sometime later, still in the same position, with a considerably wetter towel on my shoulder. I look around for Genevieve, but I don't see her right away. Turning a bit brings pain, and I cry out a little. The sound rouses her; she's been on the other side of me the whole time. "Are you all right?" she asks. "Do you need anything?"

"How long have I been asleep?"

"Almost two hours. Are you feeling any better?"

"A little. Thank you for everything you did."

"Of course. Are you planning to go in to the clinic?"

With some difficulty, I sit up. "I really should. It's the reason I didn't go to Illinois."

"I can drive you," she offers.

"Thank you. I'd like that."

In half an hour, we are out in front of the apartment building, on our way to my morning appointment. It's after 10:00 in the morning already, but not too late for the first non-dose of the day at Swift. Genevieve drops me off out front with the ever-present request, "Be careful."

"I will. I promise."

I check in and report to my regular treatment room. Shortly, I'm greeted by Greta—whose name I have managed to remember somehow. "A little later than usual today," she comments.

"Rough night," I reply. "I tried to catch up on some sleep."

Before I can say something helpful like, *By the way, my left arm's a bit pained, so please don't wrench it like a professional wrestler going for a takedown move,* she wrenches my left arm like a professional wrestler going for a takedown move. Her intention is to take my blood pressure, but my reaction ends that in a hurry.

It begins with the loudest scream I think I've ever emitted, followed by a string of vulgarities which, though not directed *at* Greta, cascade over her like the world's most unpleasant river at flood stage. It is at this moment that my actions take a sharp left turn away from rational, and I give voice to the pain and frustration welling up inside of me. I'm aware of what I'm saying, but reason surrenders to severely pissed, and it's time to blame somebody. In deference to centuries of mythos about where God lives, I look up at the ceiling, raise the arm that's not killing me, and produce a fist, which I then shake.

"What the fuck do you want from me? I got your message! I got your latest orders. In case you haven't noticed, I'm a little fucking busy right now! I can't just fly halfway across the country to do your bidding. But I'm sending somebody. Didn't you see? Didn't you hear me this morning? I'm sending someone to take care of it!"

I'm vaguely aware of Greta picking up the phone in the room and hurriedly uttering the words, "Code 22, room 9." Were I not otherwise occupied, I might take a moment to deduce that "code 22" is medical-people talk for "Patient is having a psychotic break. Perhaps you might join me in stopping him from doing so."

But no, I'm too busy shouting obscenities at the creator of the universe. "Isn't that fucking good enough for you? You have to punish me with this much goddamn pain? I'm trying! I'm fucking trying to do exactly what you want me to do! Why are you making this so damned difficult?"

I'm not sure how much longer this particular tirade would have gone on, because at the moment, two large men I don't recognize enter the room in a considerable hurry, bringing with them two things that won't end well for me: a large syringe and a wheelchair. Before I can say, "Good day, gentlemen. Is there something I can help you with?" one of them jams said syringe into my arm—*left* arm, of course—while the other eases my instantly delirious body backward into the waiting wheelchair.

The last thing I remember before slipping beneath the inky waters of unconsciousness is Greta's voice saying, "Take him to sedation."

Haze. Sounds are flanged and echoey. *Where am I? How did I get here?* Bright, fluorescent lights bathe the room. I'm lying on my back, but where? Above me, figures move back and forth as I struggle for focus. As lucidity returns, I become aware that I'm unable to move. My eyes slowly comprehend that I am strapped to the table, restrained—with my arms extended to the sides.

And like a lightning bolt, agony returns to my afflicted left arm. A cry escapes me, a mutant sound of physical anguish, helplessness, and fear that comes from a place within me I didn't know exists, a primal region of pure instinct that could give birth to enough rage to kill everyone in this room, if only I weren't tied down.

"He's coming around," a man says. "Tristan, it's all right. I'm Doctor Trask. You're safe."

The courteous thing would be for me to let him talk, but I'm not capable of this at the moment, so the screaming continues. He persists in speaking, raising his voice to be heard over me. "It looks like you're having some localized pain in your arm. What we're going to do today is called sedation therapy. It's a combination of an aerosol version of the pain reliever you've been taking for the study, combined with something to help you sleep."

I am barely conscious of what he's saying, but the words *pain reliever* and *help you sleep* sound pretty damn appealing right now, so I don't fight him.

"Try to stay calm," he continues, still talking over my shouts and sobs. "Soon we're going to put a mask on your nose and mouth. When we do, I need you to breathe as normally as you can. In between each breath, I want you to start counting down, count backwards from one hundred. Okay, Tristan, you're doing great. Here we go."

A black mask quickly covers my nose and mouth, muffling the sounds I'm making. For a moment, I have a feeling of suffocating, but soon air flows into the mask—light and slightly sweet-tasting.

"Count down for me, Tristan."

A memory stirs. *Never count down. They'll want you to count down.* The words of Stanislaw Kolodziej on the telephone to me last week, before I even knew who he was. His warning to me. *Stay in control. Always stay in control.* Yet, here I am, surrendering my control to them in just the way he warned me against.

"One hundred …" *breathe* "… ninety-nine …" *breathe* "… ninety-eight …" *breathe* "… ninety-sev—"

Without warning, without ceremony, without explanation, the world slips away from me, and I find myself in a place where there is no pain, no screaming, no chaos or confusion. Only tranquility, quantities of gentle light, plenty of air, and a feeling of floating upon it. I'm alive—at least I'm pretty sure—as I'm aware of my breathing. Looking at my own body, I see that wherever I am, I have no restraints on me, no mask on my face. There is no table beneath me and I'm wearing comfortable clothing. I am alone, and I feel no anxiety; just a powerful sensation of pleasant warmth.

Relieved, I close my eyes, and my thoughts carry me to a place that feels like the dreams of early sleep—the kind that come during those moments when you're conscious enough to remember them. I grab hold of those dream images and let them take me wherever they want to go. In some, I am flying just above the ground, arms outstretched as I look at the verdant landscape below me. I feel like I could stay here forever. If I *am* dead, then D.N. freakin' R.

My mind next takes me to a cruise ship, which is odd because I've never been on a cruise. Yet, here I am, standing at the railing of a huge, elegant vessel, looking out at the wavelets of turquoise water. Dolphins swim alongside the ship, and I swear if one of them leaps out of the water and says, "Hi, Tristan!" I will find a way to stay here forever. Stepping away from the railing, I stroll around a deck lined with lifeboats. I soon come to the bow of the ship, high above the ocean below. I stand at the railing again, cognizant of my desire to do the whole king-of-the-world thing but not needing to do it.

I'm surprised but not startled to hear a voice behind me say, "Beautiful, isn't it?"

I turn around to see an attractive woman in a white sundress standing behind me. She appears to be about my age, and she has a pleasant face. She's lovely, but it's curious—it's not in a way that seems to be the sum of her features. With some women, I think they have beautiful hair or amazing eyes or a terrific smile; maybe a great figure. I look at this woman, and it's like I'm programmed to think of her as generally attractive.

"It really is," I reply.

She steps up to the rail next to me. "Did you do the king-of-the-world thing?"

I smile at her question. "Thought about it but thought better of it."

"That's probably for the best." She looks out at the ocean as she speaks, rather than at me. "First time here?"

"It is. I've never been on a cruise before."

"You're not on one now," she replies matter-of-factly. Before I can register my confusion, she continues, "Your thoughts put you here. You sought out a place of tranquility, and this is where you ended up. A luxury cruise in the Mediterranean."

Freaky. "Does the place of tranquility come with a midnight buffet?"

She laughs a little at my joke. "It does if you want it to."

"What's your name?" I ask.

"Does it matter?"

Ordinarily, I would consider such a response strange and even rude, but she has a point. "No, I guess it really doesn't."

"Are you going to ask me next where we are?"

"The thought had crossed my mind. I ruled out heaven. I hope I'm right about that one."

"You're inside your own consciousness, and you have access to the very best parts of it, the parts where dreams live, where fantasies live, where things happen to you because you want them to." As if to demonstrate, she turns to me, places her hands behind my head, and kisses me. Bizarre as this is, I make no effort to resist, just as I wouldn't in a sexual dream. The concept of time is uncertain here, so I can't tell how long the kiss lasts. All I know is that it feels like no human interaction I've ever had. Her lips are soft and delicate, her tongue simultaneously forceful and gentle. When at last she pulls away, I have the strangest feeling of satisfaction, but several inches *above* where I expected to feel it. Amazed, I touch my midsection.

"You felt it in your stomach, didn't you?" she asks, sounding pleased with herself.

"Yes. Why would ..."

"It's because you were a bit hungry. When I kissed you, it triggered pleasant sensations in two different ways. Now you feel like you just enjoyed a wonderful dinner, am I right?"

"Let me put it this way: if you'll stay here with me, they can keep the midnight buffet."

She smiles at me, and I get the strange sensation of attachment to her, like she's been a trusted part of my life for years. "I *can* stay with you. Here or on a beach or in a rainforest or anywhere you've ever wanted to be. And anytime you want to be somewhere else, the simple act of wanting it is enough. Try it."

I close my eyes, and when I open them seconds later, it is night, and the two of us are standing in a grassy field, under more stars than I've ever seen in my life. In the distance, mountains reach up to the sky. A gentle breeze blows, and the temperature is perfect. Though I have willed us here, I still have to ask, "Where are we?"

"New Zealand," she says. "Wonderful choice. Look at the stars."

I look up at constellations that are alien to me. "But I don't understand. If I'm creating this in my mind, how can I know the stars? We're in the Southern Hemisphere, and I've never seen these stars before."

"You'd never been on a cruise ship before, but your mind filled in the details as it expected them to be. You could take us to other planets too, if you wanted, and we could breathe the air and interact with whoever lives there."

The perfection of it all is overpowering. I tilt my head back to take in the starscape, and in just a few seconds, I let myself fall back into the grass for a better view. She drops to her knees and then stretches out with me. *She.* The woman with no name and no need of one. My guide, standing in for mother, protector, lover, anything I need. She kisses me again, letting her hands caress me with a perfect knowledge of every single place I love to be touched. In response, I caress her as well, and in the back of my mind, a thought emerges: *This is a fantasy I've had for years—physical intimacy with a beautiful woman under the stars.* I don't know what to do with this information, but I feel that knowing it is significant.

Time passes; at least I think it does, as events proceed as in a dream here. She and I look up at the stars as she rests her head on my shoulder. "Are you happy here?" she asks.

"I can't remember when I've ever been happier."

She looks me in the eyes. "If there was a way you could stay here, would you?"

"What do you mean?"

"You're able to be here with me now because of what the doctors did for you. They gave you a larger dose of the pain medication and allowed you to sleep. Instead of dreaming, you opened the door to this place, this place of higher consciousness, where you can be anywhere you want to be. Where you can travel with me. If you like dogs, all you have to do is wish for one, and he can travel with us too. But today's visit ends when the medicine wears off. Then you'll return to the world you left. To the stress and the pain and the danger. Your life isn't your own there anymore, is it?"

"No. It isn't."

"You go where you're told and do what someone else commands you to do."

"Yes."

"It doesn't have to be that way. You can be here with me all the time, with no pain, none of the stress and fear."

The prospect sounds intoxicating. "What would I have to do?"

"When you leave the medical facility, they're going to give you the pain pills to take at home on your own. A month's worth, ninety at a time."

"Yes?"

"Take them all. All ninety on the first day. It's the way to return you to this place. To me."

"But ... but that much medication all at once ... I'd die."

"You would die to the other world, to the world of physical limitations. And you'd be born to this place."

Things aren't adding up all of a sudden. "But this isn't some kind of afterlife; it's an altered state of consciousness. If I die, I would have no consciousness at all, so how could I come here again?"

"It's okay," she says gently. "These are good questions. The human mind is powerful, more powerful than most people can comprehend. It allows *you* to know things that are going to happen to people before they happen. In the same way, human consciousness can transcend the death of the physical body. Once you've been here, as you are now, your mind can seek out this place and stay here unendingly, long after the physical form is just a memory. But you have to direct your consciousness here. You need to take the medication all at once to get you into the right mindset. Then, when you're free, you can escape your body and be here. You can be with me." She kisses me again, and once again the feeling washes over me, a sense of peace like nothing I've ever known. "You do want to be with me, don't you?"

"Yes," I answer, though the choice to do so isn't a conscious one.

"That's good, because I want to be with you. I love you."

"You … love me? How is that possible?"

"I've waited here for you to arrive. In a way, I've always loved you."

"But it's so fast. Do you even know my name?"

"Tristan!"

I am startled when the answer comes not from my new companion but from behind me and in a man's voice—specifically, *my* voice. I turn to the sound of it, and in the crowning disorienting moment of this particular journey, I actually see myself standing about twenty feet away, in the grassy field of a New Zealand of my own imagining.

"Don't listen to her," I tell me in a tone of lucidity and caution. "She's not real."

"No offense," I reply to my new arrival, "but of the two of you, she's the more likely candidate to be real, seeing as how you're me and all."

"You can fight this," the woman tells me calmly. "It's your own self-doubt and your own fear giving voice to your hesitation. That's why it looks like you."

"Good story," my potentially evil twin tells her, "but I'm actually the voice of the part of your mind that's conscious and aware of how much danger you're in."

Each makes a very good case. I point to my traveling companion. "But she's pretty, and she loves me."

He looks unimpressed by my latest argument. "Tristan, of the two of us, which one is *not* suggesting that you kill yourself?"

Equally good point. I rise and take a couple of steps toward myself. "Why is this happening?"

"Remember what you know about the drug," Tristan II answers. "Hallucinations; suicidal thoughts. That's where you are. Stanislaw warned you on the phone not to count down, not to lose control. But that's what they made you do. And this is where it got you. Look at her, Tristan. Really look at her. You have feelings of attachment to her, but you don't know why. You think she's beautiful, but not in a specific way. She feels like someone you should be with, but at the same time, she makes you uneasy."

The woman rises and faces him, her tone changing to a warning. "Stop it! You're confusing him."

"Am I? Or am I clearing things up?"

"I don't know who to believe," I tell them both.

"Maybe this will help," Other-Me says. With that, he looks to his left, and from out of the darkness, someone approaches him. She is young, maybe in her mid-twenties, with blonde hair and bright eyes. She looks strong, like a dancer. And though I don't know her name or her face, her presence here fills me with an even stronger feeling of inner peace.

"Hello, Tristan," the young woman says, sounding like she can barely contain her excitement at seeing me.

"Hello," I respond. "I'm sorry, but I don't know you."

"No, not yet. But you will, one day. But only if you leave here and don't listen to the person next to you."

"That's not fair!" the woman in white calls out to the new arrivals. "He's where he belongs!"

"You have to live," the dancer tells me. "To do that, you have to block the thoughts of this place. Forget the lies that make you believe it's where you belong. You're under sedation, under the influence of dangerous drugs in a medical facility in Washington, DC. You have to fight it. Force yourself to wake up. Please, Tristan. One day, you're going to be the most important person in my entire life, and I'm going to be someone you trust completely in every situation. Show me a little of that trust now. Force yourself to wake up. Force yourself. Fight this false reality with every bit of your rational mind. You've always believed that if something sounds too good to be true, it probably is. Look around you. Your mind has created the perfect place, where you can be anywhere you like, doing anything you want. You can conjure up a woman who's allegedly attractive."

"Hey!" the woman in white calls out.

The dancer just shrugs and looks at her in disdain. "But that's not the way the world works. Not our world; not any world I know of. That's why I came here. That's why *you* came here, to stop you from making a mistake that'll cost you your life."

The bubble is beginning to dissolve. Reason is returning to me, and I'm starting to know who to believe. "What do I do?" I ask. "How do I get out of here?"

"Concentrate," Other Tristan says. "Start by telling yourself that where you are isn't real and isn't possible."

"Next," the dancer says, "banish the bitch."

The woman in white looks at her with contempt. "You can just go fu—"

With a concentrated effort on my part, she vanishes before she can finish the word. Along with her, the idyllic landscape disappears as well, and I find myself in a dimly lit room. A moment's inspection tells me it is the sedation room at Swift. I look down at my own unconscious form on the table. My other self and the dancer have followed me here, so at present I am represented three times in the room, which is some freaky shit, no matter what plane of consciousness you're on.

"Good," Tristan II says, "you're back where you belong. They've undone your restraints and left you to sleep. This is your chance. Wake up from the sedation, and get out of here. Don't check out, don't talk to anybody, just go. Get home."

"Be safe," the dancer says, giving me a look of enormous tenderness and caring. "I'll see you soon."

With that, the two of them disappear before my eyes, and a single word lingers in my thoughts: *Persephone.*

Then, in a moment of consciousness unlike anything I've ever known, my perception shifts back to my actual physical body. I awaken on the exam table with a start and a cough, with full memory of what I've just been through. The room is indeed empty; the medical team must have left me alone to sleep it off. I'm thankful to find that they have indeed undone my restraints. I feel top-heavy as I try to sit up on the table, but with some effort, I manage to sit and then stand. To my pleasant surprise, most of the pain in my arm has gone. Now it's time to focus on getting out of here.

I get to my feet and take a few shaky steps before my sense of balance restores itself. As I open the door to the room, I find myself in an unfamiliar wing on the first floor of Swift. I am by no means in isolation, so I just have to move with purpose and get outside. Doing my best to clear the after-effects of the sedative, I march myself down the corridor, unmolested by the people I pass, who have no idea who I am or what I've just been through. But just before I get to the exit, Dr. Trask himself sees me.

"Mr. Shays, where are you going?"

Rather than answering, I make a vague flailing gesture that might indicate a lack of desire to talk about it. He's somehow undaunted by this, though. "We need to examine you before you leave for the …"

I assume the next word is *day,* but I'm out the door before it's out of the mouth. Remembering that I didn't drive myself here, I get my phone out and speed dial Genevieve. To my surprise, I hear her ring tone, not in the phone but nearby me. I look for the source of the sound and find that she is parked in the Swift parking lot, not fifty feet away from me. We see each other at the same moment, and she calls out, "Tristan!"

As I take a step toward her, I start to stagger again. She opens the car door and sprints over to me, which is probably for the best, as I'm beginning to understand why that doctor needed to examine me before I left. *Woozy* would be putting it mildly. Genevieve, meanwhile, is in a state of near panic.

"Oh my God, Tristan, are you all right? They wouldn't let me in. They wouldn't let me see you."

She guides me to the car and pours me into the passenger seat, closing the door behind me as she hurries back to the driver's seat. "I couldn't reach you by phone, and I didn't know how to call the facility, so I came here. But they wouldn't let me in. I told them you were inside, but they said I wasn't immediate family and it was off limits. I explained that I was getting worried because I hadn't heard from you and you'd been gone for so long …"

"Wait, wait," I utter, finally getting the words in edgewise, "gone for so long? How long was I in there?"

"Tristan, it's after 5:00. You were in there for seven hours."

"Oh my God …" Her words send a river of ice through my veins. Seven hours? "Did you call the Galesburg Fire Department?"

"I was going to, but I didn't know the address of the house. I'm sorry."

I grab my phone and see that I have eight missed calls. Five are from Genevieve herself, but the other three are from Harry Cohen. As Genevieve starts the car and begins to drive us home, I check the messages from Harry, using the speakerphone. The first is from three hours ago. "Tristan, Harry. I'm in Galesburg, and I went right to the address you gave me. I knocked on the door and rang the bell. No answer. I'm gonna grab some lunch and sit in my car outside the house, see what happens. I'll let you know. Call me when you get this."

The second message is from about an hour later. "Tristan, Harry again. Something's happening at the house. A couple of police cars showed up a few minutes ago. They're goin' to the door; knocking, ringing the bell, just like I did. No answer, though. They're walking around the perimeter, looking in windows. No probable cause, so they're not going in. That's standard procedure. Looks like they got your message after all, Tristan. Now they're back on the front porch. One of 'em's looking over here; I guess he saw me sitting in my car. He's talking to his partner, pointing over at me. Yep, here they come. I'll keep recording, in case anything gets dicey. Afternoon, gentlemen. How can I help you? *Sir, what's your business here?* Same as you, I suspect. Following up on potentially suspicious activity. I'm Harry Cohen. I'm a private investigator from Chicago. I'm going to reach for my ID now. Here you go. *Galesburg is quite a long way to travel, Mr. Cohen.* Well, I'm doing a favor for a friend of mine. He believes a lady here might be in trouble. I imagine he's the same one who called you. Name's Tristan Shays. You may have heard of him. He's quite a big deal in business. Only now he's adding do-gooder to his list of hobbies, and ol' Harry got the call, just in case there's something to it."

I have to laugh a bit, hearing this. I know exactly what he's doing, too. He's playing the concerned skeptic, making them think he doubts it, but showing them he cares enough to be there. It's a brilliant tactic for winning the cops over to his side. The recording continues.

"I was kinda hoping you boys might have probable cause to enter the residence, so we can all go in and make sure nothing funny is going on inside. *Well, sir, we walked the perimeter and did a visual and auditory inspection of the premises. We didn't find any probable cause to enter. We're going to leave a patrol unit with two officers here to see if we can contact the resident. You're probably clear to head back home if you'd like. We can take it from here.* Well, thank you, officer, but I promised my friend I'd see this through, so if it's all right with you, I'll stay here and keep watch too. *That's all right, Mr. Cohen. Just please honor the rules of jurisdiction if something does go down at this house, and allow the officers to do their work.* Will do. Thank you, officers."

There is a pause, presumably as the cops walk away from Harry's car. He then speaks into his phone again. "Well, that's where we stand. The yokelage is gonna stay camped out here for a bit, and so am I. Though I'm not sure your Spidey senses are right on this one. I'm seeing zip in the way of suspicious activity. Nobody hanging around, no cars passing the place repeatedly. Not even any sign of our little Editha, whoever she is. I'll stay with it, but I think you may end up giving me money for two scenic drives through the Illinois prairie. Call me when you get this."

"That's encouraging, at least," Genevieve says as she drives.

"I hope so. There's one more message, though."

"Play it."

With the speakerphone still on, I play the message from 5:03 p.m. Eastern Time. "Hey, pal. It's Harry. Well, it is exactly 4:03 p.m. Central Daylight Savings Time, and I can say after three hours of sitting here that Galesburg is the most boring place I've been in a long time. The cops and I have been camped out here, and there has been nothing going on. No Editha, and no bad guys. I don't know if our being here scared 'em off, but … Wait a second. Something's happening."

A feeling of fear washes over me at these words. Harry continues. "It looks like … Jesus, it is. Smoke. There's smoke coming out of an upstairs bedroom window." I listen as he pulls the phone away from his face long enough to yell to the police. "This is it! Call the fire department, and get inside that house! I'm going too." He returns to his message. "Tristan, I gotta go. This is happening just like you said, down to the minute, and I'd really like to know how you knew. I'll call you when I know anything."

Without another word, the message ends. A message he left sixteen minutes ago, while I was on the plains of New Zealand, looking up at imaginary stars with a woman whose love for me was as unreal as she was.

Chapter 8

Genevieve looks like she's in a state of shock as she mechanically drives us back to the apartment. Her eyes are vacant, and her mouth is open a little, as if traumatized. "Are you all right?" I ask her. "Do you need to pull over?"

"I don't know what I need," she says. "I honestly don't know what to do. I thought I'd lost you today. I thought they figured out who you were and decided that this was the day to get rid of you. I was sure I'd never see you again."

"No, nothing like that. I went in for my appointment, and the pain in my arm got so bad, I lashed out. They sedated me, and they gave me a strong dosage of the pain medication."

"The dangerous one?" she asks, considerably upset.

"Yes."

"Did anything bad happen to you because of that?"

Well-intentioned lie in three … two … one … "No, nothing. It just knocked me out for much longer than I expected. It did take care of the pain, though. I'm so sorry that I worried you."

"It's not *you*, it's this whole thing. The constant uncertainty. I don't know what to do. I don't know what to think. It's too much."

"I'm sorry that you're suffering because of this. Let's go back to the apartment and try to have a quiet evening together."

Our arrival at the apartment does nothing to help her anxiety. I sit at the dining room table while she paces. "I don't want you going back there," she says after a long silence.

"There's still work to do," I remind her.

"Then you need to find another way to do it. You went in there today, and they gave you that … that *stuff.* The lab called here today, with the analysis of the pill."

"On a Sunday?"

"Yeah. They didn't want to wait to give you their findings. So they told me what's in them. I wrote the names of the ingredients down, but I didn't recognize some of them. The pain reliever is a morphine derivative, but there's also a hallucinogen in there."

"There is?"

"Yes. And the lab guy said it wasn't needed for a pain reliever. He didn't see any medical necessity for a hallucinogen to be in this drug."

"That explains a lot," I muse, mostly to myself.

"So you see? You could have … I don't know … jumped off the roof, thinking you could fly."

"Gen, I'm okay. Really I am. They gave me the drug and a sedative, and I went to sleep. I had some weird dreams, but nothing that put me in danger. As for future appointments, I may have screwed myself in that department today anyway. Between my unfortunate treatment of my nurse practitioner and my hasty exit against medical orders, I don't imagine I'm anyone's favorite boy just at the moment."

"That's fine by me," she replies.

"I'll go through more of Kolodziej's e-mails tonight. I think by this point I have enough evidence that I don't need to go back to Swift anyway. I really want to find the people who are in charge of this operation and present my findings to them. But if I can't do that, I might go to the FBI and tell them what I know."

"Thank you," she says, sounding quite relieved.

"I promise you, I'm not trying to be reckless."

My cell phone rings, and I bring it out and quickly answer it. "Hello?"

"Tristan, finally."

"Harry, I'm sorry I missed your calls. The case I'm on now got complicated, and I didn't have access to communication. But I got your messages. What can you tell me? What happened there?"

"Jesus, Tristan … I don't even— I don't know where to start with this. When I sat there for those hours and didn't see anybody come or go, I thought it was a wasted trip. But then at three minutes after four, exactly when you said it would, that bedroom started pouring out smoke."

"I heard you say so on the phone. But you were there, and the police were there. You had them call the fire department. Were they able to get the fire put out?"

"Yeah, the fire guys got there in just a couple of minutes, and they were able to contain the fire pretty quick."

"Oh, thank God."

"Tristan, Editha Sayre is dead."

"What? How? If they controlled the fire, and she wasn't in the room …"

"She *was* in the room. In fact, she'd been in the room the whole time, in her bed. She'd been dead for about six hours, from the looks of it."

"What was the cause of death? Do you know?"

"Not for sure. There was no evidence of foul play. No blood, no gunshot wounds or stab wounds. In the bathroom next to her bedroom, we found a mostly empty bottle of pills, but I can't tell what they were. They're some sort of experimental trial drug or other. Doesn't give us any information to go on."

It's connected. It's all connected to this, to SODARCOM. Editha Sayre was in the trial. She probably killed herself after taking the drugs.

"Harry, I know about these drugs. This is what I'm investigating now. I'm … I guess you could say I'm undercover here in the medical facility that's running the trial. This woman must have been a patient in the study."

"Oh, she was more than that, sport. While the police were doing forensics in her room, I was checking out her personal papers downstairs. She came back to Galesburg just a few days ago from Washington, DC, where she'd been living and working for a couple of years. Seems she just got let go from a place called the Swift Medical Research and Testing

Center. I even found a page of her handwritten notes with your name on it."

"What?"

"Don't worry, I pocketed it. The cops won't see it. But this is serious, Tristan. Do you know what you've got yourself involved with here?"

"I thought I did, but maybe I don't."

"Well, the late Editha Cheryl Sayre seems to suggest …"

"What did you say, Harry?"

"Editha Cheryl Sayre. The victim's full name."

"Oh my God."

"What?" he asks.

"Cheryl. It must have been her middle name."

"You knew this woman?"

"She was my nurse practitioner. She warned me about the place, and they fired her for it. They killed her too?"

"There's no proof of that. The fire was caused by a candle that had burned down and set fire to the material around it after she had expired. As for the cause of death, it could be an OD, accidental or otherwise."

"Or it could have been an elaborate setup to look that way," I counter. "See if the police can compare her time of death to the time the candle was lit. If it was lit after she died, then it was done with the intention of setting the house on fire. These people are unbelievably dangerous. I won't say too much, because I don't want to drag you deeper into this, but this is big, Harry. Unthinkably big."

"I'm sorry I couldn't save her for you, my friend."

"It's all right. There's no way you could have." As I say these words, a realization hits me, and I talk it out into the phone. "Which begs the question, why send me to Illinois only to get there six hours late to save the person I was sent to save?"

"I don't follow you."

"The whole point of these assignments I get is to save people before tragedy strikes. But my assignment was to get there before 4:00. Cheryl … I mean Editha … had been dead since 10:00 this morning. So why send me?"

"As I recall," Harry says, "your instructions to me were 'get there and prevent the house from burning down,' so I'm guessing those were your instructions too."

"Save the house but not the woman inside it? Why? And why send me from so far away—unless ..." It's starting to make sense. "Harry, are you still in Galesburg?"

"Yeah, I'm getting dinner. Why?"

"I need you to go back into that house after the police leave."

"What am I looking for?" he asks.

"I'm not sure. But I'll know it when *you* see it. You said you found a page of her handwritten notes. I want you to look for anything official that came from her former employer."

"Okay, what's their name?"

"I don't know that either, exactly. Look for the Swift name, or for something marked SDC or SODARCOM."

"SDC. What's that stand for?"

"I don't ..."

"Right, you don't know. Stupid question. You do realize this'll cost you extra."

"I know. That's fine."

"And you're buyin' dinner. Prime rib tonight. It looks good."

"Fine. Just get a hold of whatever you can, and when you find something that looks important enough that I would have been sent to retrieve it, call me. I don't care if it's the middle of the night."

"You're the boss."

"Thanks, Harry. Enjoy your dinner. And be careful."

As I end the call, my mind reels. "What could possibly be in that house that's important enough to send me halfway across the country to retrieve it?" My words are interrupted, however, when Genevieve steps over to me and delivers a powerful slap to my face with an open palm, hard enough to knock me backward in my chair.

"What the hell?" I demand.

Her eyes dispense daggers. "That slap was to inspire the tears that should be flowing out of you right now. I heard what you said. A woman is dead. A woman who took care of you, who risked her own safety to get you the information you needed. Someone may have even killed her because of your investigation into this, and you sit there now, putting the puzzle together without a second of emotion expressed for this life cut short. *Feel this,* God damn it. Show me that whatever's brought you here hasn't stolen your humanity. Because if you don't—if you *can't* show me that these feelings are alive in you, I swear to you I'll walk out of here right now and never speak to you again."

For a moment, I sit in stunned silence, reading the deadly seriousness on her face. It takes several seconds for the full impact of her words to register. Once it does, I realize how utterly tragic Cheryl's fate is and how possible it is that I somehow had a hand in it. I drop my head into my hands, and in a moment of mixed anguish and relief, I realize that tears are indeed flowing.

"I'm sorry. It's just been … When Harry told me that, I couldn't believe it was her. I mean, I processed it on an informational level, but I couldn't allow myself to feel the grief of it."

Her tone softer, she puts a caring hand atop my head. "They killed her?"

"I don't know. Maybe. Or maybe she killed herself. Maybe it was even an accident. They found the pills from the drug trial in her home. She'd have no reason to take them. She wasn't a patient in the trial."

"And the fire?"

"It was a candle left burning. There's so many questions, and I don't think I'll ever know the answers. Harry didn't say anything about a suicide note, but if this was her doing and she intended to burn the house to cover it up, she wouldn't have left a note."

"Yes, but if the reason you were sent was to retrieve something she left for you, why would she do that and then try to destroy the very thing she brought? To me, that suggests foul play, outside influence. Someone killed her, maybe searched the house for something, and then left the candle burning."

"But why use a candle? Why not just torch the place immediately?" I ask.

"Less chance that it would look like arson. Anyone who looks into this will know that she just lost her job. A job with a secretive and controversial agency. So they let her get far away from them, they follow her, and they make it look like suicide, instead of aiming suspicion at themselves. It fits."

"What can we do? How can we make them pay for this?"

"I don't think we can," she replies. "First of all, we don't know who's responsible, and second, we couldn't prove it, even if we did. That's what makes this whole thing so dangerous: the people who are doing this are professionals. It's why I want you to finish this, take what you already have, and go to the police with it."

"I'm so close to that point, but ..."

"But?"

"Recent experiences, even today, have made me gun shy about approaching the authorities before I have something concrete, something tangible that I can present to them and say, *here, this is what you need*."

"I look at you, taking this on, and I see a man who's willing to give up his life in pursuit of this cause. Trouble is, I'm not quite that willing for you to do so."

"Well, you may want to look a little harder, dear. I've grown kind of attached to this life, and giving it up, even for a good cause, isn't something I'm eager to do. So don't worry too much."

For a moment, I catch a veiled but definite look of inner peace in her eyes. "Dinner," she says. "I'm hungry. How do you feel about Indian?"

"Sounds fine to me."

"Good. And tonight, I'm buying. You've had a hard day."

The place is called Washington Amol, and it's a little family establishment not far from the Washington Mall. We find a table in a quiet corner, and our server brings us drinks of mango and yogurt, delicately seasoned flatbreads, and entrees of lamb and chicken in the most exquisite cashew butter sauce I've ever tasted. The side dish we savor is privacy. No one is even within earshot, so we can discuss the current situation without risk.

"Assuming that everything we've seen, heard, and read is true and reliable," Genevieve says, "let's start with what we know."

I go over it in my head. "We have an agency called the SDC, also known as SODARCOM, possibly a government-funded or -sponsored agency. They've been around since at least the 1920s. They're powerful and they're secretive; able to stay out of the public eye and the press. Their possible function is to get large groups of Americans to take their own lives. They've created a drug for cancer patients that simultaneously eases their pain and induces hallucinations and suicidal thoughts. They're implicit in the stock market crash of 1929 and plotting a disruption of the mortgage industry later this year. We read about them tampering with tobacco, infant formula, food stamps, prenatal vitamins, and illegal drugs. The whole thing points to a big event in 2012, something superstitious that will reach a lot of people. Did I miss anything?"

"That's pretty thorough," she replies. "What about the parts we don't know?"

"They fall into two main categories: how and why. How is this group able to create this much chaos without being detected, and why would they want to kill 30 million Americans?"

"I think we can add *who* to the list of unknowns," she says. "Because even with all of this, we still don't know who's at the heart of it."

"Maybe, if we're supremely lucky, that's what Harry will find in Cheryl's home—something that gives us a name."

After a leisurely dinner, we return to the apartment. I go straight to the computer, to see if I have any new e-mail. Before I can check, my home page—which features current events—alerts me to a piece of news from the day, one of considerable interest. "Genevieve, come take a look at this."

She comes up behind me as I open the article, reading it over my shoulder. The headline announces: Sen. Marquez safe after thwarted attack in Florida. We exchange an intrigued but concerned look and proceed to read the article.

> U.S. Sen. Hector Marquez (D-Fla.) is unharmed after what appears to be a violent attack against him in Tampa, Fla. today. As the senator was giving a speech to a group of local fishermen, gunfire erupted from a nearby building, targeting Marquez. Due to the quick reaction of an unprecedented security team, the senator was swiftly taken to a place of safety, and the perpetrator captured and taken into custody.
>
> Marquez has had an outspoken history of protecting Florida's coastal waterways against environmental threats, and it is believed that today's attack was directly related to his position …

"So you did save him," Genevieve says, "even though he decided to go."

"So it seems. He took my message to heart. Well, that's one for the good guys, anyway."

As the evening goes on, we engage in some much-needed relaxation. Genevieve is right: at this point, returning to Swift for more treatments—real or otherwise—would be counterproductive and dangerous. And I don't dare tell her about what happened to me under the influence of the sedation therapy. I'm not sure which would be worse, her reaction to the woman in white's attempted seduction or her attempts to convince me to kill myself. Neither would be welcome news, that's for sure.

I've tried not to devote too many brain cells toward figuring out what happened to me under sedation. The part I don't want to think about is why I was so willing to be seduced by the woman in white. Yes, I was drugged, and yes, she wasn't even real. But it makes me wonder if the drug simply removed my inhibitions, allowing me to do what I secretly wanted to do all along. And then there was the second woman, the dancer. I probably made her up too, but she seemed different from the first woman. She felt like someone I know or someone I should know. The things she said—*One day, you're going to be the most important person in my entire life, and I'm going to be someone you trust completely in every situation.* How can that be? Who is she, and is she really from my future? I thought Genevieve was my future. Allowing myself to think about these implications is far more disturbing than the actual hallucination itself.

Just after 10:00, I'm contemplating making an early night of it when my cell phone rings. A quick check of the screen shows me that it's Harry Cohen calling. Just as I had about decided that he wasn't going to find anything. "Harry, you big, swinging private dick, what's the news? Did you toss the place?"

"I'd hardly call it a toss," he replies. "More of a thorough sift. I felt like I was searching for the world's most elusive set of car keys. I went through every room of that house, picked up every piece of paper I could find. Anything that seemed relevant."

"And?"

"Nothing. Not a thing in the house to be found other than that handwritten sheet of notes I told you about. And even that doesn't tell me much of anything. I was all set to call it a wash, and head out of the house empty-handed. Then I got a feeling, maybe the same kind of feelings you get, I don't know. I went to her front hall and looked at the setup there. She has a little shelf against the wall, over some IKEA-type stacked cubicles to hold shoes. On the shelf are a few letters to go out in tomorrow's mail. Only I notice the shelf has pulled away from the wall just a crack. I move the shoe cubicles from underneath, and sure enough, an envelope had dropped down behind there—an envelope to go out in tomorrow's mail. And here's the kicker—it's addressed to you, Tristan."

"To me?"

"That's right. So I'm thinkin' this has to be it. I take it to my car and open it up, and inside is a little thumb drive. Along with it is a handwritten note to you. It says, 'Tristan, You'll need this. I'm sorry I let you down. —Cheryl.' So now I'm really interested. I take it to one of the print shops with computers you can rent by the hour, and I put the drive in and see just what's so important. There's a file on there, a spreadsheet. Big one, too. It's called 'Patient Master List.' More than sixty thousand names, addresses, phone numbers on there. So tell me: is this what you were sent here to find?"

"That's it. Harry, you're brilliant. You have no idea how important that list is to me. And the sooner I get it, the better. Are you still at the copy shop?"

"Still here."

"Good. Do me a favor. Zip the file and encrypt it for safe transmission. Then e-mail it to me right away. I want to get started on this tonight."

"I'll do that. You'll also find a copy of my invoice attached to the e-mail, if you'll pardon my bluntness. This has been a longer day than I anticipated."

"For what it's worth, Harry, every name on that spreadsheet represents a life that you may have saved today."

There is a moment of silence before he offers, "Well, then I'll feel pretty good while I'm spending your money."

"Good night, Harry."

"Night. Good luck with what you have to do."

I hurry to the bedroom and tell Genevieve of Harry's amazing find. "That's wonderful!" she says. "What are you going to do with the information?"

"I'm going to write to every person on that list. I'll create a form letter using mail merge and send it to the participants. I'll draw up some letterhead that makes it look like it's coming straight from Swift. I want people to think that the agency themself has lost faith in the product. That'll carry a lot more weight than a random stranger writing to them out of the blue and telling them to throw away the pain reliever that's been sustaining them for months."

"Not everyone will believe you," she reminds me. "Some will keep taking it."

"True. But look who our target demographic is: the ones who are most likely to be having suicidal thoughts or tendencies. They're also the ones most likely to be experiencing bad side effects in general from the drug. Throw in a letter from Swift that tells them they're right, and I'm guessing that thousands will toss the pills away immediately. That's lives saved right there."

"You're actually going to use the postal service, rather than a mass e-mail?"

"Much more effective. If there was a way I could go house to house, I'd do that. Absent that option, a letter will have to suffice."

"Sixty thousand letters is going to take a ton of paper and envelopes."

"I'll call my assistant at the office. She can coordinate the effort."

"And what about the postage? Remember, you don't have a CEO's paycheck coming in now."

"You remember I told you my father invented the LED? Well, part of his legacy is that anytime anyone—my company or anyone else's—puts an LED in anything worldwide, I get a fraction of a cent. I checked my bank statement earlier. I've made $26,000 this week. So I think I'm okay on the postage."

"Okay. Strike that concern."

"But I appreciate the thought."

"Twenty-six grand for doing nothing, and you let me buy dinner?" she asks with a little smirk.

"I appreciated *that* thought too."

"Should we get some sleep, so you can write that letter in the morning?"

"If you don't mind, I want to draft it now. I'm pretty pumped up about the arrival of the master list, and I want to get my thoughts down for the text of the letter."

"Okay," she says. "I'll be in our room. If you take too long, I can't guarantee I'll wait up for you."

"All the more incentive for me to get it done quickly. See you in a bit."

She disappears into the bedroom, and I open up a new word-processing document. The first order of business is to forge some letterhead at the top, with the name and address of Swift, but not the phone number. Too many calls and the whole thing falls apart. But hey, they're a super-secret organization anyway. They wouldn't go plastering their phone number on their letterhead … I hope.

The spreadsheet arrives by e-mail, and I open it up to look at it. As promised, it has 63,819 names, addresses, and telephone numbers on it, arranged in a very orderly fashion. That'll make it much easier to do a mail merge. Seeing all those names gives me pause to think about the one I couldn't save—Cheryl herself. I try to imagine what transpired. Clearly, they found a way to listen in on her lunch conversation with me, and they didn't like what they heard. So when she got back to the facility, they must have fired her right away. It would have been completely natural for her to blame me, either internally or to her superiors. But instead, she grabbed something that she knew would help me, something exceptionally dangerous for her to have. So what did she do? She came home, back to the Midwest. Far away from the reach of SODARCOM—or so she thought. She had this file, and she didn't want to risk e-mailing it to me, so she intended to put it in the mail for Monday pickup. She would have used the only address she had for me, the one in Ocean City. But who knows when I would have been home again to get it? This proves she didn't kill herself. Important as that file was, she would have put it in the mailbox first if she had truly taken her own life.

So whatever forces have me on this insane trek decided to get the information to me sooner. But at what cost? The life of a woman who just wanted to help sick people, dying people; a woman who probably had no idea of the bigger picture behind Swift, behind SODARCOM, any of it. Until I told her. Maybe the firing came as a relief to her;

she could be free of them and start her life over again in beautiful Galesburg, Illinois—a place I'd never even heard of. Out of curiosity, I look it up online. Pictures show Midwestern small-town America. Only about thirty thousand people; a railroad hub; a couple of colleges; home of one of the Lincoln-Douglass Debates. Home of Editha Cheryl Sayre, where they'll lay her to rest next week.

The thought of it strengthens my resolve; it's time to write this letter.

August 20, 2007

<firstname><lastname>

<addr1>

<addr2>

Dear <firstname>,

My name is Dr. James Robinson, and I am on the medical oversight community at the Swift Medical Research and Testing Center in Washington, DC. We are the administrative body running the drug trial on the pain medication you are currently taking. *I'm writing to you today to instruct that you stop taking the medication and dispose of any remaining tablets you now have.* At this point in the study, we have found that a number of patients have developed serious side effects, ranging from rapid heartbeat to cardiac arrest. Some of our patients have died as a result of taking the drug, so we urge you to discontinue taking the medication immediately. We apologize for any inconvenience this may cause, but your safety must come first.

Please consult your primary care physician for the prescription of an alternative pain-relieving drug that will work for you. At this time, we have no safe alternative ready to administer. Again, we apologize.

When disposing of the drug, please do not use the sink or toilet or anything with access to the municipal water supply. We recommend that you burn the remaining supply of the drug in a safe, controlled environment.

In the next several weeks, you will receive another letter from us, including answers to questions you may have and an address you can contact for further information. Please accept our sincere apologies for any difficulties you may have encountered, and thank you for participating in our study.

Sincerely,

Dr. James Robinson

I'm very pleased with my efforts. It's compassionate yet menacing, concerned while at the same time frightening. And yes, some of the patients will continue taking it, but I'm pretty certain that anyone who's had the tiniest glimmer of a side effect will toss the stuff as far as they can throw it. Will it cause problems for SODARCOM? I hope so. I want to thwart them, now more than ever. I want angry phone calls to jam their lines; I want class-action lawsuits filed against them. I want to hurt them, because they've hurt me. I feel no shame in admitting that.

Tomorrow morning, I'll send my form letter and the spreadsheet to Kayla, my former assistant in my former office, and ask her to put the mailing together. Maybe this will cost me close to $30,000, but it's worth it. Worth all that and more. Sitting in a bank, my money does nothing but earn interest. Tomorrow I give it legs and order it to run.

Satisfied, I save my work and turn off the computer for the night. In the bedroom, Genevieve is sitting up and reading. I give her a look that tells her I want her. She gives me a look that tells me she wants me. And then, by God, we do something about it.

Chapter 9

As I awaken Monday morning, things feel different. I feel like this protracted errand may actually be coming to an end soon, and that's a relief. Still, it makes me wonder what happens after my time in Washington is over. I've left my job for the sake of being in a state of readiness when assignments come along. I'm still ready and willing to do this. I imagine I'll go home to Maryland, live in my own house. And Genevieve? I don't think we're in a place to consider anything as drastic as living together. *Although last night was very good.* I'll just have to take the relationship with her day by day, see what she wants, see what I want.

At the moment, she's still asleep, and I'm wide awake. Business hours have started at Shays Diode, and I know Kayla will be at her desk. I go to the kitchen and dial her number on my cell phone. It's good to hear her voice when she answers. "Shays Diode, Mr. Padgett's office. Kayla speaking."

"Hi, Kayla, it's Tristan."

"Tristan, oh my God! It's so good to hear from you. We were just talking about you. Are you doing okay?"

"I'm doing fine, thanks. How about you?"

"Pretty good. Esteban's really good to work for. Things have been fine. Some people were worried when you left that the place wouldn't be the same, but so far it's been good."

"I'm glad. Kayla, I'm calling because I need a favor."

"Sure. What do you need?"

"In a few minutes, I'm going to send you a letter and a spreadsheet with names and addresses—a lot of names and addresses. I need you to merge the names and addresses and create letters to send. I'll warn you now, there are more than 63,000 names on the list. I don't want you to babysit this, so please use the automated printer. I'll give you a return address for the envelopes. Let the machine do the work of printing the letters, stuffing the envelopes, printing and sealing them."

"Do you want to use the bulk mail account for postage?" she asks.

"No, not this time. Meter these first class, and pay for it out of my personal account; you should still have access to that."

"I'm guessing this is confidential, and I shouldn't read the letters?"

"It is, but you can read it. Just keep it away from anyone else at the company, please."

"So, is this top secret saving-the-world stuff?"

"Kind of, yeah."

"Cool. I think it's great that you're doing that. And I'll help with this today. I'll send you an e-mail when it's done, telling what it cost in postage."

"Charge the paper, ink, and envelopes to my personal account too."

"I will."

"Thanks for your help. I'll send you the files in just a few minutes."

"Miss ya, boss."

"Miss you too, Kayla. You be well."

I go over to the computer and prepare a confidential e-mail to Kayla. Attached are the spreadsheet and the form letter, ready to merge. In the body of the e-mail is the return address for the envelopes. With a click, my plan is underway, and SODARCOM will rue the day. Oh, they will rue.

"You're up early." Genevieve's voice from behind me startles me for a second.

"Nobody ever saved the world by sleeping in," I remind her.

"There was that one guy in France in the eighteenth century."

"Yes, but he was an anomaly."

She stands behind me as I sit at the computer. Putting her arms around my neck, she says, "How is my little fire engine of love this morning?"

"Barely able to walk, thanks to you. If you had told me what a demon you were from the beginning, I might not have been a perfect gentleman for so long."

"You're forgiven, particularly if you continue to do the things you did last night."

At this moment, I truly hope the apartment isn't bugged. "It's a deal."

"What's the plan for today?" she asks.

"It's go time. The letter is being prepped and will be sent today. I will spend the morning compiling my notes about Swift and SODARCOM. This afternoon, I'll go to the DC field office of the FBI and be the concerned citizen sharing information. Once that's over, I think our work here is done. We can probably pack up the place and head back home this evening."

"Really? That's wonderful! I'm sorry, that sounded rude. It's not that I don't want to be here with you. It's just that I'll feel a lot better when we're someplace safe."

"I understand; you don't have to explain."

"Thank you," she says.

"No problem." Then the unexpected sensation starts. "Hey, come on, that feels weird."

"What does?" she asks, sounding confused.

"Aren't you ... it feels like you're biting my neck."

"You mean while I'm talking to you and standing over a foot away?"

"That's so weird. It really feels like something's biting my neck."

"No. I'm good, but I'm not that good."

"Well, if you're not biting my neck, that could only mean—"

I don't even feel the moment when I lose consciousness. Like a light switch, I am flipped to the off position. The only reason I'm aware of it at all is that I wake up sometime later in a heap on the floor, not too far from where I was sitting. I open my eyes to find Genevieve kneeling next to me, dabbing my forehead with a wet washcloth.

"What happened?" I ask.

"You passed out."

"I did?"

"Unless this is some bizarre attempt to get me to wash your face, then yes."

"How long was I gone?"

"Fifteen minutes," she replies. "Not fifteen of my favorite minutes of the week, you'll understand. Why did you faint?"

"I don't know."

"Right before you went out, you said you thought I was biting your neck. Do you have neck pain?"

"Some," I answer.

"Come on, let's sit you up." With a bit of difficulty, I sit and face her. "Smile," she instructs.

"About what?"

"Just do it, please." I oblige. "Good. Now raise both arms." Again, no problem. "Now repeat after me: It's a pretty day."

"It's a pretty day."

"Well, it's not a stroke," she says, "thank God. I had to rule that out. Do you think it's after-effects of the sedation from yesterday?"

"I don't know; I've never been sedated before."

She slides over until she's able to rest my head on her lap. It's a comfortable position, so I make no effort to move from it. "If you'd like, I can take you to a walk-in clinic or an emergency room."

In a flash, the neck pain returns. "No, wait, it's back. I think it's an assignment. I can't turn my head, and I'm seeing images. Give me a minute."

As she puts her hands gently on my shoulders, the white ceiling acts as a screen on which I see the images of what I have to do. It takes only a minute for all the details to reach me, and when they're done, I'm left with a feeling of surprise. "Huh."

"What is it?" she asks. "What's the assignment?"

"Well, it's here in Washington, so that's a good start. At 12:35 this afternoon, a man eating lunch at his desk will choke on his food, and I'm supposed to be there to save him."

"That's it?" she asks.

"That's it. I was surprised too."

"So you don't have to disarm a bomb or stop a lion from eating a classroom full of children?"

"Points to you for creativity, but no and no. No explosives or large felines. Just a man and his piece of chicken."

"Seems almost anticlimactic," she observes.

"Yes, but tell that to the wife and children he leaves behind if I fail."

"How's the pain? Can you sit up?"

As is customary after the details of the assignment come in, the pain gives me a little break, perhaps a chance to mull over the particulars. I attempt to sit up, and with a little difficulty, I am able to do so. There's some pain when I try to turn my head, but for the most part I'm okay. "Better, thanks." With that, I return to my chair in front of the computer, and she stands next to me.

"Should we strategize?" she asks.

"Probably. I'm thinking Heimlich maneuver."

"Heimlich works for me. Or, you know, you could get there in time to say something like, 'Don't eat that chicken!'"

"That could work too. Okay, good session. I'm glad we talked."

"So what are you going to do in the three hours until your lifesaving poultry-dislodging skills are needed?"

"Just what I planned to do before: gather up information for my trip to the FBI field office this afternoon."

"Sounds good. I'll make breakfast."

With the persistent reminder of a very stiff neck, I set to work compiling my notes on Swift and SODARCOM into a format that the FBI can use. I've never used their services, and in truth, I don't know much about them apart from the probably erroneous belief that they have a division that tracks down extraterrestrials. Exciting as that prospect is, I suspect the reality is more mundane. Perhaps my accusation of 30 million counts of attempted murder will be an exciting change of pace for them. For once, I'm approaching peace officers with something more than an unsubstantiated prediction of harm to come, so they might actually do something wild like believe me. Kolodziej's e-mails will be a big help on that front, as they lay out SODARCOM's plans.

I pause long enough to think of Stanislaw, and I wonder what might have become of him. If he was telling the truth back at Swift—and I have no reason to doubt that he was—then the IV I delivered to him should have been lethal. I search online for an obituary or death notice but find nothing. Of course, with everything I've seen in the past week, it's not impossible. An organization this reliant on secrecy could easily conceal the death of one of their operatives. It makes me sad for his family, if he has one. Do they even know he's gone? I try not to dwell on the sadness of it, but Genevieve's stern warning from yesterday is still very much on my mind. I *have* been so engrossed in the puzzle that it's stood in the way of feeling some very basic human emotions, and that bothers me. This isn't who I am, but it's also not who I have to be.

Breakfast is very good. Genevieve makes french toast stuffed with bananas, served with a maple-amaretto syrup. How she comes up with this stuff I'll never know. Well-fed, I return to the task at hand, preparing orderly, fact-based presentations. It takes awhile to sort through Kolodziej's e-mails again, weeding out the ones that aren't relevant to my case. I consider adding the page from Xpoz'd TruthZ but think better of it, selecting just the old newspaper article instead. I grab a manila folder from the desk and put the pages in it as I print them.

The final page prints, and I put them all together in the folder and look at the clock to see that it's—

Shit, 11:55!

"I lost track of time!" I call out.

"You still have time. It's here in town, you said, right?"

"Yes, but there's lunchtime traffic. I've gotta go. I'll take the files and stop by the FBI after I stop this guy from choking on his chicken."

She kisses me good-bye. "Be safe."

I hurry out to the car and climb in, placing the file carefully on the front seat. I pull away from the curb rapidly, entering the light flow of traffic on the side street. So far, so good. That is, until I pull out into a main artery and find the citizenry of Washington, DC occupying the four and a half miles between me and my destination.

Four and a half miles, forty minutes. That gives me almost ten minutes per mile. No problem!

No problem when the vehicle in question is moving. But Washington has a way of clogging its streets like no other city can. A motorcade delays things for eight minutes. A group of noontime protestors slows things down for another seven. Throw in a couple of red lights, some pedestrians who think they have the right of way just because a sign says they do, and a stalled motorist turning a two-lane road into one lane, and my forty minutes quickly dissolve.

Time is painfully short as I pull up to the office building in which a man is about to have an unpleasant disagreement with poultry. Mercifully, there is a parking lot, and it even has open visitor spots. I pull into one of them quickly and sprint from the car to the building. My target is in office 306. There's no time to wait for the elevator, as I see that it's already 12:34, so I dash up the stairs and through the door marked 306.

A receptionist at the desk gets as far as "Hello, can I help ..." but as I blast by her and through the inner door, she ends the sentence with, "Hey, you can't just—" I'm sure there's more, but by that time, I'm already in the office where I'm needed, and sure enough, there's a man behind a desk with his hands grasping impotently at his neck, struggling to take a breath that just won't come.

"Stay calm," I tell him. "I'm here to help." With that, I damned heroically step behind him, pull him to his feet, wrap my arms around his diaphragm, and mightily squeeze the rotisserie-cooked offender from out of his windpipe. It sails a healthy arc halfway across the room, landing with a dull plop on the carpet.

Having succeeded, I step out from behind the desk and stand in front of him, looking into his very perplexed face. He looks to be in his early forties, fit and in good health. Granted, he takes bites of food that are too big, but everyone has their faults. At the moment, his expression conveys a combination of gratitude and wonder. "Who are you, and how did you do that?"

"Well, I'm Tristan, and how I did that is a little bit complicated."

"Do you work in the building? Did you hear me choking?"

"No, actually I came here from five miles away, and I'm here because I knew you would be in danger at this precise minute."

The receptionist's voice comes over the telephone intercom. "Sir, is everything all right?"

"Everything's fine, Maggie. Thank you. Please hold my calls for a bit."

"Yes, sir."

"I'm sorry," he says to me. "I'm Phillip Kean, by the way. *Pleased to meet you* doesn't begin to describe it. I'm still a bit stunned at how you knew to be here."

"Well, Phillip, it's kind of new to me too. Some people can play the piano. Others are brilliant surgeons. My gift—and it's a new one—is the ability to know when people are in danger of losing their lives. I get to go and try to save them."

"That's remarkable," he says, staring at me with a look of fascination. "I know this will sound conceited, and I apologize, but you've done more good here today than you may know. I'm the executive director of a group that's working to ensure vital resources for the country's population over the coming decades. If I had died here today in this absurd, ignoble way, I would never know if my group's mission will succeed. You may have preserved a lot of lives here today."

"At the risk of sounding conceited myself, it's something I'm getting used to."

"Is there somewhere you have to be?" he asks. "I'm just fascinated and would like to know more."

"I have someplace to go this afternoon, but not immediately. It's nice to talk to someone who doesn't instantly think I'm insane or trying to scam them."

"Of course. I'm sure people find it hard to believe you, even though you've come to help them. Everyone's so cynical, so greedy. They wonder what the angle is. So is this what you do? Is this your daily work?"

"It's become my daily work recently. I ran a corporation, but the missions interfered, so I stepped down to pursue this. I can live off my earnings. This way I'm free to leave at a moment's notice, just in case someone, you know, has a bad situation with some chicken."

He laughs a little at this. "Don't remind me. I'm embarrassed to have come so close to dying over a lunch entrée. I eat too fast, always have, and I suffer from a hiatal hernia, which can obstruct my airway when I eat. It's ironic, too, that you came here to save me. Part of my personal and professional philosophy is that the strength of the individual is paramount. Those who are independent and capable and self-reliant tend to prevail. And yet, here we are."

"Everybody needs a hand sometimes, Phillip."

"Tristan, may I be presumptuous?"

"I suppose so."

"Our group is well-funded, and we sometimes bring in advisors and consultants, people who report in to us with scholarly observations on society and the human condition. Your gift makes you a unique observer of the human condition. You see the things that threaten life, and you see the reactions of people when they learn of their peril. If you would be willing to file a written report to me every time you finish one of your missions, I think it would help our cause, help us serve people. I'd be prepared to offer you $50,000 a year to do this for us."

I can barely believe my ears. And it's not even about the money; this figure, which would be life-changing to some people, is unimportant to me. Far more important is that finally, someone not only believes me but wants to use this strange ability of mine to help others above and beyond the impact I have when I deliver my messages. I'd never considered the value of sharing my experiences with someone who could study their impact on society, but it makes perfect sense. Now in particular, in a moment when I'm searching for my purpose, it has found me.

"Phillip, I don't know what to say. This is a remarkable opportunity. I'd like to know more about the group and their work, but if it's as exciting and beneficial as you say it is, then yes, I would be very interested in sharing my experiences with you."

"Wonderful. Then make yourself comfortable and I'll tell you what we're about here at the Social Darwinism Commission."

In an instant, the blood leaves my face. *Social Darwinism Commission—SODARCOM.* Like the world's cruelest joke that everyone's in on but me, I have been dropped into the lair of my enemies, and I've just saved the life of their leader.

I am trying very hard not to panic, and more, trying to figure out what to do. It's important that I don't do anything stupid. Spying a letter opener on Phillip's desk, I grab it and point it at him rather stupidly.

He looks at me and at the brandished office supply. "I could offer fifty-five thousand if that would make a difference."

"Quiet! Stay right where you are, and don't move."

"Okay …"

"Social Darwinism Commission? Also known as the SDC and SODARCOM?"

"You've heard of us?" he asks in a tone of surprise. "Most people haven't."

"Yeah, well most people didn't come to Washington to go undercover at the Swift Medical Facility as a patient in your drug trial. Your drug that I had analyzed by a lab, who told me about the hallucinogen in it. The one that tries to trick cancer patients into killing themselves."

"Tristan, please. There are things you don't know ..."

"Save it, Phillip. You should be more concerned with the things I *do* know. Things about the SDC dating back decades. Things you're planning, things you're doing. You see, I got access to Stan Kolodziej's e-mails." These words bring a look of deep concern to his face. "Oh, I see that doesn't sit well with you."

"If you'll let me explain ..."

"You can explain it to the FBI. They're my next stop. In fact, if I weren't here saving your wretched life, I'd be handing over my findings to them right now."

"They already know," he says simply.

"Excuse me?"

"They know about us."

"Do they know your plans to kill 30 million Americans in the next five years?"

At this point, he quickly picks up his desk phone and presses a speed dial button. "Put it down!" I order, but he doesn't.

Into the phone he says, "I need you here now. Get back here as quickly as you can. We've got a situation in my office."

At this point, I pull the receiver out of his hands, remove the cord from the phone, and throw the phone across the room. "Who did you call?"

"An associate."

"You shouldn't have done that."

"Tristan, I know you think I'm your enemy. I know you must think the SDC is this nightmare organization bent on exterminating human life, but if you'll put the letter opener down and agree to listen to me, I promise I'll tell you anything you want to know. Then, if you want to go to the FBI or the police or the president, I won't do anything to stop you. But please, let me explain who we are and what we're doing. That's all I ask."

Keeping the letter opener in my hand, I return to the chair in front of his desk, motioning for him to sit as well. "I'm listening," I tell him.

"Thank you. First of all, some definitions. Social Darwinism is a …"

I finish for him. "A philosophy which espouses that Charles Darwin's evolutionary theory of survival of the fittest can be applied on a sociological and societal level, resulting in a society where only the most capable survive. I went to college too."

"Forgive me. I didn't mean to assume otherwise. Most people have never heard of the theory, and those who have often find it distasteful."

"I'm not exactly a fan either," I reply. "Go on."

"Our organization has been in operation in the United States since 1868. It was created by President Andrew Johnson following the Civil War. He called it the Resource Allocation Commission. The war was over, and supplies were limited. With Reconstruction, the population of the country was starting to grow again, and resources were limited. So Johnson appointed a task force to determine the best way to ensure that those in need received these resources. The group was effective, and their work continued. Of course, no one likes to be told that they're not among the needy and deserving. Some people rose up against this group, and means were needed to level the playing field."

"Is that a sanitary euphemism for killing the undesirables?" I ask.

"No, not killing. That's not what we're about here. Not in the way you think, at least. Nature is the most heinous killer of all. It claims every life that ever was and ever will be. Humans, animals, plants. Everything that *is* will one day *not be*. And nature has its reasons. Sometimes we understand them, while other times we don't. And sometimes, we very clever and industrious humans find a way to circumvent nature. Population control is an entirely natural process, a vital process for any ecosystem, even ours. But when a disease threatens to take out a weak and sickly part of the population, we develop a vaccine or a cure, and nature is thwarted. When poverty and famine work to limit the population of a region that is woefully devoid of resources, a rock star or a movie actor with a fortune and a conscience steps up, and nature loses again. Tristan, with our oh-so-good intentions, we are giving nature

155

the finger and saying we are impervious to natural selection. Listen again to those words: *natural selection.* A process that has existed for as long as there has been life on this planet. Of course, no one wants to be selected against. It doesn't end well for them. But that doesn't mean that it's wrong."

"So you and yours swoop down and play God ..."

"Quite the opposite," he interrupts. "I would argue that those who act contrary to natural processes are playing God. We are removing the barriers to those processes, allowing the necessary actions of this planet to control the human population as they should."

"Are you a government agency?"

"No, not officially. We are what's known in popular culture as a shadow organization. We accept no taxpayer money, and we have no partisanship or official government affiliation. What we do have is a pass, a sanctioning from the government, including the FBI, to operate within specific parameters, free from harassment and prosecution."

"So you very conveniently don't exist."

"Look at your own reaction after learning part of what we do. Now imagine an entire country of people, similarly informed but having only half the picture. They would destroy us."

"They *should* destroy you. Maybe instead of going to the FBI, who you seem to own, I'll go to the media, who you don't."

"Others have tried. Over the years, people have sought to expose us. We have a small team of employees whose job is to discredit these people. It's unfortunate, but we have to present them to the world as unstable and even mentally ill conspiracy theorists. I'd hate to see that happen to you. I think you're a good man, and with the work you do now, you can't afford to have people know your name and associate it with spouting wild theories. I suspect no one would ever believe your warnings again."

"Thirty million people," I say quietly. "Hitler was the most evil person who ever lived, and he killed 12 million. That makes you worse than two and a half Hitlers."

"Hitler killed people because of their religion or their nationality or their sexual preference. We're not out to kill anyone, and we certainly don't target people that way. We simply understand that there are individuals who, for whatever reason, are able to contribute more to society than others. We study these trends very carefully and find ways to work with population control techniques. Some decades, it requires the introduction of a virus into an environment. Other decades, a social event can precipitate population control, like the stock market crash in 1929."

"But why this, why now? And why so many people?"

"The population of this country just topped 300 million people. In 1980, it was 226 million. Less than thirty years to grow by 75 million people. Everyone talks about the land of plenty, the land of opportunity, but there's a crisis coming very soon. Within the next five years, things will reach a desperate level. Let's start with water. Something as simple as people watering their lawns takes up almost 70 percent of potable water nationwide, some of it nonrenewable. And what about food? Last year, 50 million Americans went hungry, many of them children. Housing? There's a huge homeless population in this country, and yet there are millions of abandoned houses that they aren't allowed to access. The media, which you wanted to run to with this story, is aware of the dire state of our country, and they've kept quiet, in the interest of not starting a panic.

"The simple fact of the matter is that nature has been disrupted. Humankind, for all the right reasons, has made leaps forward in medicine, technology, globalism, and even philanthropy. But in doing so, they failed to take into account the consequences of their actions. It's easy to descend from above as savior to a village or a country, but when the benefit gala is over, the conquering heroes go home, and what remains are human beings who now have enough resources to survive for today. We are the group that asks the question: what about tomorrow? Yes, it means we often have to make impossibly difficult decisions, but we try to do so as humanely as possible. I truly want you to know that at the core of it all, we are not a violent or dangerous organization."

I am within seconds of actually believing him when his office door forcefully swings open, and I find myself staring down the barrel of a large handgun. From behind that weapon, a voice cordially yet somehow menacingly says, "Hello, Tristan."

By this point, I shouldn't be astonished when this happens, but the sight of him once again ready to shoot me leaves me dumbfounded. "Ephraim!"

"It's funny. All Phillip had to say was the word *situation,* and I knew it would be you."

"So you've been working for SODARCOM all along? No wonder you showed up at Benton Tambril's home to collect those pills."

Phillip interrupts the reunion. "You two know each other?"

"Our paths have crossed a few times," Ephraim tells him, still—disturbingly enough—holding me at gunpoint. "I had advance knowledge that he would be coming here to investigate the drug trial, but I made sure he would be carefully watched, so he wouldn't make any trouble."

"Maybe I made trouble and you don't even know it. I know you killed Cheryl Sayre."

"Don't have the foggiest idea what you're talking about," Ephraim replies calmly.

"No, of course you don't. You would never have anything to do with killing someone and making it look like a suicide."

"Ephraim, what's he talking about?" Phillip asks, sounding dismayed at my words.

"Nothing of consequence, sir. We had to let one of our employees go for violating confidentiality rules, and Mr. Shays here has a bit of an inflated sense of personal responsibility. He couldn't find her after her dismissal, so he believes we terminated her in another sense."

"Nice cover story," I reply. "Hope it helps you sleep nights. Okay, I must be mistaken. Well, that's good. Then you shouldn't have anything to worry about. There wouldn't be anything of yours for me to find at her home ... in Illinois."

At these words, Ephraim lowers the gun a bit and gives me a look of surprise and concern. This look pleases me, as does the lowering of the gun. I should welcome it as a gift, but I can't resist the urge to mess with him a little. "What's wrong, Ephraim? Is it more difficult to see what I'm doing when I send someone else to do the leg work for me? Or are we not getting the same assignments anymore?"

"That's enough," he says, not as charmed by my impudence as I am. "It's time to go home, Tristan. We let you come here and see what we're doing. The goal was to show you that the SDC isn't evil. But as usual, you see what you want to see. It's why you're in pain when you get a new assignment; that pain is all in your head. It's your own struggle with the truth you refuse to accept: that you have no business fixing the universe's mistakes. What do you think drew me to the SDC? Finally, after years of believing that I had some obligation to clean up after the creator of this world, I found a group who understands that the opposite is true. Things happen, and people die, sometimes before we want them to. It's not our job to save them."

"Maybe I think differently," I answer quietly.

"Go home," Ephraim says simply. "You need to leave here now. You entered the drug trial on false pretenses, and I need you to leave Washington. Go back to your apartment, pack your things, and leave. Don't return to Swift. Don't talk about or write about what you saw there."

"Why, because it's illegal?"

"No, because one of the forms you signed was a confidentiality agreement, and if you share the information, the one who's breaking the law is you. Just go home or there'll be consequences."

"Phillip, after careful consideration, I've decided to decline your job offer."

"I figured as much."

"It's not too late, you know," I tell him. "You can stop this."

"Tristan," Ephraim says, using my name as a warning.

There's nothing more to say; it's time for me to leave here.

Chapter 10

I leave the office building without another word to anyone. My assignment was a success. I saved the life of a man who plans to kill 30 million innocent people in the name of population control. I've solved the mystery of SODARCOM, and I even stood up to Ephraim and lived to tell about it. But inside me, I feel dead; I feel betrayed by the one who sends me. The unanswerable question is, why send me to save someone whose plans are so unspeakably evil?

The answer I'm so desperately avoiding is that Phillip Kean isn't evil; the Social Darwinism Commission isn't evil; even Ephraim himself isn't evil. They're just doing what nature intended. What nature's creator intended. I wish I could believe it; I truly do. It would be the remedy for the overpowering angst I'm suffering right now. If I could let myself accept that this group's goals are carried out with humanity's best interest in mind, I could actually return home, not pursue this any further, and just live with the knowledge that this is happening but it probably won't happen to me or anyone I know.

If only I could.

Instead, as I drive back to the apartment, a litany is running through my mind, underscored with a drumbeat that repeats *wrong-wrong-wrong-wrong-wrong*. Too often in this world, those with power and authority subjugate the weak and the defenseless, and SODARCOM is a perfect example. *They* get to decide who lives or dies? Pardon the fuck

161

out of me? Cancer patients—easy target. They're dying anyway, just not fast enough, I suppose. Smokers, drug abusers, people on welfare, illegal immigrants. Phillip Kean says he's not Hitler because he doesn't discriminate based on race or religion. No, he discriminates based on class and income, and in my mind, that's no less insidious. I'm proud of the actions I've taken to thwart them—more so now. Those sixty thousand letters will go out, and soon SODARCOM will find itself out of the pharmaceutical business. Good riddance. Bastards.

But what now? Kill Kean? By his own reasoning, he was meant to die anyway. He's clearly in charge, and without him, the organization would lack direction. Make a statement by killing him, and others might realize that they're in danger too. But I know I can't. Killing him would make me no better than they are. Worse, in fact. I'm not a murderer. So it seems I can do nothing.

My face accurately depicts my mood as I enter the apartment minutes later. Seeing me, Genevieve draws a logical but incorrect conclusion. "Were you unable to save him?"

"Quite the contrary. That's what has me so upset."

She gets me a glass of red wine and encourages me to sit at the dining room table and explain. As I tell my tale, I see the amazement on her face with each new detail. "This has to mean something," she says when I finish. "You've seen how these assignments work. Nothing happens by coincidence. You were sent to save Kean, even though he's the head of the SDC. Maybe that means he's needed for some larger purpose that we can't see."

"I was also sent to save Kolodziej, but he wanted to die. I helped him to do that, and there were no consequences. So I don't know if I'm prepared to read anything into it just yet."

"Equally significant to me," she continues, "is the fact that Ephraim is on the payroll, and what's more, he didn't know you would be there."

"Oh, he knew. He was there with a gun trained on me inside of five minutes."

"Exactly," she says. "Kean had to call him in to the office. If Ephraim truly knows your every move, there's no chance he would have been away from that office at the moment you went there, especially if he knew you would threaten the man you were sent to save. Speaking of which, a letter opener? Really?"

"Look, I'm not a ninja. I didn't have swords and throwing stars on me, so I had to improvise. But I see your point. He only said he knew it was me *after* he saw me there. I don't think he knew about my assignment, and he certainly didn't receive the same assignment, otherwise he would have been there to save Kean himself. I think I'm rewriting the future that he expects to happen, and I like that a whole lot. It makes me unpredictable, harder for him to track."

She hesitates a moment before asking, "So what happens now? Do we go back to Maryland?"

"Yes. But there's one thing I need to do first."

"What thing?"

"I can't tell you. It's safer if you don't know."

"Tristan …"

"I know, and I'm sorry. This is the last thing I have to accomplish while I'm here. I have to strike out against them one more time. Then we can pack up and go to Maryland, and from there, we can do anything you want to do."

"I don't like this. They know everything about you now, and they know how upset you are. They'll be watching for you. If they catch you—"

"Gen, I'll be in and out before they can even organize a response. And I'll be careful, I promise. In the meantime, start gathering our things. When I get back, we can leave."

"All right," she says, sounding dubious. "Just please don't do anything risky."

I kiss her and make my way out of the apartment and back to the car. I can't promise her that, because what I have to do is risky. But I owe it to the people at Swift, both the patients and the staff. I need to do for them what I couldn't do for Cheryl: get them out of there safely. I know what's at stake, and I'm prepared to take the chance. They're wrong, and I know what I have to do.

It's too risky to park in Swift's parking lot; security cameras could let them recognize my car and stop me before I even get in. So I choose a parking spot on a side street a block away. It may complicate a speedy getaway, but it's a risk I have to take. As I approach the building, I realize that I have two possible courses of action: pretend I'm here for a regular session or burst in and do what I have to do. I'm hoping that my visit to see Kean was so recent that they haven't yet had time to notify people at Swift to keep me out. If I'm wrong, it's plan B.

I show my ID to the security officer at the front door; it's someone I've seen a couple of times over the course of the past few days. He offers a smile and a nod of recognition. I see him compare the photo on my license to my face, but I don't see him linger on the name. That's fine with me. He waves me in and wishes me a pleasant afternoon. I thank him and move on unceremoniously.

Masking my anxiety, fear, and rage, I put on a pleasant expression and approach the reception desk. A woman named Lottie is there; she's seen me before and knows I'm in the study. "Afternoon, Lottie," I say pleasantly. "Here for my next appointment."

"Oh, hello, Mr. Tristan," she replies amiably. "You can have a seat. I'll tell them you're here."

"Thank you, Lottie. I know where to go."

So far, so good.

I take a few steps down the corridor, surveying what's around me. The place is quite full. Patients sit in waiting rooms; others are accompanied by their so-called caregivers. White-coated staff members shuttle clipboards and trays and carts from room to room. *No place but here; no time but now.*

Before I can get too far, Lottie calls out to me, "Mr. Tristan, wait please. There must be some mistake. The computer says you left the treatment."

Shit. On to plan B.

"No mistake, Lottie. Please know I'm not here to hurt you or anybody." With those words, and driven by forces and circumstances I don't fully understand, I walk to the fire-suppression equipment on the wall, open the glass panel, and pull out a wooden-handled axe. It is most assuredly the moment.

"May I have everyone's attention, please?" I announce in my most oratorical voice. People stop what they're doing and look at the loud man with the axe. Funny how that works. "I'm a private investigator …" *(of sorts, by the strictest dictionary definition of each word taken separately)* "… and I've discovered that the patients of this facility are being lied to." These words move some of the staff into a posture of defense. One or two pick up phones; others band together in the corridor, in case I need to be stopped, apparently. "There is no drug study. A group called the Social Darwinism Commission is giving you pain medication laced with a hallucinogen that causes suicidal thoughts and actions."

This evokes a wave of alarmed murmuring from the patients and an attempt to calm them from the staff. "Please don't believe anything they tell you," I continue. "I'm here to inform you that you're in danger, to encourage you to leave here now, and to close this place down."

Enough talk. It's axe time.

Making sure to stay clear of people, I wield the curiously heavy object at anything that'll break—windows, chairs, computers. A water fountain dies an untimely but strangely satisfying death after a mighty blow. Staff members who were getting ready to approach me decide to back off—imagine that. I'm starting to enjoy the feel of my axe-powered justice, so I work conversation back into the equation.

"These people are not your friends!" Chop—*good-bye, table.* "They want to see you dead, along with millions of other Americans they consider inferior." Chop—*so long, laser printer.* "They've got a list of who should live and who should die, but I say—no more!" Chop—*see you in hell, meeting room window.*

An idea comes to me, and I go to the locked stairway door. "There's a second floor to this facility, but have any of you been up there? If you want to see the dark side of this place ..." With a powerful swing, I destroy the lock, and the door pops open. "Go upstairs. See the people they're storing up there, hiding them away while they slowly kill them. Help those people. They need you too."

A few of the healthier patients do venture through the door and up the stairs.

"The rest of you, run from here! Run while you can!"

I'm pleased to see some of the patients do just that. They steer a wide berth around me (as I would do around a potentially crazy person with a large, bladed weapon), but they make their way to the exit, proving that *crazy* and *correct* do not have to be mutually exclusive. The staff looks more and more irritated as my words reach their intended recipients.

A nurse says to me, "Sir, you have to put the axe down and stop what you're doing! If you don't, I'll have to call the police."

I find it very interesting that they haven't yet called the police, given the swath of destruction (which I've always secretly longed to wreak) that I have already created. But I am fully jazzed now, and there's no stopping me. "By all means, call them! I'd be very happy to pay for the damage, right after I tell them everything you and SODARCOM are doing. That's right, patients, SODARCOM. The name you see on your pill bottles. The one they won't tell you what it means. It stands for Social Darwinism Commission—as in survival of the fittest and death to those they consider weak … like human beings struggling to maintain their strength, their dignity, and their lives in the face of a disease that many of them can and will survive. So, please, call the police. I insist. And then stick around when they question me. You might just learn something."

The front door to the facility opens, but the police do not enter. Seeing what I see, I rather wish they had. Instead, I watch as Ephraim enters, solemn-faced as he looks around at the mess I've made. At the sight of him, patients and staff members—some of whom have most likely never seen him before—fall into a state of quiet awe at his very presence. I admit that I join them in this. *Motherfucker looks pissed.*

He continues moving toward me until he is standing just a few feet in front of me. He shakes his head at me in disappointment.

"Hello, Ephraim," I say quietly.

He points at the axe, and I drop it to the floor. There's no mind control or special powers at work. I just don't want to contemplate the consequences if I don't drop it. "We had an understanding," he says calmly.

In my cavalcade of bad ideas, I decide now is the time to add one more. Raising my voice again, I tell the crowd, "I'd like you all to meet Ephraim. Sorry I don't know his last name, but he's SODARCOM's enforcer. Having heard that I'm here to cause trouble, he's been sent by this benevolent scientific organization to eliminate the problem."

He pulls a very long handgun out of his belt and levels it at me. I notice that it isn't the same one he wielded at Phillip Kean's office. *How many guns does this guy have?* A gasp goes up from the crowd, and some of them duck out of the potential line of fire like extras in a Western.

"You're just making my point for me, Ephraim," I tell him, loud enough for everyone to hear. "What are you going to do, shoot me in front of all these peop—"

Peop. That's as far as I get. I'm dimly aware of him pulling the trigger and utterly unaware of anything that follows it.

I awaken flat on my back, but not where I expected to be. As I first open my eyes, my senses are dull, slow to respond. The scenery—the part that isn't spinning—looks familiar, but not in a way that's physically possible. As I struggle to move myself to a sitting position, I hear a voice from behind me. "Take it slow, Tristan."

Ephraim! His words make me sit up even faster.

"Slowly. You're going to be …"

Without a single warning, I feel prodigious amounts of vomit begin to pour out of me. Somehow, with reflexes like nothing I've ever seen before, Ephraim is there to catch it all in a five-gallon pail.

"Nauseous," he says, once every meal I've eaten in the last two weeks leaves my body. Satisfied that I'm done, he puts the pail a safe distance away and brings me a glass of water.

"I'm in my living room," I utter weakly.

"I know that," he replies.

"My living room in Ocean City. How is that possible?"

"I drove you here from Swift. What's the last thing you remember?"

"You holding a gun on me. What did you do to me?"

"It was a tranquilizer gun, the kind they use on large, unruly animals. The resemblance you were providing was close enough to warrant it." He sits in a chair opposite the sofa where I am languishing.

"You had a golden opportunity to kill me right there. Don't tell me you've found compassion."

"You saved Phillip's life. He decided that bought you the benefit of a little mercy. Besides, killing you in front of all those people would have been a bad message to send, after everything you told them."

I think back to my act of civil disobedience and smile proudly. "Yeah. Stirred up the shit a little bit there, didn't I? Might have given some folks a few things to think about."

"I'll grant you, you weren't on your best behavior," he says with that omnipresent calm. "And the axe was a nice touch. But still. Didn't anything Phillip said to you make a difference?"

"Yeah, it made a difference. It gave me the information I needed to know that my cause was just." Suddenly, a thought occurs to me, and it blocks out everything else. "Wait a minute, where's Genevieve?" I stand up, fighting a wave of dizziness, and call to her. "Genevieve? Gen!"

"Sit back down," he says. "You're still under the effects of the tranq. She's fine. She's in Washington, packing up your apartment. She has your car, and she'll drive it down here today when she's done. I drove you here myself."

Sitting (well, falling) back down, I answer, "You'll understand if I don't thank you. What did you say to her, anyway?"

"The truth: that you went a little dark and started tearing up a medical facility, so I put you in my car, and I'm driving you back home to Maryland. She seemed relieved, actually. I think she was getting a little tired of the covert operation business."

The conversation is bizarre. This man, who has thwarted me at every turn, threatened to kill me more than once—who told me that he will be standing over me when I take my last breath—is now talking to me like we're old friends. It's baffling, and I tell him as much. "I don't understand you. Why are you doing this, any of this?"

"I could ask you the same question," he counters. "At least with me, I have an explanation. I've been working for the SDC for a few years now. They pay me good money and let me do what I need to do. Sometimes that includes following you and getting creative with your plans. I work with them because I believe in what they're doing. Despite your unyielding insistence on demonizing them, the Social Darwinism Commission is acting in the best interest of the American people. But look at you. Own your own company; more money than you can spend in ten lifetimes; new girlfriend—and you put it all at risk to go slay dragons. You go rogue against the powers that recruited you. Sending someone else to do your dirty work in Illinois? What's *that* about? I'm amazed you didn't get spanked for that one."

"I'm not the one who's getting spanked for that one. Give it a few days; you'll see."

"What," he says, "the master list?" The look on my face reads as pure astonishment. "Don't look so surprised. Your little assistant at the office is dating someone in my employ. Oh, don't blame her. She had no idea. Still, you might want to put a word in her ear about how much she has to drink with dinner. Loosens her lips in all the right ways, if you know what I mean."

"Damn you."

"Don't be a sore loser," he says. "I read your letter, and I'm not even going to stop them from being mailed out. Nice wording, by the way. Good little touches of authenticity. I'll call it a learning experience, see how many people we lose from the program. Truth be told, this aspect isn't going well anyway. We were considering aborting it even before you did your little hatchet job today. I wish you could have seen yourself standing there like some demented firefighter."

"Are you finished?" I ask, annoyance evident in my tone.

"Almost. You scored a victory today; I'll grant you that. But this is a war you can't win. It's also a war you shouldn't win. No matter what your personal morals and ethics tell you, this organization is serving a crucial civic need. If you doubt that, think back to this afternoon. Would your pal, God, really send you to save the life of someone who's evil? Whose work should be stopped? Let me put it to you another way. You remember a few years back, you tried snuba diving in the Caribbean?"

"How could you possibly know about that?"

"Not important. But you do remember it. The air tanks were on the surface, and you had your mask down below. Remember how you felt when you first submerged? It took you almost two minutes to take in your first breath, didn't it? It's because your mind tells you that you can't breathe underwater; that it's not right, not possible. But if you stay down there long enough, your body fights that. It feels that mask, that regulator, and you take that first breath. Maybe you're a little panicky at first, but as the air flows into your lungs, you remember that breathing is the most natural thing in the world, and you just let it happen. That's what you have to do here, Tristan. Your mind is fighting you—telling you that what the SDC is doing is wrong, that they can't do that, and they have to be stopped. I want you to stop resisting it; let the rational side of your brain kick in. Let it remind you that this world has more people in it than it can support, and one way or another, many of them will die before they reach old age. Should it be you? Your family and friends? Your girlfriend? Or should it be drug abusers, alcoholics, chain smokers, welfare cheats, illegal aliens? You've never known want or need, but millions do, and they shouldn't have to. They're weak too, and the SDC wants to help them get strong."

"I just want you to leave me alone, Ephraim. Let me live my life. Don't follow me, don't go out of your way to thwart what I have to do. Don't drop out of the sky just to mess with my understanding of the world. Just leave me alone. Please."

He rises and stands in front of the sofa. "A lot of that depends on you. Be smart, be sensible. Stay away from the wrong crowd, and don't mix in where you don't belong. I know you see me as your enemy, but it doesn't have to be that way." He looks at me, perhaps waiting for a response. Receiving none, he continues, "Well, I should get going. Drink plenty of water for the rest of the day. You'll be dehydrated for a while."

I rise and turn to face him as he heads for the front door. "Who are you, really?" I ask.

"You'll find out soon. That's the best I can tell you."

Just over two hours later, Genevieve enters the house. Seeing me in the living room, she runs to me and throws her arms around me. "Oh, thank heaven you're here. Are you all right? Did they hurt you?"

"I'm fine," I reply. "They just tranquilized me a little more than I'm comfortable with. What about you? Are you safe?"

"I'm fine. Surprisingly so, in fact. From everything you told me about Ephraim, I was expecting him to be a lot more dangerous. He wasn't, though. He was even polite. He told me what happened with you, and he asked me to pack everything up and leave Washington; there was nothing more to do there, so I did."

"So he told you what happened at Swift?"

"Yeah. He said something about an axe. Is that true?"

"*Axe* is a harsh word. Okay, yes, it's true."

"What were you hoping to do?" she asks.

"Put them out of business. Tell people there the truth and do a little damage into the bargain."

"Tristan, you could have been arrested ... or worse."

"I know. My new buddy made that very clear. Right before he warned me to back off or there'd be consequences."

She sits next to me and gently offers, "In light of everything that's happened, I wonder if that's not a good idea. Between today's actions and the letters you sent out, I think their phony drug trial is a bust. You could spend your whole life battling them, maybe score a few hits here and there, risking Ephraim's wrath the whole time, or you could accept that they're a powerful, well-protected group. Maybe you find what they're doing repugnant ..."

"Maybe?"

"But now that you know the reasons behind it, maybe it's also possible that Kean is right, and SODARCOM is working to counteract a dangerous overpopulation scenario that would threaten millions of people, even without their presence."

I can't believe what I'm hearing. "Did they get to you too? Did Ephraim brainwash you with his propaganda?"

"I asked him why the group was doing these things, and he did take the time to explain it to me, but please don't mistake that for brainwashing. Just because you and I disagree on this point doesn't mean that I'm stupid or gullible. I know what they're doing, and I know how it sounds. But now, I also know *why* they're doing it. Throughout history, people have sometimes been tasked with unbearably awful things that have to be done, and a few have stepped up to do them. I don't want to watch them work, and I don't even want to know that it's happening. But at the same time, I'm not prepared to battle them. And I hope you aren't either."

Her words, though I know they bear no malice, still cut through me. All I can do is sit there and try to process the implications of what she has said. So I sit in silence, my head hanging low to my chest. My victory of today feels like bitter defeat. I know what the usual answer is to the question, *Is everybody else wrong, or is it me?* But damn it, what I feel doesn't feel wrong.

My silence must be longer-lasting than I realize, because at some point, I am ripped from my thoughts by her voice. "Talk to me. Let me in. I respect your feelings, and I don't want this to come between us."

"Yeah," I mutter with a little humorless laugh, "who knew genocide was one of my hot buttons?"

"You've just been through an ordeal. People throw that word around lightly, but it describes this situation. You put your life in jeopardy for the sake of saving people, only to find out that the people weren't meant to be saved. Frankly, I'd be surprised if that *didn't* mess with your head. Ever since you started getting these assignments, you've given yourself the role of protector of the human race. That's a big job. You didn't fail. You just went up against a house that couldn't lose. Now I want you to rest. Let's go somewhere, just the two of us. Somewhere with white sand, ridiculous shirts for sale, and drinks served in a hollowed-out coconut."

"Aruba?" I suggest.

"Sure. Aruba, Hawaii, Tahiti. Wherever you like."

"You buying?" I ask playfully.

"I'll buy the drinks," she offers.

"That's fair." Ease is returning to us; I need that. "I'm tired. I'm so tired."

"I don't doubt it for a second. You should go upstairs and get some sleep."

I check my watch. "It's 7:00 in the evening."

"Your point being?"

"I'm not six years old."

"And I'm not your mommy. People sleep when they're tired. Hell, the way this day has gone, I'm right there with you. I haven't had dinner yet, have you?"

"No, but I'm not hungry, really."

"Neither am I. I think it would do us both good to get out of these clothes, climb into bed, and decompress in whatever way is most effective. Then, when we're both too tired to stay awake any longer, we drift off to sleep, wake up tomorrow, and plan our tropical getaway."

"And if I get an assignment when I'm on that tropical getaway?"

"Look at it this way: when you were in Washington, you got two assignments there, so maybe they tend to send you where you already are. You could save the life of some unsuspecting Aruban."

"Genevieve, was this whole thing a mistake?"

She hesitates a moment. "Which whole thing do you mean?"

"Coming to Washington. Getting involved with something that wasn't asked of me, wasn't assigned to me."

"I don't think so. I like to believe that things don't happen by accident. When you got the call from Kolodziej, that was a call for help.

He was already in this, and he couldn't finish it alone, so you came to his aid. And you freed him."

"By killing him," I remind her.

"By doing what he asked you to do, what he couldn't do on his own. They were going to exploit his knowledge to hurt people. You kept that from happening. That's something to be proud of."

"Yes, but you said yourself, what they're doing isn't bad."

"No, I said that what they're doing might be necessary. I never said it wasn't bad. You made a statement; you stood up to an untouchable organization and said that you wouldn't sit still in the face of what they were doing. I'd bet not too many people have done that. Everyone who does gives them something to think about. So, was this a mistake? I don't think it was. Come on. Come with me. Let's put this day behind us. Tomorrow we can figure out what comes next."

Chapter 11

Home. The place like which there is no place.

Waking up in my own bed on Tuesday morning feels very good. Genevieve is still asleep beside me, so I take care not to wake her; it's barely 6:00, after all, and for the first time in a week, there's nothing pressing this morning. For all the fuss I've made about defending justice and vanquishing evil, it feels amazing to have a morning with nothing to do. Genevieve's idea about a vacation sounds great. And as peaceful as the Caribbean sounds, the idea of a cruise to Alaska is even more appealing. Apart from my drug-induced journey, I've never been on a cruise, and all the pictures and videos of Alaska that I've seen make it look spectacular.

The more I think about it, the better it sounds, so I quietly slink out of bed, use the bathroom farthest from the master bedroom, and then go to my computer and search for "Alaska cruises." Apparently, it's a very good time for them, as every cruise line imaginable is offering voyages of seven to fifteen days, some of which include rail tours of the Alaskan interior. I explore a bit, looking at the different ships and itineraries, the amenities and the extras. Cost isn't a factor, but I'm careful to avoid the highest-end cruise lines, because—truth be told—I can't stand being surrounded by too many people of wealth and privilege. They drive me out of my mind. So I find an upscale but not too upscale ship with great amenities, good food, and a fifteen-day trip from Seattle to

Alaska that includes five days in Denali. On top of that, it leaves this Saturday. I'm seconds away from booking it when a voice behind me says, "You're up early."

Frantically, I minimize the window as I try to keep from jumping out of my seat. "Morning, dear," I offer with a pleasant smile.

"What're you up to?" she asks playfully. "What were you looking at when I came in?"

"What, that? Uhh, that was porn. Yep, good old raunchy porn."

"Porn?" she repeats, clearly not believing it for a second. "So you're telling me you got up from your girlfriend's side at 6 a.m. to go look at pictures of naked women?"

"Umm … yes. That appears to be my story."

She crosses her arms in front of her. "Open that browser window. I will warn you now that if I discover you were working, the results will be very grim."

Without an option, I open the window and she looks at what I was viewing. "Alaska?" she says, her voice sounding intrigued.

"I wanted to surprise you with it, but now I think it's a good idea that you get a vote before I book it. What do you think? Two weeks in the majestic Northwest, exploring America's last frontier."

"Can we get a cabin with a balcony?" she asks.

"We can get a *suite* with a wraparound balcony."

"Let's do it!" she beams, barely containing the childlike glee that threatens to seep out of every available orifice.

About five minutes of earnest typing, and I am the proud occupant of a mini-suite on the August 25, 2007 sailing of the Hellenic Pride Cruise Lines ship *Persephone*. Genevieve seems to approve, as she showers me with gratitude and affection.

"You sure your sister won't mind watching your house for two more weeks?" I ask.

"Believe me, once she knows it's because we're on vacation and out of danger, she'll be thrilled. That reminds me, I should call her and let her know I'm all right."

"Yes, please. Let her know that I didn't get us both killed."

She sighs happily. "Alaska. I've never been anywhere near that area. Can we spend a day in Seattle, too? I've heard such good things about the city."

"Sure. We can fly there on Friday morning, spend the day, get a hotel room, and head to the ship on Saturday."

"I hope this isn't costing you too much money," she says.

"Less than you'd think. With just a few days left before sailing, they'd rather discount the suites than let them go empty. So I got a good deal. But even if I didn't, it's still worth it. My dear, if anyone deserves a vacation, it's the two of us!"

"Thank you for this."

"You're very—" Obviously, the next word is *welcome,* or even something unexpected like *pretty* or *sexy.* But for me, the next word is interrupted by drooling and falling out of my chair onto the floor, because the universe, with its impeccable sense of humor, chooses this moment to play America's favorite game, "Let's Fuck Tristan!" The pain is centered in my head this time, but it feels different somehow. With previous assignments, the pain was there, and it was intense, but this time it feels—strange as this sounds—personal, like someone is actively *trying* to hurt me. I'm aware of Genevieve crouching beside me, trying to keep me safe and comfortable; far more powerful is the sensation that someone is beating me repeatedly across the skull with a baseball bat—wooden, I think.

I start to receive details—images and facts about my mission—but these too feel different; less clear, less coherent. I struggle, despite the pain, to retain what's being sent to me. I see places, individuals, names, an address, but it's not nearly as detailed as what I'm used to—as if we have a bad connection.

As the information and the pain fade, I become more aware of my surroundings, including Genevieve running her fingers through my hair and talking softly to me. "Tristan, can you hear me? Let me know you're all right."

I look up at her. "Ow."

"Are you hurt?"

"Hurt*ing,* but not hurt."

"Was it another assignment?"

"Yes, I'm afraid it was."

"So no cruise, then?"

"I didn't say that. The assignment is in West Virginia, just a few hours away, and I need to leave very soon. If all goes well, I'll be back tonight, and we can take our cruise. Anything that tries to contact me while that's happening will get my answering service. Help me up?"

She takes my hand and lifts me to my feet. I'm a bit unsteady for a few seconds, but I quickly recover.

"What do you have to do in West Virginia?"

"There's an eight-year-old blind boy there, and he's going to wander off into the woods and get lost. I need to find him, or—if I can—prevent him from going to those woods in the first place."

"I think," she says, "this might be one of those where a call to the parents ahead of time could prevent the thing from happening at all."

"It's a good idea, but one of the pieces of information I was given is that the parents are very suspicious of strangers, especially 'city folk.' This is a very small town I'm going to, and I suspect the only way they're going to trust me is if they see me actually rescue this boy."

"I want to come with you."

"Thank you, but the instructions were very vivid this time. They told me to come alone. There must be a reason for it, and I don't want to risk it."

"That doesn't seem strange to you?" she asks.

"Everything I've been through lately has convinced me not to question such things. I promise, I'll be safe. Besides, this was going to be a day of relaxation. One of us should enjoy that, and I think it should be you."

"Tristan, if the people in this town you're going to don't trust outsiders, you need to be very careful when you bring them back their blind eight-year-old. I don't want anyone thinking you tried to take him."

"Understood. I'll be judicious." Checking the time, I continue, "We should have some breakfast, and I should hit the road. It'll take me four hours to get there from here."

Within the hour, I have bid Genevieve farewell and loaded myself into my car for the drive to Silver Spur, West Virginia. Just two blocks from my driveway, I do something I haven't done in the car in a long time: I turn the radio on. Rather than immerse myself in plans and strategies during the drive, I decide to listen to music that I enjoy. I find an oldies station and try not to take it too personally when I find that music

I enjoyed in high school is now considered "oldies." After all, it was almost twenty years ago; hardly what you'd call top of the charts now.

As the miles pass, I let the music stand in for deeper thought. The songs talk about the powerful, all-consuming nature of love and the importance of standing strong against life's troubles. They don't talk about blinding pain or mysterious assignments or lost children or government agencies that want to decimate the population—and that is exactly what I need right now, a reminder that there is a world beyond my circumstances.

Roughly twenty miles from my destination, I turn the radio off; now it's time to think about the task at hand. I begin with what I know: an eight-year-old blind boy named Michael wanders away from his family and becomes lost in an area known as Tyson's Woods. Unfortunately, I don't know the child's last name, but given that the town of Silver Spur has only about three thousand residents, there probably won't be too many blind children named Michael. His parents won't even know he's missing until I bring him back to them. How this is possible I don't even know. There must be some pretty damn bad parents out there.

The town is isolated, tucked into the Appalachians, and with that isolation comes suspicion, fear, an almost fanatical unity that rejects anyone or anything *other*. So a stranger wandering into town, looking like he's got money, and saying he's here to save a child because he gets visions from beyond—it's a recipe for making me disappear. Truth is, there's no best way to do this. I could search for the child myself before he wanders off; I could contact local law enforcement; I could try to find the parents. Each method has its advantages and its dangers. I suspect I won't know exactly what I'm going to do until I get there.

Just under thirty minutes later, I pass a sign that says Silver Spur, population 3,086. It is a wide place on a state highway, barely two miles from end to end. And it looks like it's remained the same for decades. The houses are old but well kept; there's no hint of affluence anywhere to be found. No big-box stores, no chain restaurants. I pass a small grocery store, an auto parts store, a few repair shops, a hardware store. No courthouse marks the center of town; this isn't the county seat. It's a tiny place, peopled by lower-middle-class laborers who may or may not be proud to have lived there for generations. And every single one of them I pass locks eyes with me like an animal defending its home territory. I'll find no welcome here; no sympathy, no support. Probably not much in the way of assistance.

I notice a road sign to my right that says Tyson's Woods, on a road leading to the north. I still have about an hour before the time I'm supposed to find the boy, but at least now I know where to go. Still, the time for action is approaching, and short of happening upon a blind child as I travel the town's main street, I need to make a decision. Grocery store? No, too random. Police station? Too much room for trouble if they think I'm up to something. Fire station? I like it, but unfortunately, the only fire department in town is volunteer, and unless something's burning, they're all at their day jobs. Post office? Actually, that could work. Small town like this, the post office employees would likely know everyone in town. What to say once I get there—that's the part I haven't figured out yet.

I park in front of the post office and get out of the car. I'm fairly certain that I don't look like an alien who just arrived on the planet, but you couldn't tell from the expressions of those I pass. Every single one of them stares at me with suspicion and disdain etched on their faces, every man and every woman. But no children; that strikes me as strange. Sure, the town is small, but I've yet to see a single child since I arrived. As odd as that seems, there's something I'm overlooking, some small but crucial detail that's just out of reach.

The post office is tiny, with just two customer windows, some drop slots, a couple of postage vending machines, and a wall of post office boxes. It looks to have been built in the 1920s and not renovated much since then. The floors are wooden, creaking with every step I take. The entire place has an air of antiquity about it, like walking into one of those historical theme parks out west, only this one's up and running.

Two women in their fifties stand in line at the only open window in the place, and as I approach, their postal business becomes suddenly unimportant. Neither can take her eyes off of me, and not in the way I *wish* women couldn't take their eyes off of me. Rather, they regard me much the same way they'd regard the devil if he chose to walk in on their church service some Sunday.

"Afternoon," I offer pleasantly, in a fruitless attempt to break the ice.

I am greeted, as expected, with stony silence. For a moment, I contemplate putting on a local accent in an attempt to fit in, but I quickly decide that the consequences of being found out are far worse than the implications of not being from 'round hyar. Despite the reception, I decide to address both women and the elderly man behind the counter at the same time. "My name is Dr. ... Watson," (for some reason), "and I'm from the Sacred Angels School for Blind Children in Maryland. I've come to talk to a local family about getting their little boy, Michael, enrolled at our school. But I've done something kind of careless. I left my file in my office that gives the family's name and address. I do know that they live here in Silver Spur, and their little fella is Michael. He's eight years old. Do any of you know the family I'm talking about, by chance?"

The two women look at each other, and by the identical look of horror on their faces, you'd think I walked into the local diner and asked for an eight-year-old child slow-roasted and served on a kaiser roll with barbecue sauce. Though the pair is rendered speechless, the postal employee isn't. "Eglantine, run find Sheriff Paul. Tell him we've got another one comin' askin' about Michael."

One of the women scurries out the door. After a few seconds' thought, her friend follows at a brisk pace, leaving me alone with the man. The prospect of "Sheriff Paul" coming to talk to me is not a good one—although if anyone in town could give me an answer, it would likely be him. I could run, but nothing would make me look guiltier. Instead I try to coax some reason out of the person who thought it's a good time to go fetch lawman. "Sir, I promise you, I mean no harm to the boy, his family, or anyone here."

"Dr. Watson, is it?" he asks, in a tone that indicates that his bullshitometer is spiking in the red. "Would you have any identification to prove that? Or did you leave that in your office too?"

"You said 'another one asking about Michael.' Was someone here before, asking about the same boy? A stranger? Maybe someone you didn't trust?"

"You stay here. Sheriff'll sort this out."

"Please, Mister ..." I find a nametag on his vest. "Ogilvie. The reason I'm here is because the others were here first. They might mean

181

some harm to Michael, but I swear to you on a stack of bibles that I'm on the side of right."

"Evil don't think it's evil," he says simply.

Before I can engage him further—and much sooner than I would have thought reasonable—the women return with a tall man of about thirty, wearing a khaki uniform and wide-brimmed hat. Even without the badge on his chest and the gun on his hip, I wouldn't need three guesses to know who was facing me. And if the town weren't small enough to have the whole place carpeted, I might've had some extra time to prepare for this introduction. As it is, I have to wing it.

"That's him, Sheriff," one of the women says, quite unnecessarily, in my opinion. Given the choices present, I am quite obviously "him."

"Sheriff Paul, I'm guessing," I say pleasantly, with a smile of appeasement that would charm the nits off a monkey. He's having none of it.

"That's right. Who would you be?"

A fair question, given the impending need to prove it. The postal worker answers in my stead. "He told us he's Dr. Watson from some kinda school."

"Dr. Watson?" the sheriff says. "Guess that makes me Sherlock Holmes then, does it?"

To extend the metaphor properly, that would make him Inspector Lestrade, but I don't press the point. "My name isn't important," I reply, knowing full well that it is important to them, along with that pesky little matter of impersonating a doctor. Come to think of it, I *was* given an honorary PhD by my alma mater a few years ago. Wonder if that'd be enough to ward off trouble. "What *is* important, and what I need you to believe, is that I'm here to help. I don't know who came here before or what they wanted, but what I do know is that there's a child in town, an eight-year-old boy named Michael, and he might be in danger. I came here to help his parents and protect him from harm. If you need to put me in handcuffs and take me to the station, I'll go. Hook me up to a lie detector, and I'll tell you the same thing. I'm not dangerous. I just have information that can help this child."

For reasons I can't understand, one of the women leans in toward the other and whispers a single word: "Sears."

What the hell does that mean? Is it the boy's surname? The name of the people who were here before? A sale on refrigerators and lawn mowers going on today? Much as I'd like to ask, Sheriff Paul interjects at this point. "You need to go," he says simply. "Leave town. I don't know where you get your information from, but there's no eight-year-old blind boy in Silver Spur."

It worked. I gave it a try, and it worked. "Sheriff, I never mentioned that the child was blind. He is, but I'm curious how you knew that."

Interestingly enough, the sheriff does not look proud of me for executing my little ruse so successfully. Instead he looks at me with an expression suggesting that he's pondering the different cavities on my body where the barrel of his gun would fit conveniently. "Let's go."

I allow him to follow me out of the post office and into the street. "What aren't you telling me?" I ask him. "What is it you couldn't say in front of those people, but you can say in front of just me?"

"This your car?" he asks.

"Yes."

"I want you to get in it, and I want you to drive back to wherever you came from. And if you hear of anyone else wantin' to come to Silver Spur, you tell them they're not welcome here. We're not some sideshow for your entertainment. Go on out of here. I'll be watchin' the streets this afternoon, and if I find you still in town, I may just run you in and see if there's some laws you've broken. Now go on."

Without another word, he gets into his patrol car across the street and drives off. *Curiouser and curiouser.* For a man who didn't say much, Sheriff Paul has given me plenty to think about. *We're not some sideshow for your entertainment.* Okay, Dr. Watson, what does that mean? It suggests that others have been here before me, asking about the blind child. But more than that—it's like they've made the place a tourist attraction, and the locals don't want it to be. How could a child do that? Does he have two heads? Can he flap his arms and fly? He's important enough to send me here to save him, but why?

I realize that the odds of finding an Internet café in town are nil, so I give Genevieve a call, hoping she can do an online search for me. The signal is very weak, cutting in and out, but I place the call. Her phone rings four times and goes to voicemail. "Hi, it's me. I'm in West Virginia, but I'm encountering a cone of silence. I think they're covering something up. When you get this, please give me a call. I want to look up this town and see what's going on."

And so I stand at the curb of a mostly empty street in the center of this tiny town, alone and without outside resources. The sheriff's warning to leave still resounds in my ears, which means only one thing: I need to make my way to Tyson's Woods discreetly. *What, I'm going to let a little thing like the law stand in the way of doing what I need to do?* I get back into the car and head for the turnoff to the woods, making sure that the sheriff's car is nowhere near me as I make the turn. Safely out of sight, I proceed for three and a quarter miles, watching as the roadside foliage gets progressively thicker. Before long, I am in the middle of a substantial grove of deciduous trees, which serve to very effectively and unfortunately block out a good deal of sunlight. The later in the day it gets, the harder it will be to find a missing boy.

Ahead on my left, I see a sign: Tyson's Woods State Forest, West Virginia Division of Natural Resources. The road in is paved and well maintained, but conspicuously absent is any sort of staff presence. Unlike a state park or national park, Tyson's Woods appears to be a hands-off operation, which will make my efforts that much more difficult. There'll be no one to help me if things go wrong. *Unless ...* I bring out my phone and confirm my fear: no bars. The weak signal I had in town has faded away out here. "Well, shit."

If privacy was high on my list of wishes for the day, I'd be in paradise. There is literally not another soul around—which strikes me as odd. Michael supposedly wandered away from his family to get lost in these woods, a family that isn't here now. Three miles from town is too far for the child—a blind child, I might add—to walk on his own, and I scarcely believe the parents were visiting here earlier and left the place without being damn sure their handicapped son was in the vehicle with them.

As I park in the main parking lot and get out of the car, I start to wonder if maybe the sheriff was right. Maybe there is no blind child. I'm just about ready to believe that I got my information wrong, when suddenly I hear it—laughter ... a child's laughter. The sound is unmistakable as it echoes through the trees, which is lovely and atmospheric but makes it damn difficult to track the source.

I cup my hands around my mouth and call out, "Michael? Michael!"

More laughter is my reply; this time it sounds like it's coming from a hiking trail to my right. I head in that direction, continuing to talk to him. "Michael, my name is Tristan! I'm a friend of your parents. They're worried about you, and they asked me to bring you home to them." *Yeah, that doesn't sound creepy or anything. Maybe I should add "in my windowless van full of puppies" to complete the motif.*

Ahead on the trail, I hear the sound of scurrying footsteps, so I follow. Again, something feels wrong. *Scurrying—that's what it is.* These sound like the footsteps of a child running. Would a blind child alone on a trail be running? For some reason, I look at my watch and see that it's 1:45 p.m. Inside my mind, aching to come out, is a realization—something so simple, so obvious, but what is it?

Another round of laughter from ahead of me on the trail breaks my train of thought, and I find myself running to catch up. No matter how fast I go, I can't seem to catch him or even see him. How can a blind kid be so graceful?

Graceful. As I run, my mind runs even faster. *Graceful. Graceful, full of grace. Who's full of grace? Who? Michael. Who? Child full of grace. Which child? Sunday's? No—no ... Tuesday's child is full of grace. Tuesday. This is Tuesday, and it's 1:45 p.m. No children in town. Why no children? Why? Where?*

"Oh my God ..." I stop dead in my tracks. "School. They're all in school."

Of course. Something so obvious but just out of reach. The children are all in school. School systems aren't waiting for Labor Day to start the year anymore; by mid-August, most are in full swing. My schedule has been so insane, I lose track of the days, but an eight-year-old child—even a blind one—would be in school on a Tuesday afternoon. He wouldn't be able to get away by himself. Even if they went on a field trip here, they wouldn't leave him behind. He couldn't be here. So what have I been chas—

My thought is cut short as I look down the trail and see him standing there—a boy of about eight, wearing a plaid shirt and cut-off denim pants. His shoes are very old and worn out, and he wears no socks. His face is dirty, and his eyes are two drops of cloudy milk, looking but not seeing as he stares at me.

"Michael," I say quietly.

His response is that same laugh that has been echoing through the trees. Without a word, he turns and runs further down the trail. *So he is real. I can catch him now. He's close.*

Determined not to lose sight of him, I sprint once more, hoping to catch up. He navigates each turn on the trail as if he can see it perfectly. I stay behind him, as the trail climbs a steep hill. The boy is tireless; not so for me. Not one for regular exercise, I quickly become winded, struggling to keep pace with him. On the right, the trail skirts a cliff with a drop that increases with each hundred feet I travel. I can see the danger, but how can he? One wrong turn, one misstep, and he could easily go over.

"Michael!" I call out, panting. "Stay where you are. There's … there's dangerous cliffs here."

He doesn't reply, just laughs again and continues leading the pursuit. But I'm gaining on him; I can feel it. I lose sight of him less often, and soon I am just a few paces behind him. Just as I finally feel confident that I can catch him, he turns to the right, stepping off the trail. He stands still for a moment, right at the cliff's edge. Then he turns to me again. Before I can say anything, he continues forward, stepping over the edge and into the unsupporting air.

"No!" The word is an act of futility, for the unthinkable has already happened. As I scramble to the edge and kneel to look over the side, he has disappeared from view, down a drop that I now see is at least sixty feet down to a rocky valley below.

I can't fail him. Not after everything that's happened. Maybe he landed somewhere soft. Maybe he's all right. I can get down to him.

There's no time to plan; I look around for a handhold and prepare to descend the cliff wall to save this child. Just as I reach out to begin the descent, a hand grabs my shoulder from behind, and I am pulled forcefully away from the cliff and thrown to the trail firmly on my back. I see stars for a second, and when my vision clears, I find myself looking into the face of a very angry Sheriff Paul.

"What did I tell you?" he demands through gritted teeth. "What did I say about leaving here?"

"He fell," I answer, fear lacing my words. "He fell, he fell, he fell!"

"Yes," Paul says, "he fell. Look at me. Look at me. July 2, 1985. Right there, at that cliff. Michael Scofield fell."

"What?"

"On that spot, in these woods, that little blind child died—twenty-two years ago."

His face is just inches from mine, and everything tells me he's speaking the truth—but how? I'm so disoriented, so uncertain of everything. He must realize this, because his tone softens, and he helps me to my feet. "Come on. Stand up."

Gradually I rise, finally able to stand steadily. "What's happening here?"

"Are you all right to drive yourself back to town?" he asks.

"I ... yeah, I think so."

"I want you to follow me in your car. I'll take you to someone who can explain it."

He helps me back down the trail; to my surprise, I have run more than a mile into the woods, chasing a child I was certain was there. It's disconcerting to think that I was wrong, not to mention more than a little confusing. One thing eludes me, though, so I ask him. "How did you know I would be here?"

"You had a look on your face when I told you to leave town, a look that said you weren't planning to. When I didn't find you in town, I knew you'd be here. They always come here."

"Always? You mean this has happened before?"

"Yes. Conjur Man will explain."

"Who's—"

"Hush now," he says, as if I were the age of my intended quarry. "Save your strength. I expect you're feelin' a bit sick." *Come to think of it, I am, actually.* "There's haints in these woods will play havoc with your system."

We return to our respective vehicles, and I am given a police escort back to town. I'm pleased to see that he skips the lights and siren and simply leads the way to a street just two blocks from the post office where we met. He parks out front and I next to him, and he leads me into an old, weather-worn storefront with a simple, hand-painted sign above it that says "Conjur Man." I have only the vaguest idea what that means.

Once inside, the air feels a bit close. There is an aroma I can't quite place—nutmeg, maybe; I'm not sure. My head is still gently swimmy from the experience at Tyson's Woods. Before I can give it too much thought, a man emerges from the back room, through beaded curtains (of course) to stand before us. He is tall, dark-skinned, bald-headed, and wearing aviator sunglasses and a vibrant dashiki that is reminiscent of a giraffe or a leopard's pattern.

"Good afternoon, Sheriff Paul," he says pleasantly in a very metered baritone. "You've brought me a new client?"

"Another one from the woods, Conjur Man," the sheriff says. "I was able to stop him before he got hurt, but I think he needs to talk to you."

"Thank you, Sheriff. I'd be happy to. Have a pleasant day."

"You too, Conjur Man."

The sheriff takes his leave, and the shopkeeper gestures for me to sit at a round table that occupies a corner of his front room. "You're welcome here," he says calmly, sitting opposite me. Without even asking, he offers me a cold bottle of water, which I graciously accept. "My name is Keswegi Umbi."

"Better known as Conjur Man?" I reply.

"This is rural West Virginia. Many people here struggled with my name, so they resorted to 'Boy' or less-gracious epithets. I borrowed from local folklore, presenting myself as one of the seers of legend."

In an instant, it occurs to me—the word the woman uttered in the post office. Not Sears, but *seers*. Something tells me this town gets its share of them.

"Thank you for meeting with me," I say to him. "My name is …"

"Tristan Shays," he finishes without missing a beat. "Yes, I know."

"Okay, that's weird."

"Your mind is like a powerful transmitter, Tristan. You're different from most who come here. And I must apologize that our little town has drawn you out under false pretenses."

"I have so many questions," I reply.

"You came here because you believed a child was lost in the woods, a blind child named Michael Scofield. So you went to the woods to try to save him. You followed the sound of his laughter; perhaps you even saw him. Then he led you to a cliff, and you believe he fell over the side of it. Please stop me if anything is inaccurate."

"No, everything is right on target."

"You were ready to go down that cliff after him, but the sheriff stopped you. I imagine at that point, he told you the truth: Michael did fall down that cliff, twenty-two years ago."

"What happened to me here? Why did this happen?"

"Michael is what the mountain people call a skin dancer, a spirit who can inhabit his former body. Some call him a haint, a ghost. In life, Michael was a powerful seer. Ironic for a blind child, but it allowed him to get by without the use of a cane or anyone to help him."

"How did he fall?"

"He was on that trail with his parents. It wasn't as well-groomed and maintained as it is now. Michael was chasing a small animal, the way young boys do, and he ventured too close to the edge. Before anyone could stop him, he tumbled over and died on the rocks below. Those woods were his favorite place, and when his escort came to take him to the other side, he ran away. So now he stays here. His parents would go to those woods to be near him, and he appeared to them. Then, last year, his mother died, and his father stopped going. I believe Michael is finally ready to go to the other side, but his escort has long since given up trying to find him. So the boy reaches out to anyone sensitive enough to hear him, and he asks them to come and find him."

"But then why did he run away when he saw me?"

"Because he's still a child, and it's still a game. Part of the rules of that game are *catch me first*. Many have tried; no one has succeeded. A few have gone over that same cliff."

"No wonder the sheriff wanted me to leave. This town must be like Disneyland for psychics."

"I admit, it helps me to stay in business, along with many of the more mundane shopkeepers here. But there is some danger, and it is an invasion of our privacy, the sanctity of our home. So we do what we can to control the crowds."

"This may be the strangest thing that's ever happened to me," I admit.

"That's quite a statement, given what you've seen and done recently. These past weeks have changed you."

"You can see all that?"

"Yes."

"Then tell me, *please,* why is this happening? If you see these things, then you know what I've been through. The part I don't understand is why. What did I do to be chosen for this?"

"For one with such a gift, you see very little. This is your birthright. An honor bestowed upon you from centuries past."

"My … I don't understand."

"You're one of a few—very few—with such gifts. The world is full of individuals who have abilities beyond those of other people. But you—what you are shouldn't even exist. Modern religion is founded on the belief in an infallible God, a being so powerful and wise that it never makes mistakes. And yet they do occur, and you are charged with fixing them. Ponder that, Tristan. God says to you, 'I didn't mean for this to happen, and if it happens, I am fallible in man's eyes. Please prevent it.'"

"But so many bad things happen even without me and my kind. Doesn't that show his fallibility?" I ask.

"We see these things as *bad* from our human experience. But if no one is sent to stop them, then we must accept that they were meant to happen. Floods and earthquakes and hurricanes kill thousands, and we see this and think *this can't be right.* But death is as natural as life, and everything happens in its season. The people you were pursuing this very week told you the same thing. Sometimes, circumstances work against God's will, and his earthly messengers are called upon to right things again. What you see as a burden, Tristan Shays, is an honor. You are truly blessed."

"So why does it hurt so much every time?"

He reaches across the table and puts a hand gently on my forehead. The residual pain I'm feeling disappears at his touch. "Shakespeare said, 'There is nothing either good or bad, but thinking makes it so.' See the burden, and you will feel the pain; see the blessing, and you will feel the joy."

"I've failed sometimes."

"I know," he says gently, "but not because you didn't try. If God himself is not flawless, how can man expect to be? You will fail sometimes, and sometimes you will succeed. You must always look at those around you with a discerning eye. Some who you believe you can trust will deceive you; others you doubt may prove to be allies."

"How will I know?"

"By listening to the innermost voice."

"I could go back out to those woods," I tell him, "try to contact the child again and escort him to the other side."

"That's very caring of you, but no. Others will come, and someone will succeed. Escorting a soul to the other side is a very special task, one that requires an expert. Someone will come and help him cross when he's ready."

"Come with me," I answer, somewhat surprised by my own words.

"Where would you have me go?"

"Wherever I go. You obviously have a gift, one that would help me to succeed at what I have to do. You could leave this town, go somewhere you'll be respected, valued."

"I was born here," he says. "My great-great-grandparents were slaves in this area. When they were freed, they chose to remain here. My ancestors were beaten, brutalized, spit on by the people of Silver Spur, West Virginia. And now, *their* descendants won't make a move without asking me if it's a good idea."

"So you stay here to repay their cruelty with kindness."

"Sometimes. Sometimes it's just fun to fuck with their heads." At this, he offers a knowing smile, and I can't contain the laugh that's built up inside me.

"Oh, I like you."

"Every now and then, the good guy gets to do something bad. So thank you for your offer, but this is where I belong. Besides, you have someone to accompany you, someone with a gift."

"I suppose I do." I rise and get a hundred dollars out of my wallet, handing it across the table to him.

"You don't owe me anything," he says. "You were brought here."

"I believe in paying someone for a service of value," I reply, continuing to offer the bill.

He nods a little and takes it. "Then I accept. Thank you."

"Thank you for your help."

I turn to leave, but he calls to me. "Tristan." I pause and look back at him. "Be careful."

"Will do."

About fifteen miles east of Silver Spur, in the silence of my car, I am startled by a sound—a signal from my phone that I have voicemail. I check the screen and see that Genevieve has called. Without even listening to her message, I call her back. She picks up right away. "Are you all right?" she asks.

"I'm fine. I'm on my way home. I couldn't get a signal where I was."

"Was it a success? Were you able to find the child?"

"It's kind of a long story. For now, I'll just say that things are fine, and I can't wait to see you again. How about you? How was your day?"

"It was remarkable. Something happened today—something good, and I want to tell you all about it, but it should be in person. When will you be home?"

"It won't be for about four hours."

"It's okay," she says. "It's important enough that it can wait."

Chapter 12

Owing to rush-hour traffic congestion, it is late evening before I return to Ocean City. I'm quite tired as I pull into the driveway; today took a lot out of me and gave me a lot to think about. I marvel once again at the fascinating people I've met since this whole thing started. People I would never have encountered otherwise. Latest addition to the list, Mr. Keswegi Umbi, the Conjur Man of Silver Spur, West Virginia. With a single touch, he was able to take my pain away—yet another reason I wish he could come with me. Human analgesic.

In a way, his words served to take some of my pain away too. Would it be possible for me to look at these assignments as the blessing he says they are? And if I do, will that really stave off any further agony? I've tried, really tried to consider myself fortunate to have this opportunity, and yet, with each new assignment comes the wave of crippling pain. If there was a way to do the assignments without the misery, that would be perfectly acceptable.

My birthright. What could that mean? I don't recall any of my ancestors leaping into action to save strangers. That's the kind of thing you remember, I suspect.

Only seconds after entering the house, I am enfolded in Genevieve's arms. "Welcome home," she says. "I'm glad you're here, and I'm glad you're safe. Are you hungry?"

"No, thanks. I ate something of uncertain origin on the drive home."

"Come, sit in the living room with me. You can relax for the rest of the evening, can't you?"

"I believe so," I reply, following her to the sofa, which feels much more comfortable than the driver's seat of my car after so many hours.

"I did get your message earlier, but your phone went to voicemail when I called you back, so I wasn't able to be of much help. So what happened out there? What did you think they were covering up?"

I tell her the strange tale of Michael Scofield and the Conjur Man, and she hangs on every word. With her background in the paranormal, my every exploit must be like the greatest story hour she's ever attended. It's nice to have someone who believes it all without doubting. My answers to "Hi, honey, how was your day?" might result in considerable disbelief from most people, I have to admit.

"That's so weird," she says when I finish my story. "Why you, do you think? I mean, you were so far away from there, and this thing happened more than twenty years ago. Why would you be sent there now to try to help?"

"Wish I knew. The way Conjur Man described it, this happens all the time. There are more people than I thought who have gifts of this nature, and the boy's spirit calls them to come to him. I wish I could have met some of the others, to hear their stories. Apparently, there are people who help spirits cross to the other side—that's what they do. God, what must that be like?"

"Sounds pretty grim," she retorts.

"That was a terrible joke."

"Yeah, kind of."

"So, you said on the phone that something remarkable happened today, but you wanted to tell me in person. Now I'm in person, so tell me."

"Okay. I need you to hear me out, because this will sound strange, but it's true. I was on the Boardwalk in Ocean City today, just looking at the shops and relaxing. From out of nowhere, I hear a voice behind me say, 'You're in pain.' Well, I wasn't in pain, but I turned around, and someone was behind me, talking right to me. 'I'm really not,' I said, and this person said, 'Not for yourself, but for someone close to you.'"

"Ephraim," I reply with some concern. "Was it Ephraim?"

"No, that's what I thought too, but this was a woman. I made sure, because I know he's used disguises before. But this wasn't him. We sat at a table and talked for an hour. She's like us ... she has gifts. They used to be very extreme—to the point where she couldn't live a normal life. She was a clairvoyant, and she could see people far away who were suffering and dying. Only, unlike you, she didn't see these things until they were actually happening. So there was no way she could help or prevent it. It was like being a constant witness to suffering every waking hour."

"Sounds horrible," I offer quietly.

"It was. She couldn't work, couldn't have normal relationships. She was exhausted from everything she saw in her mind. And she knew it was real, because she would see the news the next day, and the images she'd already seen were there. Now she's all right again. She's still sensitive to the feelings of others, but only when she's near them. That's how she knew to talk to me."

"So what changed for her? How did she get past all the other stuff?"

"That's what I want to talk to you about," she says with an excited smile. "She learned about a research group that's made amazing strides in the area of psychic and paranormal abilities. She went to see them, and they treated her; they were able to suppress the images that were plaguing her, so she could live her life again. She gave me their information, and I called them today. I told them about you, about what you've been through, and they want to meet you tomorrow, to meet both of us. They think they can help you."

"Genevieve, I don't know. After what I've just been through with SODARCOM, the thought of putting myself in the hands of strangers, of a secret, experimental group ..."

"That's just it. They're not secret or experimental. I looked them up online. They're privately funded, nonpartisan, and dedicated to educational and healing purposes."

"So who are they and where are they?"

"They're in southern Pennsylvania, just a few hours' drive from here. They call themselves the Gnothautii Society."

The name doesn't ring a bell at all. "No ... thought—?"

"Gnothautii. It comes from a Greek phrase meaning 'know thyself.' They started out as a literary society, but over the years, the literature they studied dealt more and more with psychic abilities and the paranormal. When other branches of the society disbanded, this group stayed with it. You can look them up. I spoke with them at length, and I got a very good feeling about them. The woman I met, Karolena, says they saved her life."

"How, exactly, do you see them helping me?" I inquire.

"In whatever way you need. If you don't want to do these assignments anymore, we'll tell them, and they can suppress the visions. Or if you want to keep taking them but you don't want the pain that goes along with it, I suspect they can help you with that too."

Her words definitely give me pause to think. I'm finally reaching a place where I feel like this is my calling—like I *could* dedicate my life to helping people. But the prospect of doing so without mind-numbing pain as an incentive is tempting.

"Wow, that's … that's a lot to consider. This past week has given me quite a bit to think about. At first, when I got these assignments, I considered them an imposition, an intrusion on my life. I kept asking, why me, why this? But now that I've done more of them, and I see the difference that I can make, I'm starting to make peace with the concept and the reality. Then there's the pain. I hope you never know the kind of pain that I experience with these. Every time, I think it couldn't be worse than the last time, and then it comes, and I'm wrong. If they could really let me carry out these assignments without that pain, that's something I'd be interested in. I suppose I could go talk to them tomorrow. After all, it's not like they're going to force the treatment on me, right?"

"Exactly. I imagine they'll talk with you, listen to your experiences, and determine the best way of helping you. Whatever you decide, you have my unquestioning support. It just kills me a little each time I see you suffer, and I never want to see you in that much pain again."

Her face shows complete earnestness. How can I refuse? "Let's do this, then."

"Wonderful. I'll let them know we're coming, and I'll tell Karolena as well. She wanted to know if her suggestion was helpful." She kisses me. "Thank you for trying this. Please know that I'm doing this with your well-being in mind."

"I do. I really do."

Later in the evening, Genevieve excuses herself to take a shower. I should add at this point that I trust her completely, I really do. It is not doubt of her that motivates me to go quietly to my computer, get online, and look up the Gnothautii Society—which is harder to spell than I expected, knowing only the sound of the word. But I do find them, not in some scammer file or in any "Xpoz'd" anything, but in their own professional, respectable website. It talks about their literary history, their leadership, past and present, the split that occurred decades ago between the original members and those who wanted to pursue the new path. A separate page describes their goals and activities.

The Gnothautii Society, it says, *is rooted in the exploration of the untapped potential of the human mind, a field of study known as psionics. Unlike modern skeptics, we believe that human consciousness can far transcend the limits of so-called "normal" thinking. We believe in the potential of every human mind to discover and utilize extrasensory abilities and trans-perceptual thought.*

Funded by a private consortium of researchers and philanthropists, the Gnothautii Society does not charge individuals for consultations or treatments. We do require appointments, and we will determine a course of action based on an initial intake interview. For the privacy of all parties, we prohibit any audio or video recording devices during any interaction with clients.

Our services are diverse, encompassing traditional and non-traditional tests for psychic abilities, out-of-body travel, channeling, brain scans, and sensory dep

Genevieve emerges from the bathroom, and I quickly close the window before I can finish reading; I don't want her to think that I'm suspicious of her recommendation. Besides, what I've read seems legitimate. Tomorrow will be that initial intake interview, and that should give me plenty of information about whether they can be trusted.

WEDNESDAY, AUGUST 22, 2007

After the exploits of yesterday, I sleep very well. In brief moments of consciousness in the night, I'm aware that Genevieve has fallen asleep in my arms, and I like that. I feel like this is where she belongs and where I belong. She has managed to lower my long-standing defenses and make me forget my unfortunate fear of intimacy. We're not like traditional couples; we don't display overt affection publicly, we don't call each other by cutesy pet names, and we don't shower each other with gifts.

But in a way, she *has* given me a gift. Today is her contribution to my well-being. She sought out a way to take away my pain and still allow me to pursue my new calling. That's worth more than a wristwatch or a tie or a bottle of cologne. That's a gift of life itself, and when we're on our cruise next week, I'm going to celebrate her as I find a way to offer her a gift of equal meaning.

By 7:00 a.m., we're both awake and out of bed. There's a drive of almost four hours ahead, so an early start is important. Breakfast is light but satisfying. Neither of us packs an overnight bag; everything we need to do, we should be able to do in a single day. If not, hell, maybe we'll stay overnight at a nudist colony. No need for a change of clothes there.

Making our way to the car, I head for the driver's side, but she stops me, extending her hand. "What?" I ask.

"Keys, please. You drove all day yesterday. It's my turn."

"I really don't mind driving," I remind her.

"Neither do I, and your car is much nicer than mine. So give 'em over."

"And if I refuse?" I ask playfully.

"I just won't tell you where we're going."

"You fight dirty. Here." I hand her the ring of keys. "Knock yourself out."

She settles in behind the wheel, and we're underway. The temperature is only in the seventies, after a week of high heat and humidity, so we're able to drive with the windows open. The breeze feels good, and—despite my near insistence on driving—it's nice to be the passenger for a change.

Traffic on the bridge is typically heavy for a weekday morning, but once we get through it and start heading north, we both relax, and the talk turns to this weekend's plans. Genevieve smiles broadly and says, "Just a couple more days until our cruise."

"Very exciting stuff," I reply, smiling back at her.

"I really don't know much about Alaska. I don't know what to expect when we get there."

"Well," I answer, "strictly from what I read, we'll sail from Seattle, up the western coastline of Canada, until we reach the southern tip of Alaska. Once we're there, we'll stop in a couple of small towns and spend the day in port, exploring. We'll also spend one of the days on the ship sailing by the glaciers."

"Oh, that sounds amazing. Will it be freezing cold?"

"It sounds like the average daily high will be about sixty degrees. Evenings will be cooler, so you'll want to pack some warm clothes. But the ship has a spa with heated tile beds. I'm not exactly sure what that feels like, but I suspect I'll spend hours finding out."

She gives my hand a loving squeeze. "Thank you for this. I promise not to be the kind of girlfriend who takes advantage of your financial situation. It's one reason I didn't want to ask about vacations and things like that. I needed you to know that it's not the reason why I'm here."

"Hey, hey, listen to me. I never suspected that for a moment. Please don't worry about that. And if I ever do have concerns, I won't keep them to myself. I'll tell you, so we can work them out. Just like I want you to do. Fair enough?"

"Fair enough. Tell me more about Alaska."

The drive continues, and I have to admit, all the talk of our upcoming vacation makes me wish we were starting it today. But there's one more piece of business to attend to first. The Gnothautii. I want to believe that these people can alleviate my suffering, allowing me to examine each new assignment as it comes in; letting me decide if it's worth my time and effort to intercede. Of course, one thing the pain does is make each decision obvious. There is no deliberation; I do this or I suffer. I *don't* do this, and someone else suffers and probably dies. That alone should make the choice simple. Yet it doesn't. Is it really human nature to risk your life to save a stranger? I mean, if it were a friend in peril, or God forbid Genevieve, I would act without hesitation. But someone I've never met? Someone I'll never see again? I simply take it on faith that the person I'm saving is a good person. I give you Phillip Kean as a for-example. A man whose very reason for being is horrific to me, and yet I saved his life. What about if the circumstances were reversed? If I were the one in peril? Would someone be sent by God to save me? It makes me wonder.

"You're awfully quiet," Genevieve accurately observes. "Everything okay?"

"Just thinking about the day ahead. Wondering what's going to happen."

"I'll be there with you the whole time. If something makes you uncomfortable, just say stop, and we go no further."

"Thank you. I appreciate that."

After a couple of minutes of silence she asks, "How should we pass the time?"

"I don't know. What do you think?"

"We could play twenty questions," she suggests.

"Twenty questions … with a psychic? I'm not falling for that!"

We manage to find some pleasant diversions that don't offer my gifted companion an undue edge. In between, we talk about the future—about what happens after the cruise. Neither of us is certain about what we want in the long term, but for now, being together feels like the right thing to do.

Despite my ongoing offers to share the driving, she insists on taking us the entire way to Pennsylvania. "You can drive us back, if you really want to," she says. "Although, if they do any kind of treatment today that leaves you tired, we can always get a room for the night."

Just before 11:30 in the morning, we enter the city of York, Pennsylvania. Genevieve follows a sheet of written directions that lead her to the outskirts of town, to a one-story building with its own small parking lot. I notice that there are no nearby businesses or homes; I suppose I didn't expect them to have a storefront in a shopping mall, but I was hoping for something a little less isolated.

My apprehension must be evident on my face as we're parking, as Genevieve asks, "You all right?"

"Yeah, just the same jitters I got when my mother took me to the pediatrician decades ago. I'll be fine once we're inside."

We exit the car and walk hand-in-hand into the building. A sign in the lobby says Gnothautii Society, founded 1849. No other companies are listed or shown, suggesting that they are the building's sole occupant, further suggesting that somehow, this group can afford the rent or mortgage on a building of about three thousand square feet. Privately funded, but by whom? Researchers and philanthropists, the website said; so why does that make me nervous? Why does the whole thing make me so nervous?

Before I can postulate an answer, we are greeted by a thirty-something man with thick glasses and a severely receding hairline. "Hi," he says. "Are you Tristan?"

"That's right. Tristan Shays."

He looks at Genevieve. "And you are?"

"Genevieve Swan. I'm Tristan's companion. I was told it was all right for me to be here."

"Yeah, that's fine. I'm Eric. Dr. Eric Paloma. Nice to meet you both."

"A receptionist with a PhD?" I muse.

"Oh, sorry. I'm head of research here. A receptionist is an expense we forgo; we don't get much walk-in traffic. When the door sensor told me you were here, I came out. Why don't you come on back and we can sit. Can I get you something?"

Genevieve shakes her head, and I reply, "No, thanks. I'm here for the information."

He escorts us back to a small room with a rectangular table surrounded by six chairs, and we all have a seat. "I imagine you have questions," Dr. Paloma suggests.

"One main question, with smaller questions around it," I answer. "What do you plan to do to me?"

He gives a pleasant smile. "That sounds a bit ominous. The reality of the situation is less so. We want to get a better sense of what's happening chemically in your brain, so we'd like to have you take an EEG, maybe an MRI. You're part of a very elite group of people, Tristan. There are thousands of psychics in the world; maybe even millions. We're still not sure. Most aren't aware or aren't interested in their abilities. Many others dismiss it as coincidence or fluke. Some use it to make a living, and others quietly carry these gifts around, utilizing them when they need them. But you … what do you know of your circumstances?"

"Not a lot," I answer. "I know that a month ago, I started receiving these visions, showing me people who were in danger—who they are, where they are, what's going to happen to them and when. I didn't realize at first, but I'm sent this information because I'm supposed to warn them; I'm supposed to stop these things from happening. If I don't, I feel overpowering pain somewhere in my body, which subsides as I get closer to the person I'm supposed to warn."

"Fascinating," he says. "I've met other messengers, but you're the first who experiences the pain."

"Messengers?" Genevieve repeats.

"That's the nickname they've been given in psi circles. Usually, they have a strong religious background—understandable, knowing who they all are …"

"Wait," I interrupt. "What do you mean, *knowing who they all are?*"

"You really are going about this without background knowledge. Of the five messengers I've met before you, four were descendants of Old Testament prophets."

This I did not expect. "Seriously?"

"That's what they told me, anyway, and given that I didn't suggest the possibility, the fact that all four of them brought it up tells me that it's the truth as they understand it. Down through the centuries, the offspring of the biblical prophets retained the ability to see the future, and God—or somebody—employed them as messengers on Earth." He pauses to reflect on the astonished expression on my face. "Wild stuff, huh?"

"My mother was a lawyer," I answer quietly, for reasons I don't quite know.

"That leaves the question: what do you want to happen? If we're successful in isolating the proper chemicals and frequencies inside your brain, we can suppress the visions. You won't know when someone's in danger, and you won't have to help."

I have to admit there's a part of me that thinks this is a very appealing prospect. No more missions, no more assignments. Bad things will happen to good people, just as they have since the beginning of human history. Only Tristan Shays won't be dropping everything, risking arrest, scorn, and bodily harm to set things right.

But then I think of my father, of everything he achieved and accomplished. He helped to invent a whole new form of illumination, and then he founded a corporation to bring it to the world. What would he say if he knew I was given this gift, this opportunity, and I chose to reject it for the sake of convenience? The look in his eyes would speak volumes. He'd lock eyes with me, and in a tone devoid of both pride and judgment, he'd simply say, *You do what you have to do.*

Despite the risk, despite the disruption of my life, this is what I have to do. *Thank you, Dad. I needed that reminder.* "Dr. Paloma, Genevieve told me that you might be able to alter things in a way that I still receive the visions but I don't feel the physical pain associated with them. Is that a possibility?"

"It is," he says, and I note a hint of either hesitation or disappointment in his voice before he continues, "but it will be more difficult. In working with other messengers, we have some valuable information about what part of the brain is active when the visions are coming in, so we can isolate that area and find ways to block the visions. But as I said, you're the first to experience physical pain in association with them, so we're breaking new ground. We don't want to make you incapable of ever feeling pain; that would be dangerous. So we'd need to do deeper-level scans to find what areas of the brain are responsible for the pain signals, and then work to suppress those."

"Would that work?" I ask.

"In theory, yes. There's plenty of historical precedent for pain-suppression techniques. The tricky part is isolating the pain that stems from these visions. You came here from some distance away, isn't that right?"

"About four hours' drive, yes."

"With your permission, I'd like to start on the tests and scans today, to see what we can determine. Are you willing?"

I look at Genevieve and she at me. This feels fast, but it's also the next logical step, and if I take time to think about it, I'll have driven four hours for a ten-minute interview. "Just the tests today?" I ask.

"Yes. We'll need some time to study the results and work out a plan of action based on them anyway. But at least with the tests behind us, we'll have spent our time wisely today, and the next time you come up, we'll be ready to proceed."

"Then … I guess … yes. Okay, let's do the tests."

"Very good. If you'll wait here for just a couple of minutes, I'll let the rest of the team know, and we'll get things set up for you."

He leaves the room, and Genevieve and I exchange mutual looks of astonishment. "This is … uhhh …" I'm unsure how to finish the sentence.

"Descended from biblical prophets?" she says. "You never told me."

"Well, that's because no one ever told me."

"You never traced your family history?"

"Once, years ago. I think I was able to go back five or six generations to good, solid, Protestant European stock. Salt of the earth, that kind of thing. I suspect I would have remembered if somebody told me I came from Bible folk."

"Do you believe it?" she asks.

"I don't know. Tell me something like that six months ago, I would have laughed it off. Today, I'm more firmly entrenched in the *anything's possible* camp."

"Even more reason to keep taking the assignments."

"Might I remind you what they used to do to the prophets? Spoiler alert: it involved stones."

"Hopefully things are a little more civilized today," she offers in consolation. "If they can take the pain away and let you keep receiving the visions, I can see this being a life for us. You helping people; me by your side, helping you. Trips to lovely, peaceful places in between. Tell me you could be happy with that life, and I'll pledge to you right now to stay with you."

For several seconds, I look squarely, intently into her eyes. I'm anxious about hesitating too long before answering, lest my delay read as unwillingness. Yet she is patient; nothing in her expression suggests a need to hurry. It's very clear that she wants me to give the answer that I mean with all my heart. Shortly thereafter, I do.

"I could be very happy with that life."

Smiling wider than I've ever seen her, she leans in to me and begins a kiss that lasts a very long time, long enough that the door opens and Dr. Eric Paloma walks in on us. He's stopped in his tracks, and we part politely. "Sorry about that," I offer. "This is what happens when you leave two teenagers alone together."

He doesn't reply, but there's a strange look on his face, almost as if he wishes he hadn't seen this. Not in the way people sometimes do when they see their parents being affectionate or some such thing, but more like—I'm not even sure what. Regret, maybe?

"We're ready for you," he says. "If the two of you would like to follow me."

He leads us out of the room, deeper into the building, past meeting rooms and rooms filled with the trappings of science. We end up in a large room that looks like an operating theater. In the center is a table long enough and high enough to accommodate a person. Around it are a dozen or more electronic devices, some with computer monitors, others with wires and electrodes and dials. I notice LEDs on practically everything. My work arrived here long before I did.

Elsewhere in the room are computer terminals, a crash cart, video cameras, and a wall lined with devices I couldn't even begin to describe for their intricacy. Dr. Paloma introduces two other men, both in their late twenties. "Mr. Shays, Miss Swan, this is Dr. Sanjay Raju and our assistant, Majudd Kalmar."

"Nice to meet everybody," I say weakly. "Though I gotta tell you, the décor gives off kind of a mad scientist/secret lair/laboratory of evil vibe. Sorry."

The three of them laugh a bit at this; I suspect it's not the first time they've heard it. "Occupational hazard," Paloma says. "The equipment we use doesn't come in pastels with wide-eyed cartoon bunnies on it."

"Understood," I reply.

Majudd tells us, "I'm going to need to hold on to cell phones and anything in your pockets, both of you. The equipment is very sensitive, and we don't want anything altering the readings."

We give him our belongings, which he places in a plastic bowl, carrying them out of the room. Paloma steps over to me and says, "Okay, Tristan, let's get you up on the table, please." I follow him to the table, climb on, and lie flat on my back. To my surprise, he reaches underneath the table and produces sturdy leather straps, which he proceeds to secure around my wrists and ankles.

"Whoa, whoa," I say to him, "bondage isn't really a first-date thing with me."

He laughs. "Don't worry. It's to help keep you from moving around during the scan. Even when people tell us they'll hold perfectly still, they usually end up fidgeting, and that can add hours to the procedure."

I allow him to tighten the restraints, though I'm beginning to get a decidedly uneasy feeling. I notice that he has not attached a restraint to my head, which—thinking about it—would be the one area of my body he'd *least* like me to be able to move. I watch as he goes to a wall phone and dials three digits. "You can come in now," he says into the phone before hanging up. I assume he's inviting the head of the testing team.

A minute later, following a strange silence shared by everyone in the room, I learn the truth. A door into the room opens, and a woman walks in—a woman I've seen before. Genevieve is the first to acknowledge her, in a tone of familiarity and welcome. "Karolena, I'm so glad you could be here."

The woman utterly disregards her, walking straight to Eric Paloma's side. "Is everything ready?" she asks him.

His reply is delivered in a tone of subservience and even fear. "Yes, but I don't know if this is a good idea. I don't know if this is right."

She turns to him and gives an icy stare. "Listen to me very carefully. It's important that you understand one thing: I created this facility. This is my project, and I am the *only one* who says what is right and what is wrong. If you think I'm wrong, *you're* wrong. You'll always be wrong. And I'll always be right. Don't even try to argue with me. I'll win. The response I'm looking for is *yes, ma'am*."

"Yes, ma'am," he utters quietly.

The woman turns to me, putting on a smile I can only describe as dangerous. "Tristan Shays," she says, "how very nice to see you again, particularly in this supine position."

In the corner of my eye, I see Genevieve rise from her seat. "Karolena, what is this?"

"Someone sit her down and keep her there," she orders. "I'll deal with her in a minute." Her eyes never leave my face as she says this. Across the room, Majudd returns Genevieve to her seat.

"Senator Marquez's aide," I think aloud.

"Aide-de-camp, please," she corrects in a playful tone. "Hector is so trusting of his people. A shame he doesn't know them better."

But my realization doesn't end there. "That voice … I've heard it before. When Genevieve was channeling—you spoke to me."

"How flattering of you to remember. You see, this is why it's risky to play with the spirit world. You never know who might tag along. And now, here we are, all together at last. How did you enjoy your trip to West Virginia, by the way? Oh yes, that was a little gift from me, too. I needed you out of the picture yesterday, so I could have a meet-and-greet with your friend. Very nice of you to oblige."

My foray into the fucking obvious leads me to say, "You set me up. You set us both up."

"You have no one but yourselves to blame. You're waaaaaaay ahead of schedule on sticking your nose in where it doesn't belong. You've been on our radar for a month now, ever since your little 'gift' began. But we were perfectly content to let you go about your business for now. That is, until you showed up at the senator's office and interfered."

Things are starting to make sense. "So you're part of the cartel that wants to kill him. Of course, what better way to keep track of his actions than to have someone on the inside."

"It's not about killing him," she corrects. "That's an avenue of last resort. It's about converting him. Kill him, and another of his mindset steps up to oppose us. But converting him to our cause by any means necessary is far more effective."

"I don't understand. Why are you doing this? You have what you want. I'm not a threat to you. Genevieve isn't a threat to you."

"Oh, you silly boy." She runs her fingers through my hair in a way that makes me very uncomfortable, particularly because I can do nothing to stop her. "You're so new at this. You think so linearly. A problem isn't a problem if it never gets the chance to *be* a problem. There are some very powerful people watching you very carefully. The fact that you were selected to warn the senator has convinced them that you need to be removed from the equation."

Genevieve stands and shouts, "No!"

"What did I say?" Karolena asks in a tone of annoyance. Majudd quickly silences Genevieve again.

"You've lured me here so that your so-called research institute can kill me. How very philanthropic of you."

"Kill you? There's no need to kill you. If I wanted to do that, I could have done it in Washington. You're here because these men can remove the part of you that makes you a threat to me and mine. You'll still be alive, if you can call it that. I imagine there'll be a lot of drooling and adult diapers, things like that. But on the bright side, you'll never be bothered with these annoying visions again."

I'm getting nowhere with her, so I turn—as best I can—to Dr. Eric Paloma. "You don't have to do this. You said yourself, you don't think this is right. Is it the money? Is it because this woman funds you? Let us go, and I'll fund your research fully for ten years."

He looks at me, then at her, then back at me. When next he looks at Karolena, the resolute hostility on her face removes any possibility of his siding with me. "It's more than the money," he says apologetically. "Consolidated Offshore's psi cartel is the reason we're here. They're very powerful, very influential."

"And they're paying you to destroy lives," I remind him.

"We do a lot of good for people. We've opened up new frontiers of the human mind. I know that's no consolation to you, but I promise you, we'll be very humane in what we do today."

"That's enough," Karolena interrupts. "Start the procedure. You have until the end of the day. I'll come back tonight, and we'll find a place for poor Mr. Shays to live out his declining years after the stroke that incapacitated him so severely."

The seconds that follow are like an unpleasant hallucination. The imminent fate that awaits me makes my heart race, my breathing erratic, and my eyes cloud over with the tears that are threatening to flow. On top of that, the straps holding me are tight and painful, keeping me from moving in any helpful way. A sound fills my ears, echoing throughout the room, a cry of rage. Disoriented as I am, I don't know exactly where it's coming from, but I know the voice. It is Genevieve Swan, and I perceive her in the distance as a blur of motion. Fueled by her desire to keep me safe, she is racing to my aid. The woman

I love is coming to save me, and for an instant, I pity anyone who tries to stand in her way.

In the periphery of my vision, I see her approach, a look of powerful, primal hate in her eyes as she charges toward the people who hold me captive. I watch as Karolena turns to face her attacker, and from out of somewhere—I'm unsure where—a dark shape appears in her hand. In the fraction of a second it takes my brain to realize what it is, there is no time to cry out a warning. Karolena, her back to me, points the gun at Genevieve and fires. The gunshot is impossibly loud at this close range, and I squeeze my eyes tightly shut against the horror, but not before I see Genevieve thrown backward across the room and to the polished concrete floor.

I cannot see her, but worse, I cannot hear her. No words, no sobs, no cries for help; just a terrible, certain silence that tells me everything I never wanted to know.

She will die. Someone you love. And she will be the first of many. The words from the dream I had on the day we met. For a month, I silently prayed that Genevieve would not be the person to die. But now I know. She is gone. No tearful farewell; no hand held tightly in mine as she quietly slips away after years together; no last words of love and gratitude. Just an unspeakable, violent end in a chamber of horror that she led us to in the name of alleviating my pain. In this moment, I am in more pain than I've ever been in before.

The tears are pouring from my eyes, and anguished sobs escape my lips. As the ringing in my ears subsides, I hear Karolena's voice, as cold and emotionless as ever it was. "Get rid of *that,* and get to work. I'll be back in eight hours."

Through clenched teeth, I cry out with rage of my own. "Run from here! And you'd better pray that they kill me. Because if there's a spark of life left in me when they're done, I swear to the God who sent me that I will kill you with my own hands, Karolena!"

She exits the room without a word in response, and immediately, I feel myself begin to tremble uncontrollably. How I wish I could leave my body, the way I did under sedation therapy at Swift, and go somewhere—anywhere but this place, this moment. Closing my eyes against this waking nightmare, I am left with only sound, the sound of men's voices. *Who* is saying *what* becomes immaterial, as they have all fused in my thoughts into one culpable enemy whose mission is to take everything away from me. I cannot even fight them; all I can do is listen as they discuss the surgical theft of my life.

"We have to get started. We don't have much time."

"Did you see that? Did you see what she did?"

"Yes, I saw. Which is precisely why we do exactly what she says. You're delusional if you think she wouldn't do exactly the same thing to any one of us. We knew the risks when we affiliated ourselves with Traeger's cartel. Today we know exactly what those risks entail. Now help me prep the patient for the procedure."

"Are we using general anesthesia?"

"No, just a local. We need him conscious, so he can respond to our verbal prompts."

"Look at him. He's shocky already, and we haven't even started yet."

"Of course he's shocky. Think of what he's just seen here. Prepare a mild sedative to control the tremors. But remember, we need him conscious and coherent."

"Right away."

One of the men leans close to my ear and speaks in a quiet tone that suggests compassion. I think it is Paloma, but I don't care to open my eyes and look. Because fuck him, compassion and all. He killed my Swan, just as sure as if he pulled the trigger himself. "Tristan, I'm so sorry. Really, I'm sorrier than I can possibly express to you. This wasn't supposed to happen this way. Believe me, if there was a way I could accept your funding, I would. But the cartel … they've turned this organization into a weapon to use against their enemies. You saw Karolena—she's evil. That's the only word to describe her. Pure evil. If we defied her, she would kill us. I know I should stand up and do the right thing, but I'm afraid. That's the terrible truth. I'm so afraid."

"Pushing Propofol, 2 mcg/ml."

Within seconds, the trembling that racked me begins to subside. A slight fogginess overtakes my mind, but the words remain clear.

"Push the local anesthetic next. Let's get him numb. Prep the drill and get the Barnhart Device ready."

The sedative washes over my consciousness like nepenthe, keeping me in a place halfway between lucidity and dreams. Mercifully, it dulls the edges of the memory of Genevieve's murder and leaves me just aware enough to know that a great injustice has taken place. New sounds take the place of the voices—a heart monitor, an electric razor, a drill. At one point, I realize that I am being injected, after which I feel nothing above my neck. I am beyond caring what happens to me.

Time passes; I'm sure it does. That's what time does. But in what quantity, I have no idea. My eyes are closed, but I am awake. Around me, men are working, if you could call it work. Their goal is the destruction of my mind. I want to sleep, but try as I might, I can't.

Voices return. "Tristan, can you hear me?"

I don't speak; I will not speak. But I open my eyes, struggling to focus on the masked, white-gowned figures encircling me.

"Tristan, we've inserted a probe into your brain." He continues in a tone of covertness. "There's a way to salvage this, but we need your help. We don't have to do as much damage as Karolena wants. We can suppress the visions but leave you with the parts of your mental faculties that will allow you to have a normal life."

"What are you doing? Are you out of your mind?"

"Shut it, Majudd. I can't take away this man's future just because he's inconvenient to the cartel. You can cooperate with me, or you can step out."

"This is on *your* head, then."

"All right, Tristan. In order for this to work, we need you to respond when we ask you questions. If it's too hard to speak, you can just blink once for yes, twice for no. Do you hear a high-pitched sound?"

I hear the sound. I hear it quite clearly. But I don't speak. I don't blink. I won't help them. I don't care what this costs me.

"I don't understand it. He should be hearing the sound. Go deeper, and turn the device up to twenty."

The sound intensifies, but still I won't grant them an acknowledgment. If they kill me, so be it. Life doesn't matter now.

I drift, a conscious but absent participant in my own vivisection. I hear the voices continue, with added frustration at my lack of either willingness or ability—they seem unable to tell which—to assist them. Sounds from the various instruments increase in volume and pitch. My thoughts begin to destabilize. I lose the sense of where I am, what day this is, why I am here. I feel the desire to leave, but I don't know how. *Did I walk here? Did someone bring me? I think so, but who? I can't remember.* I can't remember what happened before I was put on this table. I just know that I feel dizzy, and I'm not supposed to talk.

Why am I not supposed to talk? I open my eyes enough to see doctors operating on me. *Am I sick? Am I hurt? If they're operating on me, why am I awake?* I open my mouth to ask the doctor, but suddenly I feel a terrible tightness in my chest, like a great weight has been placed on top of me. Pain radiates throughout me, and I hear an awful collection of sound. Machines are beeping loudly, alarms go off, and the doctors' voices rise to a frantic pitch.

"He's crashing!"

"EEG functions are highly erratic. I'm getting only alpha wave readings. Where's the other readings? We should be getting readings across the spectrum."

"We can't worry about that now. Get the crash cart."

"But he's not in V-fib."

"Get the goddamn cart over here!"

My eyes are open now, but I can barely see. My blood feels like needles of ice as it thickens in every part of my body. Each breath is agonizing as I struggle to take in enough air.

This is where it ends. This is how it ends. Surrounded by people and yet alone.

My thought is interrupted by a terrible sound, adding to the symphony of already terrible sounds—a metallic crash against stone. More light enters the room. A door has been kicked in, or at least I think so; things are fading away from me.

Voices again. "How did you get in here?"

"Oh my God, it's not possible!"

"Please, you don't have to do this! We're trying to save him!"

"No, don't! Please! We didn't mean to hurt you!"

Explosions, small ones. Gunshots, maybe. My eyes are failing; all I see is light and dark. The white-gowned figures are gone. Standing above me is a single individual, dressed in dark colors. The police? My rescuer, perhaps? My mouth moves in what I think I remember to be a smile, but I don't know if I even succeed at that. Agonizingly, I draw in a breath, let it out, and realize that another is not coming.

Silently, I let the blackness wash over me.

Then suddenly, there is awareness, as if someone has opened up the floodgates of sensation. It begins with a piercing sharpness in my chest, and then the feeling that someone has liquefied hornets and is pouring them through my every vein. My breath returns, rapid and imprecise, but filling my lungs with the oxygen needed to keep my brain alive. Sound returns next, a man's voice, talking to someone, somewhere. "I have a medical emergency, and I need helicopter transport. I have a thirty-four-year-old male who crashed during an unauthorized intracranial medical procedure. I've resuscitated him with adrenaline, but he's a long way from stable. I need ground-unit paramedics to assist me, and a med-evac to take him to the best neurosurgical center in the area. I'm in York, at 18500 Palisade. ... Thank you."

Someone's trying to save me.

The man puts a hand on my shoulder. "You hold on. Help is coming, Tristan."

Epilogue

Darkness. Emptiness. An absence of sensory input. *Am I dead?* A breath; another. *I'm alive, but …*

With some effort, I open my eyes. The first thing I notice is how dry they are. As they flutter open, the light is so bright that it hurts. *But what light? Where am I?*

I reach for any memory that precedes this moment, but they are slow to come. Maybe more details of my surroundings will help. I see the rest of my body, lying in a bed, covered with a white cotton blanket. My arms are bare, and wires lead from me to various machines in the room. The light that assails my eyes comes from fluorescent tubes lining the ceiling.

A hospital; I think I'm in a hospital.

I'm momentarily startled when a man's face enters my field of vision. He is standing over me, smiling at me. In hushed tones, he says, "Hey there. Welcome back. I'm glad I was here when you woke up. How do you feel?"

My first attempt at speaking yields only a very dry cough.

"Wait, wait," he says. "Let me help." He pours water from a plastic pitcher into a plastic cup and hands it to me. My arm feels weak as I bring the cup to my lips and take a long swallow, which also hurts going down.

"Thank you," I respond weakly. "Where am I?"

"The intensive care unit at Johns Hopkins Hospital in Baltimore. Best care money can buy."

"How long have I been asleep?" I ask.

His answer is nothing short of astonishing. "Nine days, my friend. For a while there, we weren't sure you were going to come back to us. You were hurt pretty bad."

Nine days? How can that be possible? "I don't remember what happened."

"That's okay. You've had a pretty traumatic brain injury, and some things will take a while to come back. For now, all you need to know is this: You went to see some people to help get rid of pain you've been feeling. But they weren't good people. They didn't know what they were doing, and they botched things. You almost died on the operating table. Luckily, I was able to show up in time to help you. I had you brought here."

"Thank you. How did you know to be there?"

"When I found out where you went, I thought it was a good idea for me to go there. These same people hurt me pretty bad several years ago, and I couldn't live with myself if I let them hurt you too."

"I have the dimmest memories of all that. Flashes, glimpses."

He asks an important question. "Do you remember who you are?"

It takes me a moment. "Tristan. Tristan Shays. Though I don't know how much more than that I can tell you right now."

"That's okay," he says pleasantly. "You just woke up after a really horrible ordeal. We'll play catch-up later."

"Thank you again for saving me. And I'm very sorry and very embarrassed at the next question, but I think it's necessary. Could you please remind me who you are and how we know each other?"

"Of course. My name is Ephraim Shays. I'm your second cousin on your father's side."

Though it offers no familiarity to me, I don't want to appear rude. "Ephraim, of course. Please forgive me for forgetting."

"Nothing to forgive, Tristan. Nothing at all."

"Have you been with me this entire time?"

"Off and on. I was hoping to be here when you woke up, so you'd have a familiar face—in theory, anyway—to greet you."

"What happened to the people who did this to me?"

"I made sure they won't hurt anyone ever again. There was another person there the same time you were. Unfortunately, she was killed."

"That's terrible," I reply quietly.

"Her family was notified, and a benefactor set them up with 10 million dollars for their loss."

"That's quite a benefactor. Wish I had someone looking out for me that way."

"Funny you should say so," he says pleasantly.

"What do you mean?"

"I've been looking for a reason to resign from my job. When you got injured, I found that reason. I have enough money to live on, and you're not ready to be on your own yet. I'm going to stay with you and take care of you full time until you're well again."

"Ephraim, I … I don't know what to say. That's incredibly caring and generous, but I don't know how I could impose on you that way."

"You're not imposing. I'm offering. Family comes first. Besides, I have a feeling it's very important that I stick close to you for a while."

Printed in the United States
by Baker & Taylor Publisher Services